Ghost in the Polka Dot Bikini

A GHOST OF GRANNY APPLES MYSTERY

Ghost in the Polka Dot Bikini

Sue Ann Jaffarian

THORNDIKE
CHIVERS

This Large Print edition is published by Thorndike Press, Waterville, Maine, USA and by AudioGO Ltd, Bath, England.

Thorndike Press, a part of Gale, Cengage Learning.

The text of this Large Print edition is unabridged.

Other aspects of the book may vary from the original edition.

Set in 16 pt. Plantin.

LIBRARY OF CONGRESS CATALOGING-IN-PUBLICATION DATA

Jaffarian, Sue Ann, 1952–
    Ghost in the polka dot bikini : a ghost of Granny Apples
mystery / by Sue Ann Jaffarian.
        p. cm. — (Thorndike Press large print mystery)
    ISBN-13: 978-1-4104-3462-3 (hardcover)
    ISBN-10: 1-4104-3462-1 (hardcover)
    1. Actresses—Fiction. 2. Santa Catalina Island (Calif.)—Fiction.
3. Large type books. I. Title.
PS3610.A359G485 2011b
813'.6—dc22   2011003965

BRITISH LIBRARY CATALOGUING-IN-PUBLICATION DATA AVAILABLE

Published in 2011 in the U.S. by arrangement with Midnight Ink, an imprint of Llewellyn Ltd. Woodbury, MN 55125-2989 USA.

Published in 2011 in the U.K. by arrangement with Llewellyn Worldwide Ltd.

U.K. Hardcover: 978 1 445 83722 2 (Chivers Large Print)
U.K. Softcover: 978 1 445 83723 9 (Camden Large Print)

Printed in the United States of America
1 2 3 4 5 6 7 15 14 13 12 11

For Susan Groeneweg.
Thank you, dear friend,
for all your years of friendship
and for tagging along with me
to Catalina.

ACKNOWLEDGMENTS

Thanks to the usual suspects: Whitney Lee, my agent; Diana James, my manager; and all the good folks at Llewellyn Worldwide/ Midnight Ink for their continued support, talent, and encouragement.

Thank you, also, to the Los Angeles County Sheriff's Department–Catalina Division, the *Catalina Islander,* Island Express Helicopter Service, and all the wonderful folks I met while on the island doing research.

ONE

The woman frolicking in the waves was underdressed for November, even for a ghost. Emma Whitecastle watched as the curvaceous, bikini-clad spirit dashed in and out of the waves, as carefree and untouched by the morning cold as a porpoise. Emma, on the other hand, pulled her jacket together and zipped it up close under her chin before hovering over the cup of hot coffee she'd picked up from a bakery around the corner. She'd had a restless night, tossing and turning most of it, so just after five thirty she dressed quietly in jeans, a sweater, warm socks, and sneakers, and headed for the beach to watch the sunrise, leaving behind a sleeping Phillip Bowers in their hotel room.

It was Thanksgiving weekend. Kelly, Emma's daughter who was attending Harvard, hadn't come home for the short holiday, opting instead to spend it at a friend's home in Connecticut. Emma's parents were on a cruise through the Panama Canal. Phil's boys, both a little older than Kelly, were with their mother, and his aunt Susan and uncle Glen were visiting their daughter. That left Phil and Emma to fend for themselves over the four-day holiday.

Catalina had been Phil's idea. Emma had been to the vacation spot located just twenty-six miles off the coast of Southern California many times while married to Grant Whitecastle, the bad boy of TV talk-show hosts. During those times, she'd either stayed in the finest island hotels, like the former Wrigley Mansion, now known as the Inn on Mt. Ada, or on the yachts of Grant's show-biz friends. When Phil first proposed the trip, he'd booked them at the Inn on Mt. Ada, but Emma didn't want to stay anywhere she'd stayed with Grant. As Phil ticked off the names of the best hotels, Emma had said no to each.

Phil had been frustrated. "You can't go through life avoiding everywhere the two of you traveled. If you do, we'll never go anywhere."

He'd been right. But he hadn't been right about why Emma felt the way she did.

"Are you sure you're over him?" Phil had asked, the vein in his neck as taut as pulled rope, bracing himself for news he didn't want to hear.

Emma's divorce from Grant Whitecastle had been finalized at the end of last year. Technically, she'd become a single woman on January first, just eleven months ago. She and Grant had been separated about a year and a half prior to that, but the marriage had been on the rocks almost from the time he'd hit it big with his tacky, tabloid-style talk show. Even before they'd been formally separated, Grant had impregnated Carolyn Bryant, his B-movie, party-girl mistress. Grant had married Carolyn on the first weekend in the new year in a splashy wedding attended by much of Hollywood. Photos of the bride and groom with their toddler son, Oscar, had assaulted Emma from every supermarket checkout stand. And that's how Emma knew she was over Grant Whitecastle. The photos elicited nothing from her except pity for Grant, for the life he'd thrown away in his quest for fame and his lust for a sleazy wannabe out to grab any man with a big name and a bigger bank account. He'd lost her, damaged the bond with his daughter, even lost the respect of his own parents. He'd pretty much flipped them all the bird — in public.

Kelly had been reluctant to attend her

father's wedding, but in the end she did, reporting back that even though it looked like Hollywood had turned out for the circus event, it was more out of deep-seated support and respect for Grant's parents, George and Celeste Whitecastle.

George Whitecastle was a multi-award-winning director and producer who counted Clint Eastwood and George Lucas among his closest friends. George's parents, both now dead, had been Hollywood legends. And Celeste had been a famous starlet, known for her beauty and grace. She'd even been dubbed the next Grace Kelly. And, like the late Princess of Monaco, Celeste had given up her budding career for love and family.

Emma knew that Kelly's summation was probably correct — that most of the A-list guests at the wedding had been there for George and Celeste. Even though Emma was no longer married to Grant, she was still on the fringe of show business, having her own modest talk show on television, and gossip managed to filter down to her. Grant Whitecastle was respected for his runaway ratings, not for himself. The minute those ratings dipped, he'd be kicked aside like a pair of old, worn sneakers, just as he had kicked Emma aside.

No, Emma was over Grant Whitecastle. She'd stopped loving him long before the divorce was final. What she tried to explain to Phil Bowers was that she wanted to make new and happier memories with him. Many of her past stays on Catalina had not been pleasant ones. Even on the small island, Grant had managed to cat around, and many of those luxury hotel rooms had been scenes of arguments and despair. In the end, she'd finally agreed to the Hotel Metropole, where Phil booked them into a lovely mini suite with a balcony facing the ocean.

Emma took an appreciative sip of her coffee and studied the ghost playing in the surf. She'd first seen the spirit yesterday. It had been Thanksgiving morning, their first morning on the island. After breakfast, she and Phil had gone for a morning stroll to explore the beachfront shop windows before the village of Avalon was fully awake. The ghost of the young woman had been sitting on one of the tiled benches, her eyes closed, her pretty face turned toward the slow-rising sun as if soaking up rays at high noon in July. As they had passed by, the ghost had opened her eyes and looked at Emma with a frank curiosity as solid as the bench on which she sat. She said nothing, but several steps later, when Emma looked over her shoulder, the ghost was still staring after them.

Catalina supposedly had many ghosts in residence, the most famous being that of Natalie Wood. The actress had drowned while yachting off Two Harbors, the other main town on the island. The accident had occurred over Thanksgiving weekend in 1981, and since then many people have claimed they've seen the ghost of the popular movie star walking the beach. While on the island, Emma planned to do some research into the local spirits and legends for a segment on Catalina for her weekly television talk show on paranormal theories and activities. Catalina's rich paranormal history dated back to its original Indian inhabitants and included colorful stories about the Chicago Cubs baseball team, who used the island as its spring training camp for nearly thirty years, and the golden era of Hollywood, when movie stars like Clark Gable and Errol Flynn considered it their playground.

Emma was fairly new to the world of spirits and ghosts, only discovering her ability to see and speak with them last year when the ghost of her great-great-great grandmother, Ish Reynolds, better known as Granny Apples, had come to her for help to prove her innocence in the death of her husband, Jacob. At first skeptical, Emma reluctantly embraced her ability to see the dead and helped Granny. It was during her investigation into Granny's death that she'd met Phil Bowers. Shortly after, she was offered a chance to host the talk show — the Whitecastle name, no doubt, giving as much, if not more, weight to the producer's decision about hiring her than her abilities.

The show, which aired Thursdays opposite Grant's daily talk show, was doing well and had a solid following after its first short season. It was currently on hiatus but had been picked up for another run with more episodes. Unlike Grant's show, Emma's did not pander to sensationalism, gossip, or tacky subjects but instead featured lively debates involving experts, scientists, and skeptics, as well as historical data and stories. And not only did it cover the world of spirits, but other fields of paranormal study as well. Her show, simply called *The Whitecastle Report,* was well respected for its research and even-handed presentation of its subjects. It was a reputation Emma took great pride in — and great pains to protect.

As for her own paranormal talents, even though Emma saw ghosts all the time, she kept her personal abilities out of the limelight as much as possible. To her relief, spirits didn't crowd around her like a swarm of pesky flies. Usually, they just went about their business. Sometimes they took casual note of her, and sometimes they interacted with her. Since yesterday morning, Emma had seen the young, bikini-wearing ghost several times, including during Thanksgiving dinner at the country club, where the spirit, dressed in her flirty dotted and ruffled bathing suit, had flitted from table to table unnoticed while guests dined on turkey and pumpkin pie. The spirit hadn't spoken to Emma yet, just studied her with a playful interest, like a puppy with a tilted head.

It had been thoughts of the ghost that had given Emma a restless night and beckoned her outside at sunrise.

As the darkness turned gunmetal gray, the ghost continued to play in the surf. Her image was hazy, like a column of smoke molded into the shape of a woman. She'd been blond in life, her figure curvy, with large breasts, a tiny waist, and a sweetheart bottom. However she had died, it'd been while wearing the bikini; thus, she was forever clad. And she had died young, possibly in her mid to late twenties.

When the ghost turned and looked toward the town, Emma raised a hand and gave the spirit a friendly wave. The ghost smiled and waved back, totally untroubled about being seen. Turning back toward the sea, she waved again before disappearing into the waves lapping at the pier pilings.

"Brrrr," a familiar whispery voice said from behind Emma. "Makes me cold as a witch's titty just looking at her."

Emma continued looking at the spot where the young spirit had disappeared. "You're a ghost, Granny. You don't feel cold."

"But I remember it. Felt it plenty in my life. Hunger, too. There were winters in the cabin, didn't know which would claim us first before spring, the cold or starvation."

As a shiver went through Emma, she took a big drink of her coffee. Usually she could tell when Granny or another spirit was near by a sudden chill in the air, but in the cold of the damp sea air, Granny's arrival had gone unnoticed.

"You know that ghost, Granny? The one just now on the beach?" She turned to look at the spirit of Ish Reynolds, the woman who'd been known as Granny Apples because of her expert pie baking.

Just as the young ghost was bound for

eternity to wear a bikini, Granny Apples would always be dressed in pioneer clothing consisting of a long-sleeved blouse and long, full skirt. Granny had died over a hundred years ago. She had been a tiny but strong woman with braided hair circling her head like a crown and a pinched face weathered by years of working out-of-doors. Granny had been only forty-one years old when she died, but the hard life and the attitude of her times made her seem older.

"Can't say that I do," the ghost answered, keeping her face to the sea.

"She keeps appearing to me. I think she wants something."

"Has she spoken?"

"Not yet. She just watches me in a friendly manner, almost like she's trying to remember me from somewhere."

"Maybe she's an old schoolmate who's passed on."

Emma swallowed some more hot coffee. "No, I don't think so. From her appearance, I'd say she might have died sometime in the sixties. That's the *nineteen* sixties," Emma clarified, tossing Granny an impish grin.

The ghost pursed her lips in annoyance. "I ken what you mean. They didn't wear bathing costumes like that in my day."

"Did you notice her hairstyle? The way

it's teased on top, with the ends curled upward? That was called a flip. And her bathing suit looks a bit old-fashioned, with the polka dots and ruffles."

Granny crossed her arms. "Humph, glad I was dressed when I passed. Hate to think of spending eternity with my backside hanging out like that."

Granny's observation caught Emma's attention. She smiled, glad she hadn't yet met any ghosts who'd died in the nude.

The town of Avalon was tucked into a crescent-shaped bay on Catalina Island. The main street that ran along the beachfront was appropriately named Crescent. High hills stood on either side of the bay like sentries. Daylight crept over one hill, while fog rolled over the opposite one. They met in the middle like tenuous lovers, shrouding the sea in a hazy veil. Palm trees along the beach were ringed with tiny lights, and many of the shopfronts and hotels already had their Christmas lights up and lit. At night, it had been magical walking along the festive beach hand in hand with Phil. This morning, the lights faded into the swelling dawn, handing the baton of a new day off to the sun.

Both behind and in front of Emma, the town was starting to stir. Ahead of her, people staying on the numerous boats and yachts moored in the bay were waking. She caught sight of a bright yellow rubber dinghy making its way from one boat to the pier like a duckling swimming off on its own for the first time. On the long pier that housed several tourist businesses and restaurants, she could make out people going about the chore of opening for the day. Along Crescent, a few folks were out for early morning strolls or heading to work. Behind her, she heard the soft *thunk* of metal against pavement, followed by a gentle swoosh. Turning, she saw a man, bundled in jacket and gloves, sweeping the street and sidewalk with a broom and caddy, moving deliberately along Crescent, scanning for wayward trash and debris. Catalina was very clean, and its citizens took great pride in keeping it that way. It was one of the things Emma had always enjoyed about the island.

"Mighty beautiful place."

Emma started. She'd almost forgotten about Granny. The ghost was perched on the far edge of her bench, still looking out to sea.

"Never saw the ocean til I was dead."

"Never?"

The question surprised both Emma and

Granny. Swinging their heads in unison to their left, they saw the young ghost — the woman from the beach — standing just a few feet away. In addition to her bikini, she wore a small bow clipped to the right side of her hair — nothing else. It was the first time Emma had seen her so close or heard her voice.

"Came from Kansas," Granny continued, as if she spoke to this new spirit every day. "Settled in the mountains once we got to California. That's where the gold was, so that's where my man stayed put."

"I'd just *die* if I couldn't go to the beach." Through the ghostly whisper, Emma discerned a young voice that held an almost childlike quality. She changed her estimation of the woman's age at death to be her early twenties. "Growing up, all I ever dreamed about were California beaches. And now here I am." The young spirit twirled with glee like she'd won a prize at a carnival.

Emma and Granny looked at each other a moment before Granny cocked a thumb in Emma's direction. "This here's my great-granddaughter, Emma."

"Great-great-great granddaughter," Emma corrected. She drank the last of her coffee in one final gulp and tossed the cup into a trash bin that stood next to the bench. She knew Granny was sensitive about her age, even in death, and Emma loved teasing her about it.

"Whatever," Granny replied, rolled her eyes. Emma frowned at the response, thinking Granny was picking up far too many modern bad habits. Granny returned her attention to the other ghost. "Emma's a friend to those on the other side."

The young ghost looked from one woman to the other — from the dead to the living and back again — her face glowing and guileless in the growing morning light.

"My name's Tessa — Tessa North." Before either Granny or Emma could say anything, the young spirit added, "Am I really dead?"

Two

"Wait a minute."

Their suite's bathroom had a whirlpool tub bordered on one side with sliding doors that could be opened to expose the tub to the bedroom and the warmth from the fireplace. Phil, who was shaving, turned from the mirror to stare at Emma through the open sliding doors. She was sprawled on their king-size bed in a fluffy terrycloth robe, telling him about her encounter with Tessa North. After returning from her sunrise rendezvous with the two ghosts, Emma had warmed her bones in the tub, where she'd been joined by a playful Phil.

"Are you telling me that this ghost doesn't know she's dead?"

"It's more like she's not sure about it. Like she's confused."

He pointed his razor in her direction. "But you think she died in the sixties?"

"Yes, at least from her hairstyle and bathing suit. She looks like something out of one of those old teen beach movies. You know, the ones with Frankie Avalon and Annette Funicello. Weren't those from the sixties?"

"Sure were." Phil grinned through tracks of shaving cream. "When I was a kid, my first major crush was on Annette Funicello." He winked at Emma. "Man, could she fill out a bathing suit." Emma made a face at him. He laughed and went back to shaving.

"Too bad you can't see ghosts, Phil. The figure on Tessa North makes Annette look downright dowdy."

Phil rinsed his face, then turned back to Emma while drying off with a hand towel. "Really?" He raised an eyebrow.

"Think Pamela Sue Anderson, but naïve."

Both his eyebrows shot up. "Hmm, maybe you could arrange a special vision for me."

Shaking her head with amusement, Emma got off the bed, removed her robe, and started to dress. "Fat chance, cowboy."

Phil dashed out of the bathroom and gently tackled Emma, the two of them falling back down onto the large bed. Emma giggled as he straddled her, holding her arms above her head. "You old fool, get off me."

From his perch, Phil Bowers studied his

prey. Dressed or undressed, the sight of Emma Whitecastle never ceased to take his breath away. Tall and willowy, with short, blond, flirty hair, she wore her forties well. He adored every inch of her, including the fine lines edging her crisp blue eyes and generous mouth. And he loved that her intelligence and sharp wit kept him on his toes. She was everything he'd ever wanted in a woman, even if she did come with a sidecar of things that went bump in the night. He'd learned to adjust to the unconventional side of Emma Whitecastle, just as she'd learned to accommodate his stubbornness.

Phil leaned down and trapped Emma's mouth with his own. They both smelled of soap and tasted of toothpaste. His kiss was long and demanding. Emma settled into it, her own lips parting in welcome. When he let go of her arms, they instinctively went around his neck in an embrace.

"You two are worse than a couple of field rabbits."

Phil Bowers felt, rather than heard, the slight gasp as it escaped Emma's lips. It wasn't a pant of passion, but rather a slight pause or change of mind before she turned back to the matter at hand. For a fleeting instant, Emma had lost her focus mid-kiss.

When he felt the cold draft on his bare back, Phil was pretty sure why. He rolled off of her.

"I thought Granny wasn't supposed to come into our bedroom. You know how I feel about putting on a show."

Emma sighed. She wasn't about to lie. Even though Phil Bowers couldn't hear or see Granny Apples, he'd become very astute about knowing when the spirit was present. He even talked directly to the ghost on occasion, although Emma had to relay Granny's replies.

He didn't wait for Emma to respond. "Granny, you know you're not to intrude on our intimate time. And don't pretend you're not here. I can feel you."

"She doesn't usually, Phil." Emma got off the bed and pulled her robe back on. In spite of the flickering flames in the fireplace, with Granny in the room, the air had turned chilly.

Ghosts need energy to materialize, much as a flashlight needs batteries to shine. They extract that energy from the heat in the atmosphere around them, causing the air to turn cool or even cold as the heat is absorbed into their physical presentation. But like all energy, it was used up quickly, and their apparitions soon needed to disappear to recharge.

"Isn't he a little old to be carrying on like a prize stud?" As the ghost materialized, Emma saw her gray image perched on the edge of one of the upholstered chairs across from the bed.

Emma looked over at Phil Bowers. He'd gotten off the bed, the towel he'd been wearing falling to the floor in the movement. Ghost or no ghost, he didn't replace it. He was a fine-looking man in his early fifties, tall and strong with wide shoulders and a slight middle-aged spread. His face was rugged, divided by a thick, graying moustache; his head was bald. His eyes danced when he laughed or teased, which he did often. Phil was a very successful attorney with a practice in San Diego and a family ranch in Julian, where Granny was from. He was solid and dependable and embraced no pretense, nor did he tolerate it in others. He was the opposite of her trend-chasing, looks-obsessed, headline-grabbing ex-husband. Grant Whitecastle was smoke and mirrors; Phillip Bowers, a load-bearing wall.

As both the ghost and his lover watched, Phil walked to the dresser, pulled out clothes, and started dressing. Emma looked over at Granny. The ghost was trying to keep her eyes averted in an attempt at modesty, but Emma saw her sneak appreciative looks Phil's way. In spite of her snappish comments, Emma knew that Granny liked and admired Phil Bowers and did her best to comply with his wishes about respecting intimate boundaries.

Emma walked over to the ghost and took the matching chair next to her. "What's up, Granny?"

"It's that Tessa girl. I think we need to help her."

"You mean *I* need to help her, don't you?"

"I said *we*. I mean *we*."

"Don't get testy. Did you talk to her?"

"Little fool thinks she's on some sort of never-ending holiday."

"And what's wrong with that? She appeared happy enough."

"She's not sure she's dead, Emma. She needs help."

"Did she tell you anything about what happened to her — about the last thing she remembers?"

"Is this about the bikini ghost?" Phil stood nearby, listening to what sounded like a one-sided conversation while he threaded a belt through the loops at the waist of his jeans.

"Yes. Granny thinks we should help her

realize her situation. The girl may not fully understand that she's dead."

Phil picked up his boots and plopped down in the chair where Granny was sitting, going through the ghost unawares.

"Humph!" Granny disappeared, popping up on the bed.

"You know he didn't do that on purpose, Granny."

"I'm not so sure." The ghost crossed her arms and scowled.

Phil looked at Emma, then at the place where she'd refocused her eyes. It dawned on him what had happened. "Damn it, Granny, if I can't see you, how do you expect me *not* to go through you?" He pulled on one boot. "Hard to believe this beach bunny hasn't caught on in all this time that she's not among the living. Didn't it occur to her after the first ten or so years? Didn't she wonder why she wasn't hungry or thirsty — or why she can swim in November without being cold?" He pulled on the other boot.

"She seems a bit tetched to me," Granny offered. Emma relayed her words to Phil.

Emma got up and shed her robe once more. "I don't think she's *tetched,* as you put it, Granny. But she does seem naïve, almost childlike." This time, Emma suc-

29

ceeded in getting dressed without interruption, thinking and talking as she clothed herself. "I think on some level Tessa does know she's dead, but she's in denial about it. Maybe that childish behavior is part of her defense mechanism."

Finished dressing, Phil sat back in his chair, waiting for Emma. "Maybe she needs a ghost shrink."

Emma stopped dressing and looked at Granny. Granny looked back. "Milo," the two of them said at the same time, but Phil only heard Emma.

"I was kidding, Emma."

Emma pulled on her sweater and reached for her cell phone. "Kidding or not, who better to tell us what may be going on with this ghost?" She scrolled through the phone's address book and selected Milo's number.

Milo Ravenscroft was the clairvoyant who had connected Granny with Emma, then mentored Emma through the process of accepting and learning about her special gifts. It was also Milo who had recommended Emma as the host of the paranormal talk show. He was a short, nerdy man in his forties who lived in a modest house where the western boundary of Los Angeles bordered Santa Monica. He was a well-known clairvoyant but opted for a quiet life outside of the limelight. Emma respected him for that.

After Milo answered and pleasantries were exchanged, Emma used the speaker feature on her phone and got to the reason for her call.

"It is very possible, Emma," Milo told her, "that this spirit is in denial about her death. Sometimes, for various reasons, spirits do need help going to the other side. And they all need to cross over, even if they choose to come back to visit, like Granny."

"But how can we help her?"

Phil ran a hand over his smooth skull in frustration. "Oh, boy. I can see this romantic weekend going south real quick."

"I'm not sure, Emma," Milo continued, "without meeting her myself. But try to find out what happened to her at the time of her death. Maybe something traumatic occurred."

Phil leaned forward in his chair to be heard through the small speaker. "You don't consider dying traumatic?"

"Of course it's traumatic, Phil." Milo laughed lightly. "But something very unusual might have happened to make her block it out or deny it. While spirits don't have the same sense of time and location — or even sense of surroundings — that we

31

do, they were still real people at one time. Just as we don't fully understand the true depth of the human mind, we have even less understanding of what happens to that mind at the time of — or after — death."

Phil shook his head. "Tell you what, Milo. Why don't you come on over here and hold a few couch sessions with this Tessa ghost?"

"I would find that quite fascinating, Phil, but this weekend is out of the question for me. I'm in Chicago right now and won't be home until Tuesday. Tell you what, though, Emma: find out what you can about Tessa, and when I return, we'll put our heads together."

"Okay," Emma agreed. "If she reappears, I'll see what I can learn."

"Is Granny there?"

"I'm here, Milo." Still uncomfortable with some modern conveniences, the ghost hovered with caution by the phone held by Emma.

"Granny, see if you can get Tessa to come to the mainland for a session. You might have to guide her over when we do it. Almost fetch her, if you will. I'll bet she died on Catalina and hasn't left the island since."

"Ah." In his comfortable seat, Phil stretched, raising his arms over his head, clasping his hands together, and extending them as far as he could. Finished, he added his two cents. "May I ask a question here?"

Milo paused. Granny and Emma turned to Phil and waited.

"Has this ghost even asked for your help? She might be happy just the way she is. If so, why upset her apple cart?" When no one replied, Phil continued. "She's already dead. It's not like you're going to change her situation by meddling."

Granny was the first to turn her attention toward the sliding doors that led to the balcony. Emma's eyes followed. Phil turned in his chair to look too, but only because Emma had. He saw nothing. Granny and Emma saw the young spirit. She was standing just outside on the balcony, looking in. Her earlier smile had been replaced by a frown.

"You guys there?" Milo called from the phone.

Emma pulled the phone close to her mouth and whispered, "Tessa North just appeared."

Emma motioned to the young spirit to come in. Phil got up out of his chair and moved to the other side of the room. With the bathroom sliding doors still open, he sat on the edge of the whirlpool tub and watched, keeping his senses alert. He wasn't sure what was about to happen, but he was pretty sure he wouldn't understand much of it. With further encouragement from Emma, the young ghost walked through the glass doors and entered the room, making it even cooler. The change in temperature was something Phil did understand. He knew a new spirit had entered the room. His stomach growled. Whatever was going to happen, he hoped they'd make it snappy so he and Emma could get to breakfast. Ghosts may not need to eat, but they did.

He hoisted one booted leg across the opposite knee. "I'm guessing now might be a good time to ask her if she wants that help or not."

THREE

After Granny and Tessa North disappeared, Phil and Emma had a late breakfast at Jack's Country Kitchen, then resumed their weekend plans with a long walk uphill to the Wrigley Memorial and Botanical Gardens. Though cool and damp that morning, the fog had burned off, leaving the air warm with a crisp accent.

Holding hands, they followed a small map of the city, wandering first down Catalina Avenue to Tremont Street, then along Tremont until it intersected with Avalon Canyon Road. Along the way, they passed small, colorful houses, many built in the shotgun style, standing eaves to eaves on the limited soil. At Avalon Canyon Road, they turned left, leaving behind the more densely populated area. According to the map, at the end of Avalon Canyon Road, they would find the botanical gardens. Phil had wanted to rent a golf cart, the most common mode of transportation on the island, but Emma had held her ground, citing that they needed the exercise.

"Didn't we get enough exercise back at the hotel last night?" Phil shot her a sly look. "And this morning?"

"And didn't *you* just fill up on biscuits and gravy? Not to mention sausages and a three-egg omelet."

"And enjoyed every morsel." He winked at her. "Hey, Fancy Pants, not my problem if you don't eat red meat. A sausage or two might do you good once in a while."

"Yuck. My blueberry pancakes were just fine, thank you."

Fancy Pants was the nickname Phil had tagged her with when they'd first met. At that time, he'd meant it as a negative moniker, but now it was his pet name for her. And as the nickname had moved from negative to affectionate, so Emma's feelings about it had changed from annoyance to enjoyment.

They walked a few more steps, passing the island's fire station. "Odd, isn't it?" she observed with a smile. "I'm the city girl and you're the country boy, yet I'm the one who wants to hike and spend time outside."

"I spend plenty of time outside on the ranch. Right now, I'm on vacation. Didn't realize I'd be on a forced march."

"And aren't you glad I had you change your boots for athletic shoes?"

Phil growled with pretend annoyance. Emma saw physical exercise as a form of entertainment, while he saw it as a means to get things done, like working around the ranch he shared with his aunt and uncle, Susan and Glen Steveson, or spending time on a treadmill because his doctor had ordered him to do it. But as much as he groused, he really did enjoy the activities he shared with Emma and had never felt better.

Emma laughed. "I'll make it up to you."

"You bet you will, Fancy Pants." He stopped her in her tracks and planted a big kiss on her mouth. She melted into his strong, warm arms.

"I'll make it up to you about Granny, too."

"No problem there, so long as she's not in the peanut gallery when we're feeling frisky. And as long as I don't end up at the bottom of your priority list."

"Not a chance, cowboy." Emma's smile turned quickly into a frown. "Seriously, Phil, do you mind very much about the ghosts?"

Phil Bowers looked into her clear blue eyes, feeling his heart swell at the kindness and affection — and love — radiating from them. He stuck a hand into his pants pocket and fingered the small box he'd put there earlier.

"Not really. I'd mind it more if you were boring. And, Emma Whitecastle, you are anything but boring." After looking around, he changed his mind and removed his hand from his pocket, using it to cup her cheek instead. He kissed her quickly again before they resumed their walk.

"So," he said, after they'd walked a few more yards, "what's the deal on this new ghost? Remember, I only heard your side of it."

He had asked about it over breakfast, but Emma stalled, saying she'd tell him when they weren't in such a public place.

The ghost of Tessa North had been reluctant at first, but she soon relaxed in their presence. With curiosity, she'd looked at Phil, who was staring in her direction.

"He can't see me?" Her question wasn't one of concern, but of interest.

Emma shook her head. "No, he can't. And he can't hear you either, but he knows you're there. He's a good friend of mine and Granny's." When Tessa said nothing more, Emma added, "Is there something we can do for you, Tessa?"

The ghost shrugged and moved away from the balcony doors. She drifted over to where Phil sat, as if testing whether or not he could see her, then moved closer to Granny and Emma.

"Granny asked me if I knew I was dead." She shrugged again, lifting her shoulders high with exaggeration as only the young can do. "I know I'm not like you, Emma, or like him." She pointed at Phil. "At least not anymore. But is this what being dead is like? Playing at the beach every day? Where are the angels? In Sunday school, we were told angels came to get us and take us to God."

Emma smiled at the young ghost. "You are dead, Tessa. You are a spirit now, able to come and go as you like."

"But you need to pass over to the other side," Granny insisted.

"Granny's right, Tessa. I'm not sure what's on the other side. Maybe God, maybe angels, maybe nothing but peace and bright light, but there does seem to be an orderly way of going about it. You can always come back here to visit, just as Granny does."

"But I can't go anywhere. I have to stay here and wait."

"Wait for what, Tessa?" As Emma asked the question, she noticed Phil become more alert, trying to fill in the blanks between her conversation and what he couldn't hear.

Granny drifted closer to Tessa North. "What are you waiting for, child?"

"For Curtis." Tessa said it as if it explained everything. When she received only blank looks, she added, "He told me he'd come back." She looked worried. "If I go somewhere, he might not be able to find me."

"Who's Curtis, Tessa?" Emma kept her voice in mother mode, speaking to Tessa as if speaking to her own daughter.

The ghost cast her eyes downward. Her blush was evidenced by her manner rather than by her colorless and hazy cheeks. She looked up and beamed. "He told me he loved me. He told me he'd come back."

Emma moved over and sat down in one of the chairs. "Let's talk about this, Tessa."

Following Emma's example, Tessa sat in the chair closest to the balcony. Granny stood near her. Phil watched Emma, noting that she was as comfortable talking to the air as she was speaking with him. When they'd first met, he'd called her psychotic; now he thought her amazing.

"Tessa," Emma began, keeping her voice kind and soothing. "What do you last remember? About being alive, I mean, and about Curtis?"

Tessa gave off a big sigh and scrunched

her pretty face as she tried to remember. "We were on the boat." A frown materialized across Tessa's brow. "Everyone was upset by the news and wanted to get away to relax."

"What news, Tessa? Do you remember that?"

"Of course I do. Everyone was upset about it."

"Who's everyone?"

Turning her face to Emma, Tessa looked at her in surprise. "Why, just *everyone.* Don't you read or listen to the news?"

Emma tried not to smile too much lest Tessa interpret it as mockery. She'd learned that spirits often have no sense of time or history. It could be that Tessa had no concept of how many years had passed since her death. She was still pretty sure Tessa was from the sixties, so she dug deep into her brain to unearth major news events of that decade. Since Emma wasn't born until the sixties, all the information at her disposal would have been learned from history books and stories told by people like her parents. She recalled that the sixties had been turbulent years — the Vietnam War, protest marches, the assassinations of both President Kennedy and Martin Luther King, the Cuban Missile Crisis — with any number of things that could have made big news.

"What specifically upset Curtis, Tessa?"

When Tessa spoke, her eyes were wide. "They were there, you know — at the Ambassador Hotel — when it happened."

The Ambassador Hotel. That definitely struck a chord in Emma's memory bank. She rooted around to grasp it clearly before speaking. "The Ambassador Hotel? You mean Curtis was there when Robert Kennedy was shot?"

When Phil and Emma reached the botanical gardens, Emma dug a water bottle out of the small backpack she was wearing and handed it to Phil. She dug out another for herself.

Phil took a drink and wiped his mouth with the back of his hand. "So now we know about when this Tessa died."

Emma nodded while she took her own drink.

"Kennedy was shot in June of 1968." Phil took another drink of water before continuing. "I was in junior high at the time. School was almost out for the summer. I remember it well."

"According to Tessa, this Curtis was at the Ambassador, attending the party for Kennedy. Said he was very upset for days after and came to Catalina on his boat to relax."

"Curtis who? Did she give you a last name?"

"Nope. Every time I asked, she dodged the question — and not very skillfully. It was almost like she was afraid to tell me."

"It might have been Curtis who killed her."

"Could very well be. She doesn't remember much right now, but she might regain bits and pieces of what happened as we talk. The last she remembers is that Curtis told her he'd come back for her."

Instead of his usual cowboy hat, Phil was wearing a ball cap to protect his scalp from the sun. He took it off and wiped the top of his bald head with a bandana from his pocket. "Hmm, she could have been hurt, and he went to get help but never made it back."

The sun was high in the sky now, and the morning haze was a memory. "That's a good possibility." Emma put on her sunglasses and studied the rugged terrain around the gardens. "I'm with Milo on the theory that Tessa died here on the island. And since she's wearing a bathing suit, it's probably a safe guess that she died in or near the water. I can't really see her up here or somewhere else away from the beach, can you?"

"Not if she's wearing a bikini."

Emma watched as Phil tipped his water bottle back again. "You're enjoying this, aren't you?" she asked him.

"Loving it. Catalina's a great place."

"I don't mean that. You're getting into the whole thing with Tessa, aren't you?"

He pointed a finger at himself. "Who, me? Nah." But his grin told the truth.

"Come on, Bowers," Emma teased, poking a short polished nail into his chest. "Admit it. You wouldn't be asking questions if you weren't interested."

"I'd be more interested if I could actually see the little hottie."

Emma shook her head in mock disgust and headed for the entrance of the botanical gardens. "Men. Even death doesn't slow you down."

Phil trotted after her. "Hey, hey, hey — in case you haven't noticed, I'm far from dead."

Emma and Phil spent the next couple of hours walking the gardens, their arms wrapped around each other's waists, enjoying their time together. There were many other visitors besides them, including whole families enjoying the long Thanksgiving holiday away from the bustle of city life. It made the two of them think of their own children.

"How about we all get together for Christmas in Julian?" Phil suggested. "Kelly, my boys, your parents, everyone. Aunt Susan would love it as much as we would."

Emma flashed him a big smile. "Ah, you read my mind. It can be the official launch of my cabin."

Shortly after Phil and Emma had met — and after she'd proven that Granny had not murdered her husband — Phil and his family had deeded the property once belonging to Ish and Jacob Reynolds to Emma. It was a small parcel directly across from the Bowers ranch. Emma had elected to build a vacation home on what was once Granny's homestead. Except for interior touches, the "cabin" — a three bedroom, two-story mountain retreat with two fireplaces — was nearly finished. She'd already spent some time there, and her mother had come down to help with the decorating, but Emma had never had her entire family down to Julian. Christmas would be the perfect time. Her mother and Phil's aunt had become friends, and she had no doubt her father, a retired heart surgeon, would fit right in with Phil's uncle Glen. And Kelly might enjoy the getaway before returning to her studies.

"Christmas in Julian? Hotdog!"

With a start, Emma turned to find the ghost of Granny Apples standing just behind her. She scowled. " 'Hotdog'? Where in the world did you pick up a phrase like that?"

As Emma talked to thin air, Phil noticed a few folks stare at her as they passed by. He gallantly shifted his position so that they would think she was talking to him. Emma talked so naturally to Granny that she often forgot about the living taking notice. It amused him to be her cover when it came to the spirits, though often the topic of conversation didn't suit how he wanted strangers to perceive him.

"I heard it on TV — that show your father watches."

Emma knew what show Granny was referring to. It was an old sitcom from the late fifties. Her father loved the show and watched reruns of it almost every afternoon. Granny often watched television in the den with him. She was especially fond of NFL games.

Although Paul Miller believed in Granny's existence, he wasn't keen on the idea of a ghost hanging around his wife and daughter. At first, Emma and her mother, Elizabeth, tried to keep Granny's presence a secret, but Dr. Miller was not a stupid man, and it wasn't long before he realized that the ghost of Granny Apples had returned and set up part-time residence in his home. He finally accepted her presence as he might an annoying mother-in-law. In the past year, he and Phil Bowers had had several conversations about it over beers, deciding it was part of loving the women in their lives.

"You are watching entirely too much TV, Granny." Emma kept her voice low and looked up at Phil as she spoke, grateful for his willingness to play along.

"I have a lot of history to catch up on. Seems to be the best way to do it."

"*Hotdog* is not history. It's slang, and outdated slang at that."

"Whatever." The ghost drifted off.

Phil knitted his brows in curiosity. *"Hotdog?"*

Emma waved a hand at him. "I'll tell you later." She followed the image of the ghost.

"Granny," Emma hissed at the spirit. "Have you talked anymore with Tessa?" Phil sidled up to Emma and linked an arm through hers, creating an image of the two of them sharing a tête-à-tête.

Granny drifted over to a nearby bench and sat down in the middle of it. Emma and Phil followed.

"Scoot over, Granny, or Phil will sit right down on top of you."

"Humph." The ghost crossed her arms across her chest but moved to the end of the bench. Phil and Emma sat down, with Emma in the middle.

"So, Granny, did you learn anything?"

"The girl's still saying nothing about this Curtis fellow. I think he's the one who done her in."

"Why do you think that?"

"I get the feeling he's the last one to see her alive. He told her to wait until he came back — said he was going to fetch help."

"So she was hurt?"

"Seems so. She doesn't remember much about it, except that there was a lot of blood and her head hurt. She remembers that. And that Curtis said he was going for help."

Emma leaned in toward Phil while she talked to Granny. "That doesn't sound like he killed her. He was going for help."

The ghost got up and moved within Emma's line of vision, her arms crossed in front of her to emphasize her point. "But he never came back, did he?"

FOUR

As they walked back toward Avalon Bay, Emma relayed to Phil the little information Granny had gleaned from Tessa. Granny had disappeared shortly after they'd left the gardens.

"Okay, let's review what we know so far."

"Spoken like a true lawyer."

Phil grunted. "What can I say, an occupational hazard."

Emma ticked off the facts in her head as she said them out loud. "First, we're pretty sure Tessa died here on Catalina, close to the water. We know she came here in June of 1968 on the boat of a man named Curtis. Somehow she was hurt, and Curtis went for help. He never returned."

"Correction," Phil interrupted. "We don't know that he never returned. He could have returned and it was too late. She might have already died from whatever injuries she'd received."

"You have a good point there."

"Counselor."

"Excuse me?"

"Counselor. You have a good point there, *counselor.*"

Emma shook her head and tried to suppress a laugh. "Have you ever noticed that when it suits you, you're an attorney, but any other time, you prefer to be thought of as a rancher?"

"I was a rancher long before I was an attorney. I only put the attorney hat on when it's needed."

"Like now?"

"Now seems as good a time as any to put all that analytical thought processes to work, doesn't it?"

"Correct . . . *counselor.*"

Phil put an arm across Emma's shoulders and pulled her close. "Now you're catching on."

"Okay," Emma continued. "To our knowledge, or from what Tessa told us, Curtis never came back, or she doesn't think he ever came back. And her ghost has lingered here all these years waiting for him."

Emma pulled her cell phone from her backpack and started dialing. Phil watched her with a raised eyebrow. She threw him a coy smile. "What's the use of having a research assistant if you don't use her?" He touched the side of his head with an index finger, letting Emma know that was smart thinking.

When Emma's call was answered by a voicemail recording, she said, "Jackie, it's me, Emma. When you get back into the office, can you do some research on a Tessa North? She would have been born sometime in the late forties. Probably lived in the Los Angeles area in the sixties, died June of 1968. I'm afraid that's all I have right now. Thanks a lot. Hope you're having a great holiday."

Jackie Houchin had been assigned to Emma by the studio. When her show was first being put together, Jackie divided her time between *The Whitecastle Report* and a weekly travel show. She was young, smart, and committed to a future in television, but Jackie had wanted no part of *The Whitecastle Report* when she'd first come onboard. Convinced that Emma was no different than her famous, hyped-up ex-husband, Jackie had been sure Emma's show would be nothing more than an hour of quackery. It had taken many months of patience and perseverance on Emma's part to prove to the young, serious woman that she was dedicated to producing a quality show with an objective view of people's beliefs in the paranormal. Jackie was still a skeptic when it came to such things, but she eventually became a fan of Emma's and threw herself into her work, wrangling guests and researching ideas she and Emma had for future shows. Together they made a formidable team, although Emma still had not enlightened Jackie about Granny's presence or her own talents.

Emma turned her attention back to her conversation with Phil. "Granny believes this Curtis killed Tessa. That he hurt her and left her to die."

"That's another possibility. In which case, it would explain why he might not have returned with help. It will be interesting to see what Jackie finds out. There might be some old obituary or even news about her death."

"And there would be a death record. Catalina is in the county of Los Angeles. I'm sure Jackie will turn something up like that." They were almost back to town when another idea stopped Emma in her tracks. "You know, Phil, on an island of this size, it can't be that common for people to die without notice, especially a tourist. I wonder if the police would have records on it."

Phil consulted the map. "The island is

policed by the Los Angeles County Sheriff's Department. There's a station here in town." He studied the town map again. "Looks like it's right across from where we caught that tour bus yesterday." They had reached an intersection. Phil looked up and studied the street signs. "If we turn left here, then right at Sumner, it should bring us right to it."

"Who knew?"

Phil looked up from the map. "Who knew what?"

"That a man would actually consult a map."

Phil folded the small map and gently slapped Emma on the behind with it. "Get going, Fancy Pants. There's a ghost waiting to go wherever it is ghosts need to go."

The police station looked like any typical municipal building in any other town, except that it was unusually compact. Stepping up to the counter, they were greeted by a small woman with very short dark blond hair. She wore the crisp uniform of the LA County Sheriff's Department. The name tag above her pocket read *Weaver.*

From her wallet, Emma extracted a business card. "Hello," she said to the woman, handing her the card. "I'm Emma White-castle. I host a TV show called *The White-*

castle Report. I'm doing research for a new show on ghosts of Catalina Island and was wondering if you could help me."

If Deputy Weaver thought the request odd, she never showed it, keeping her face as blank as a clean slate. "If I can."

"I understand a woman by the name of Tessa North died on Catalina about forty years ago. Would you have any records on that?"

"Deaths are recorded with the Los Angeles County Recorder's Office."

"Yes, I understand that," Emma explained. "We're in the process of obtaining those records. But if Ms. North's death was suspicious in any way, or if the sheriff's department was called in about it, would you have any records?"

"No, I'm afraid not," Deputy Weaver said with a slight shake of her head. "The sheriff's department came to the island in 1962, and our early records are not accessible. Anything prior to 1962 would have been handled by the former city police department, and I'm not sure they kept those records or where they would be kept if they did."

"We believe Tessa North died in 1968."

The young officer shook her head again, but her face remained unmoved. "I'm afraid records going back that far would not be readily available. But you might try the newspaper."

Phil moved closer. "Catalina has its own newspaper?"

"Yes, sir. *The Catalina Islander.* Comes out every Friday. It's been around almost a hundred years. If someone died on the island, even forty years ago, they would have noted it."

Deputy Weaver consulted a sheet near her desk and jotted something down on a sticky note. She handed it to Emma. "Here's the address and phone number for the paper. The office is over on Marilla, not far from here, but you should probably call first. I'm not sure how they've archived old issues, but they might be the best place to start. Another place you might try is the hospital, although I'm sure their records would be confidential."

After thanking the officer, Emma and Phil stepped out into the sunshine. "That was a good idea," Phil said, "sending us to the newspaper."

"Yes." Emma dialed the number on the note the deputy gave her but only received voicemail. Maneuvering through the voice-mail tree until she reached the editor, she left a message asking for a return call. After, she looked at her watch. "Wow, it's almost two o'clock. No wonder I'm hungry."

"Okay," Phil said, taking her arm and leading her down the street. "You marched me up the hill, now I'm going to march you down to the bay. Let's try that restaurant with the patio overlooking the water." He received no argument.

Over a lunch of bay shrimp salads washed down with cold beer, they sat side by side and stared out at the cheerful, sunny bay full of bobbing boats. Some were small, others full-blown yachts; most fell somewhere in between. Many of the boats' dinghies were gone, now tethered to docks at the pier while their owners visited the island for the day. The boats in the bay were moored in orderly rows like a neighborhood of tract houses separated by streets. All bows were pointed away from the island. Emma watched with interest as the harbor master's boat cruised up and down the watery paths, occasionally stopping at a boat or calling out a greeting to someone on a deck.

"Phil, do you think the harbor master could help us identify Curtis?"

Phil tilted back the remainder of his beer and motioned to the waiter to bring them a second round. "Doubtful. The records are too old, and all we have is a first name. Not to mention the records might not be public." After the waiter brought them two more beers, Phil glanced around the patio. "No sign of Tessa?"

"Not since this morning in our room."

"Are we alone, or is Granny around?"

Emma looked around the patio, noting that it was half filled with other diners. "Except for these folks, it's just us."

Smiling, Phil leaned back and fished something out of his pants pocket. He put it on the table in front of Emma. It was the small square jeweler's box he'd fingered earlier while they were walking. Emma gulped, worried about what was inside.

"Emma —," Phil began.

She cut him off with nervous stammering. "Phil, we've talked about this before. You know how I feel about you, but I'm not ready to make a commitment. Not to you, not to anyone." The words tumbled out of her, somersaulting onto the table, where they pooled liked spilled water waiting to be mopped up. "I was married nearly twenty years. So were you."

"But Emma —"

Again, she didn't wait for him to finish. "We both need time to rebuild our lives as individuals. To see where we're going before deciding if we're making the journey together."

Phil Bowers got up from the table. Emma went silent. Looking out at the bay, he took several deep breaths before sitting back down at their table, this time across from her. The box remained between them.

Phil fixed her with stern eyes and leaned back. "You finished?"

She wasn't. "I just don't want either of us to get hurt, Phil. We're both still raw from our respective divorces. I have Kelly to worry about. You have your boys."

"Just let me know when you're ready to listen." He took a long pull from his fresh beer and turned to study the boats again. A nearby couple looked over at them, then turned away.

They sat in silence. Phil polished off his beer. Emma picked at the label on her bottle. When the waiter came by to see if they wanted another round, Phil waved him off and turned back to Emma.

"Usually it's me who jumps to conclusions," he told her. "Not sure I like this change of roles."

Emma started to say something, then snapped her mouth shut when she saw the look in Phil's eyes — a mixture of amusement and annoyance, with the balance in favor of the latter.

"Emma, I love you, and I believe you love me, but I know neither of us is ready for a long-term commitment yet. As much as I'd love to spend every waking moment with you, it's just not possible right now with us living so far apart. You have your new career as a ghost wrangler, and I have my law practice. But I didn't realize it precluded me from buying you something nice once in a while."

Emma looked down at the small box, realizing too late she'd made a big mistake. All she could do was chew on the foot in her mouth. "Obviously, I've made the wrong assumption."

"Yes, Fancy Pants, you have." He gave a soft chuckle. "But, trust me, after this, if I ever do propose to you, I'll bring along a whip and a chair, just in case."

She looked up at him, her eyes starting to fill with tears. "I'm sorry I spoiled your surprise, Phil. It was stupid of me. I behaved abominably."

"No, Emma." He reached across the table and took her hands. "You behaved like someone still in a world of hurt and worried about being hurt again, contrary to what you say about being over Grant Whitecastle. You may be over him, but you are not over your divorce. We were both cast aside, and we both need time to lick our wounds. Fair enough?"

She gave him a small smile. "Fair enough."

He released her hands and picked up the box. "Of course, it would have helped had this *not* been a ring box, but it was the only box they had that fit what's inside."

"I don't deserve it now, Phil."

"Hush, darling. Let's just rewind the last ten minutes or so. Okay?"

She cleared her throat. "Okay."

Phil got up from the table. He stuck the box back into his pocket before sliding back into the booth next to her. After a few seconds, he dug back into the pocket of his jeans and produced the box, placing it in front of her.

"Got you something, Fancy Pants."

Doubt clouded her brow. "You think it's that easy to forget and move on?"

He looked into her lovely but still-watery eyes. "Most things in life don't come with the opportunity of a do-over. This moment does."

Her heart filled with relief as she leaned over and kissed him hard on the lips. In spite of his outside gruffness, Phil Bowers was one of the most decent and kind men she'd ever met.

After the kiss, Phil urged her to open the box. "I was going to give you this tonight at dinner, but earlier today, when you asked if I minded about the ghosts, I decided it would be fun to give it to you now."

Emma opened the box. After a few seconds of disbelief, she laughed out loud. Several people turned to look at them again before returning to their own business.

"Where did you ever find this?" she asked, still surprised. Nestled inside the box was a small brooch shaped like a ghost. Not the kind Emma saw, but along the lines of a bed sheet with eyeholes. Its body was outfitted with pavé diamonds. Two tiny sapphires staked out the eyes.

"I found it in a jewelry store near my office. Part of an upscale Halloween collection, no doubt." He took the pin from the box and fastened it to Emma's shirt. "Guess we're pinned now. Is that okay?" He winked at her.

"So it's true — you really don't mind the ghosts."

"I think of you and Granny, and even the others, as a package deal."

"Kind of a *love me, love my ghosts* thing, huh?"

Phil leaned over and kissed Emma's forehead. "Now you're catching on."

FIVE

"Phil, look at this."

They were in a small bookshop on Crescent Street. Emma had picked up a couple of books on local ghosts and was browsing through them, deciding which ones were worth buying, when a tidbit of information in one of them caught her eye. She carried the book down a nearby aisle to where Phil was checking out the latest paperback thrillers.

Phil read the heading of the paragraph indicated by the tip of Emma's finger. " 'Bikini Ghost.' " He looked up at Emma. "Is this our ghost?"

"Sure seems so."

Phil adjusted his reading glasses and read the small paragraph. "For years, longtime Catalina resident Mrs. Sandra Sechrest claimed that a ghost wearing nothing but a polka dot bikini has been haunting the beach in Avalon near the pier. To date, no one but Mrs. Sechrest has reported such sightings."

Phil took off his glasses and looked up at Emma. "So you're not the only one who has seen her."

"But why me, Phil? The other spirit sightings in these books have been witnessed or confirmed by several people, but Tessa was only reported by this Sechrest woman. Look here." Emma indicated the next paragraph. "According to this, the author tried several times to validate the ghost in the bikini but could not, and it states that the apparition is only mentioned in the book as a possibility. These other two books on spirits don't even mention Tessa at all — they only cover the usual historical sightings."

"How can you be sure Tessa is the ghost this book is referencing?" Phil grinned. "Who knows, there might be a whole bevy of dead bikini beauties out there."

Emma screwed up her face. "Somehow I doubt that."

She checked the first few pages of the book for a publishing date. "This book was published about five years ago. I wonder if Mrs. Sechrest still lives on the island?"

While purchasing the books, Emma asked the young clerk behind the counter if she knew a Sandra Sechrest. She did not but added that she was fairly new to the island. As soon as they returned to their hotel room, Phil plopped down on the bed with his new novel while Emma called information and asked for the number of a "Sandra Sechrest" or "S. Sechrest." There was no listing.

As soon as Emma settled down next to Phil to read her own new purchases, her cell phone rang. It was a man from the *Catalina Islander,* the local newspaper.

After a short introduction, Emma got down to why she'd called. "I'm looking for information about a death that would have occurred on the island in the late sixties, June of 1968 to be exact. I was told your paper might have archive copies going back that far."

"We do, but the copies are archived at the Catalina Island Museum. It's housed in the ground floor of the Casino."

"Would it be possible for me to look through them?"

"I'm sure they'd let you, but you might want to call first and make an appointment." He gave Emma the number.

Before disconnecting, Emma had one final question. "Excuse me, but have you lived on the island a long time?"

"Most of my life."

"Do you know Sandra Sechrest?"

"Yes, of course. Most everyone knew Sandy Sechrest. She was a colorful local fixture here on the island."

"Was?"

"Yes, Sandy died two months ago."

"I'm very sorry to hear that."

"Don't be. Sandy lived a long and happy life. She died of natural causes at the age of eighty-four."

"I picked up a book today that mentioned something about her seeing a ghost in a bikini. Do you know anything about that?"

The man laughed. "I've heard that story several times — not sure how much of it I believe. Sandy was a delightful but eccentric woman. After her husband died, she lived alone in a small cottage here in town, just blocks from the beach. Every day, rain or shine, she would walk to the beach to watch the sunset over the bay. Did that right up until the day she died. People often heard her talking to herself, especially when she sat watching the sunset. Guess she was chatting with her dead husband." The man's tone was one of affectionate amusement.

Emma's brain went on alert. "Did she always sit in the same place to watch the sunset?"

"Sure did. It was one of the benches near

the pier — on the right side of the pier if you're looking out at the sea. She was there every day like clockwork. Still miss seeing her. That's how we knew something was wrong. The day she died, she didn't show up. Someone went to her home and found her dead. Her heart had given out just a few hours earlier."

After the call, Emma made another, this time to the Catalina Island Museum. A recording informed her that the museum was closed until ten the next morning.

Phil had stopped reading and was watching and listening. "Good news or bad news?"

"A little of both. The good news is the papers are archived at the museum, and we can probably research them tomorrow when the museum opens. The bad news is Sandra Sechrest is dead. She died just two months ago at the age of eighty-four."

Emma left the bed and walked to the balcony doors and opened them. Stepping out onto the balcony, she gazed out across the beach and sea while her mind sorted through its own archiving system. Sandy Sechrest was the only person who had claimed to see a ghost in a bikini. And every day, Mrs. Sechrest had watched the sunset from a spot on the beach near the pier.

Emma turned her head to the right and tried to study the beach down by the pier, down where she had first seen Tessa North that morning. The sun was setting. She checked her watch. It was about four thirty. On a November evening, sunset would be very soon. As if in agreement, the twinkle lights in the palm trees came to life against the waning daylight. Emma shivered in the growing cold.

Dashing back into the room, she grabbed a jacket and made for the door to the suite. "Want to see the sunset?" she asked Phil over her shoulder as she yanked open the door.

Phil hopped off the bed, snagged his own jacket, and ran after her. "This a romantic stroll or another march?"

"I have a hunch. Hurry up or we might miss it."

Emma crossed the street in front of the hotel and moved fast along the beachfront toward the pier. Phil caught up and matched her long, quick strides.

"Miss what?"

"Sandy Sechrest."

"But I thought she was dead." When Emma gave him a quick glance, he added, "Oh, I see."

"According to the man from the newspaper, for years, every day at sunset, Sandy Sechrest came down to the beach to watch the sunset. It's just a hunch, but you never know."

They covered the distance from their hotel to the pier almost at a jog. Once at the pier, Emma slowed down and started scanning the various benches that looked out toward the ocean. What she saw made her screech to a stop.

"Wow."

"Wow what?" Slightly winded, Phil stopped beside her.

For a full minute, Emma didn't say anything. She wasn't sure how many there were, but it seemed Sandy Sechrest wasn't the only one who enjoyed watching the sunset. In the fading daylight, the shimmering outlines of spirits came into view like sequins scattered on a gray velvet gown. She turned slowly in a circle, taking in the section of beach they'd just passed, as well as the section ahead of them. The spirits — male and female, young and old — were all turned toward the sea, all watching the end of the day. Here and there were the living also watching the sun say good night, oblivious to the dead amongst them.

"What is it, Emma?"

She leaned in close to Phil so the live folks

nearby couldn't hear her. "There are many ghosts here right now — perhaps a dozen. They're scattered up and down the beach, watching the sunset like it's some sort of ritual."

Phil jerked this way and that, craning to see something, but he couldn't. "Are you kidding me?"

She shook her head. "I don't recall seeing them last night."

"Last night at this time," he reminded her, "we were having an early dinner at the country club." He pulled Emma close and whispered, "Do they know you can see them?"

"Not sure. But if they did know and were afraid, I wouldn't be able to."

As if answering Phil's question, one of the spirits nearest Emma turned and looked at them. It was a bent old man with a full beard. He nodded to Emma and gave her a quick impish wink, causing Emma to laugh.

"What?" asked Phil.

"They know. One of them, a little old gnarled man, just winked at me."

"You mean a ghost just hit on my girl?" Phil chuckled. "Not sure I like that. Doesn't he know we're going steady?"

"Smart alec."

"Hey, maybe you can fix the old geezer

up with Granny."

Emma took Phil's hand and started tugging him forward. "Come on, let's see if we can find Sandy."

"You have any idea what she looks like?"

"No, but I know she was very old when she died and should be on or near one of the benches on this side of the pier."

It wasn't difficult for Emma to spot a likely candidate as Sandy Sechrest. The ghost of an elderly woman sat on one of the tile benches. Her hair was white and worn in a short pixie cut on top of a round, wizened face. She was short and slightly plump, dressed in baggy trousers and a loose man's shirt with the sleeves rolled almost to her elbows. The shirt was plain except for stains that looked like paint splatters. Her face was turned to the sea, chin up, eyes closed, as if in prayer. At her feet sat a cross-legged Tessa North.

Next to the old woman sat a young live couple, bundled against the cooling night, kissing. Tessa looked up and waved happily at Emma. With her chin, Emma indicated the couple. Tessa caught on and nodded back with a giggle, as if keeping a delicious secret.

"You find her?" whispered Phil into Emma's ear.

Emma turned into him and wrapped her arms around his waist. "Yes, I think so," she whispered back. "On that bench over there with the necking couple. Tessa's sitting on the ground in front of the spirit of an elderly woman."

Shortly after, the young couple left arm in arm. With Phil in tow, Emma approached the ghost of the old woman on the bench.

"Mrs. Sandra Sechrest, I presume?"

Six

"Just Sandy, please." The eyes of the older ghost opened and fixed on Emma and Phil. "You must be Emma, and this must be your gentleman friend." Although her voice came out in the usual ghostly sounds, the words were direct and clear, with just a hint of the slight vibration that comes with age. "Tessa's told me a great deal about you."

The young ghost at her feet shot a smile at them both before popping up and running toward the waves, where she disappeared.

"Ah, youth," sighed the older ghost. "Even in death, their exuberance both entertains and tires me."

"May we join you, Sandy?" Emma asked.

"Yes, of course."

Emma sat down on the bench and indicated for Phil to sit next to her, placing him between her and the spirit. "Do you mind if Phil sits between us? That way people will

72

think I'm talking to him instead of to thin air."

"Good plan. I know for years folks thought I was crazy."

"So you could see and hear spirits before you died?"

"Yes, all my life, even as a young girl. People thought I had imaginary friends. When I got older, I learned to be more cautious."

"Were you afraid people wouldn't believe you?"

The ghost chuckled. "More like I was afraid they *would*. I had no need for either the scorn or the folderol that would come with it."

Emma looked out over the bay. "I know what you mean."

"I daresay you do, Emma Whitecastle of *The Whitecastle Report*."

Emma leaned around Phil to shoot Sandy a look of surprise. The ghost gave her a warm, knowing smile.

"Problems?" Phil asked. Emma shook her head slightly but kept her eyes on the ghost.

"I knew who you were as soon as Tessa gave me your name," Sandy told her. "I've seen your television show. Think it's first-rate. And you're very skillful at keeping your personal talents out of the limelight. To most, you're probably just a lovely and talented show host. But I knew the moment I first saw you onscreen that you had the gift."

Quickly, Emma gave Phil a summary of the conversation.

When she was done, Sandy asked, "You finally divorced from that scoundrel Grant Whitecastle?"

"Yes," Emma answered, no longer surprised at what Sandy said. "Nearly a year now."

The ghost looked Phil Bowers up and down. "I see you traded up."

Emma snorted with laughter.

"What?" Phil asked.

"She said you're an improvement over Grant. Said I traded up."

Phil glanced at the ghost. Even though he couldn't see her, he winked in her direction. "Damn straight she did. Nowhere to go but up from that fool."

With the sun officially down, the air was getting cooler. Phil drew Emma into him for warmth, holding her tight.

"Sandy," Emma continued, "I saw a small entry in a book about your sighting of a bikini-wearing ghost. But there was no mention of her in the other books I saw on Catalina spirits."

"That's correct. A few longtime friends knew I could see the spirits. The man who wrote that book was a friend and island resident. He passed away about a year after its publication. When he asked my permission to include it, I said yes, as long as he didn't sensationalize it."

"How long have you known about Tessa?"

"I started seeing her spirit many years ago. As far as I can tell, almost as soon as she died."

"In the late sixties?"

"That would be about right. For years, my husband and I came down here every evening for the sunset. One summer night, Howard and I were sitting here enjoying ice cream cones, and there Tessa was, playing in the surf plain as day."

"Could your husband see her?"

Sandy shook her head. "No. He didn't have the gift. But he knew I did and made his peace with it." She again looked Phil over. "It helps to have an understanding mate."

Emma turned her head toward the surf and waited a moment before speaking again. "I don't think Tessa has crossed over yet, Sandy. Have you?"

"My, yes. Couldn't wait." The ghost's voice took on excitement, and a wide smile crossed her hazy face. "But even before I died, I knew I'd come back here again. Howard and I still watch the sunsets together most nights, though he's not as diligent as I am."

"But what about Tessa? Have you encouraged her to cross?"

"Yes, I have. I've tried to explain to her that it's a simple thing, but important, to complete the process, like checking in and being accounted for, then she can come back. But she's stubborn. She's waiting for a man and is sure he's returning to her right here in Avalon." The ghost sighed. "I think she's afraid if she crosses over, she'll either miss or forget him."

"Tessa died forty years ago. If the man she's waiting for was in his twenties, then he'd be in his mid-sixties now, possibly older. He could already be dead."

"I don't think he is, Emma. Just a feeling I have."

"Did she tell you his name?"

"Only name she ever said was Curtis."

Emma passed along the information to Phil. "So," he said, "we're looking for a man named Curtis, who is older and used to come here on a boat."

Emma addressed the ghost. "Sandy, we want to help Tessa. Is there anything,

anything at all, you can remember that might help us find this Curtis? I think he's the key to helping her."

"Not this minute, but if I do, I'll find you. I'd like the child to move along as much as you would. I know it sounds odd, but she's become like a daughter to me over the years."

"Doesn't sound odd to me at all, Sandy. I have a daughter almost her age. I've wanted to help Tessa as soon as I first saw her." Emma paused. "There's something both sweet and tragic about her, isn't there? Something that brings out the maternal instincts."

The ghost looked at Emma and nodded. "Yes, there's definitely something going on beneath that naiveté. Makes you wonder what her story is. Something tells me it's a doozy."

After Emma conveyed the latest batch of conversation to Phil, they fell silent for a few minutes. Phil and Emma cuddled against the cold, Sandy gazed off into the sea; the three of them settled easily into comfortable companionship.

Emma broke the silence with another question. "Sandy, do you have any idea how or exactly where Tessa died?"

Sandy glanced at Emma, then looked back

at the ocean, her lined face screwed in concentration. "I'm not sure she even knows or remembers herself. She could have blocked it out or is in denial. I just recall her saying something about a loud noise and a blow or something hitting her. And blood. She did say there was a lot of blood. She's always said Curtis was getting help and coming back."

"We're researching the back issues of the newspaper tomorrow. Maybe there's something there that could tell us something."

The ghost shook her head. "Doubtful. I've read every issue of that paper since I've been able to read, even when I went to the mainland to live for a short while. A death on an island this size is always big news, especially the death of a tourist. There was never anything about Tessa's death in the paper, I'll almost guarantee it."

"That would mean she didn't die on the island then."

"There was never any mention that I recall about a bad accident involving a young woman either. Ever since I first met Tessa, I've been trying to figure out what happened to her."

Emma's mind tumbled over the possibilities until it settled on a hit. She sat at attention as she addressed the ghost. "Are you saying it's possible she died and her body was never found?"

The spirit of Sandy Sechrest got up and drifted a few feet, its image starting to fade.

"What I'm saying is, I'm glad you're here, Emma Whitecastle. If anyone can help Tessa, it's you."

"I'll do my best. If you remember anything and can't find me, try to find a spirit named Granny Apples. She's helping."

"I've already met Granny. She was with Tessa earlier." Sandy grinned at Emma. "That ancestor of yours is quite a pistol. Said she needed to find a TV. I sent her to that bar over there." The ghost pointed toward a beachfront cantina. "Didn't know they had television in her time." She laughed.

"They didn't. It's a modern bad habit she's acquired, along with a few others."

"Seems she's a Chargers fan." Again, the spirit laughed, this time with gusto. "Just when you think you've seen it all."

"The Chargers aren't playing today," Phil said after the spirit of Sandy Sechrest disappeared and Emma filled him in on the rest of the conversation. He and Emma were still on the bench. Huddled together, they watched the soft glow of evening break over the waves.

"Granny doesn't know that, Phil. I doubt my father discusses football season schedules with her." Emma gave off a slight chuckle. "I'm not even sure he realizes she watches the games with him."

"Maybe we should go to a game and take her along."

Emma sat up and looked at him with amusement. "You want to create a monster? Right now she thinks it's a game played inside a little box, like a movie. She'd be haunting the locker room if she found out it's real and found her way there."

"Never know, might help their game."

Emma got up from the bench and tugged on Phil's hand. "Come on," she said with a giggle, "let's go see if she's still in that bar. How does an Irish coffee sound?"

"Like medicine for my cold, achy bones. Lead on, Fancy Pants."

Seven

Granny Apples wasn't at the bar watching TV. Neither did she show up later that evening. Nor did Tessa or Sandy. Phil and Emma spent a relaxing, ghost-free evening and Saturday morning. After breakfast, they walked down to the Casino and the museum.

Built in 1929, the Catalina Island Casino is the most recognizable landmark on the island and graces the majority of postcards sent by visitors. Despite its name, there was no gambling. The magnificent, circular, Art Deco building got its name from the Italian meaning of the word *casino* — gathering place. Housing a grand ballroom and a movie theatre, as well as the Catalina Island Museum, it was the main venue for events on the island. During the island's glory days, it hosted many of the famous big bands and talents like Glenn Miller and Harry James. Even today, people flock to the island to attend special dances and events at the Casino. Although Emma had been inside the Casino many times, its overwhelming beauty and size never failed to stun her into reverence.

Sandy had said she'd never seen anything in the newspaper that could be linked to Tessa North, but Emma still wanted to go through some of the back issues surrounding the time of Tessa's death. She found nothing about a death or accident during the time period, nor did she find anything in the weeks or months following about a body being found. In all, their trip to the museum produced a big zero, except that Emma spotted the ghost of a woman dressed in finery from the early 1900s wandering the museum. It was one of the spirits mentioned in the book she'd picked up the day before.

"Did you see this?" Phil pushed an old newspaper in Emma's direction. "It's about Sandy Sechrest."

Emma studied the article. It was short in length and reported that island artist Sandy Sechrest was having a showing of her work at the Lighthouse Gallery.

"She's a painter," Emma said. "Makes sense. The shirt she was wearing appeared to be covered with paint splatters." She took note of the date on the paper. "Apparently, she was painting years ago and was still at it when she died." She looked at Phil. "How interesting."

"Wonder if any of her paintings are still around."

Before leaving the museum, they asked the curator about Sandy Sechrest.

"The Lighthouse Gallery closed down many, many years ago," the woman reported. "But Sandy's work is still being sold in several of the present galleries. She was well known for painting scenes of life here on the island."

After walking back to the main part of town via Casino Way, they consulted their guidebook for art galleries. At the first they struck out, but the owner directed them to another gallery on the next street over, saying that gallery had several of Sandy's paintings currently on display.

The second gallery was larger. There appeared to be a single clerk, and he was tied up with an older couple considering an original oil seascape. The clerk nodded at Phil and Emma when they came in and said he'd be with them shortly. They strolled the shop, which ran long and deep into the building. On the walls were many paintings, all by local artists, according to posted plaques. Most were of nature, with seascapes being the most common theme.

"Here's one, Emma." Phil was standing in front of a large oil painting in an ornate frame, peering at the plaque through his reading glasses. The painting was of Avalon Bay. There were a few boats moored in the bay, and from the clouds and sky, it appeared to have been a stormy day. "It says it was painted in 1997."

Emma read the plaque of the painting next to it — one depicting a fire ravaging a canyon. The painting was both beautiful and terrifying, and so realistic you could almost feel heat from the blaze radiating off the canvas. "This one was painted in 2007." Emma looked over at Phil. "I remember this fire. It almost destroyed the island."

"Most everyone was evacuated to the mainland, but I stayed."

Emma turned to find the ghost of Sandy Sechrest standing behind her.

"I painted several scenes from the fire, but they never sold well. People want happy and serene. They don't want to be reminded of catastrophes. But I felt the need to memorialize it. After all, it was part of island life."

Before answering, Emma glanced over at the store clerk. He was still busy with his customers near the front of the store. "You died while painting, didn't you, Sandy?"

The ghost smiled. "Yes, died with my boots on, so to speak. Was working on a wildflower scene when my heart gave out. Wouldn't have wanted to go any other way."

The ghost drifted deeper into the store. "There are several more of my paintings here, but this is the one I'd like you to see." She stopped in front of a medium-sized oil of Avalon Bay during the height of summer tourism. The bay was filled with moored boats. The sun was high. But the painting focused on the people filling the beach. They sat on towels or in beach chairs or cavorted in the surf. Children played with pails and shovels. The plaque said it was completed in 2006, but something was off.

"The clothing," Emma said, glancing from the painting to the ghost. "It's wrong for the time period during which it was painted."

"Very observant, Emma." The spirit moved closer to the painting. "It's of the time when I first saw Tessa. I wanted to preserve it. Should have painted it years before."

Emma pointed to a prominent and familiar figure standing knee deep in the surf, one arm in the air waving playfully at something or someone. The figure in the painting wore a pink polka dot bikini and a flip hairstyle. "That's Tessa."

"Yes. It's what I recall seeing just after she started showing up. Of course, I took liberties with the color of her swimsuit, since I couldn't tell what it was by looking at her spirit. Always thought it might be pink though." Sandy stopped studying her painting and faced Emma. "Something happened to that girl, Emma, something terrible. I'm certain of it. I should have looked into it myself back then, but I didn't. I painted this so she wouldn't be lost and forgotten forever. Call it her epitaph."

Emma showed the painting to Phil and relayed what Sandy had said. When she turned back around to the ghost, she was gone.

They were at a small beachside restaurant, relaxing and having a bite of lunch, when Granny popped up unexpectedly. "Movies." The ghost said the word in a blunt manner, like it'd been chopped off from a whole sentence. Startled, Emma started coughing on the bite of sandwich in her mouth.

"You okay, darling?" Phil handed her a glass of water.

Emma took the offered water and took several large swallows, clearing her throat.

"I'm fine," she choked out as she dabbed her moist eyes with her napkin. "Granny just surprised me mid-bite, that's all. You'd think I'd get used to it, wouldn't you?"

"Maybe we can put a bell around her neck, like on a cat. Or set up a special ring tone, like on a cell phone."

Emma and Phil laughed. Granny Apples scowled. "I ain't no darn cat. And while you two have been lollygagging, I've been working."

Emma looked around to make sure no one was within earshot, but they were the only people currently on the patio. Most were dining inside, where it was warmer. "We've been working, too, Granny. We've talked with the ghost of Sandy Sechrest. We're beginning to think Tessa's body was never found."

"A person doesn't just misplace a body." Granny twisted her pinched face from side to side and pursed her lips. "Seems to me that means murder."

"Quite possible. So, Granny, what did you say about movies?"

"Movies. Talking pictures. I think they have something to do with Tessa."

"Did she mention them?"

Granny moved her head up and down in short, mechanical movements. "Spent some time with the girl. She was chattering about motion pictures. Something about breaking them. My land, that lass can jabber — at least about everything *not* having to do with Curtis or why she's dead."

Emma gave Phil a quick summary.

He thought a minute. "Could Tessa have meant breaking *into* the movies?"

Emma turned back to the ghost. "Did Tessa say she was in the movies, Granny? Was she an actress?"

Granny gave the question serious thought. "I just recollect her saying that breaking movies was exciting."

Emma whipped out her cell phone and punched the speed dial for Jackie Houchin. Again, she reached only voicemail. "Jackie, on that info I need for Tessa North, also check to see if she might have been an actress. Probably was just starting out in the sixties."

After closing the phone, she said, "Good work, Granny. That information could be a very big help."

"Humph, glad some of us are working. How long is this holiday of yours anyway?"

"We're going home tomorrow morning, Granny."

"Good. I'm worried about Archie."

Their waitress came by to refresh Emma's

iced tea and Phil's coffee and to leave their check. Emma waited until she went back inside before speaking again to Granny.

"Archie? What about him?" Archie was the Scottish Terrier belonging to Emma's family. He'd been placed in an upscale doggie hotel for the few days Emma was gone. "Is he okay?"

Phil put down his coffee. "What about Archie?"

"He's lonely." Granny crossed her arms. "It's not good for him to be cooped up like that while you're off gallivanting."

Emma smiled, more to herself than to Granny. Like her, the dog could see and hear Granny. Emma had learned that most animals could see spirits, though few paid them any mind. But Granny and Archie had developed a close bond. At home, the ghost and the dog played together in the back yard almost every day.

"Nothing's wrong with Archie," Emma told Phil. "Granny misses him is all."

"Don't be ridiculous," huffed the ghost. "It's just a silly animal."

Phil turned in the direction Emma was looking. "Why don't you pop in and visit him, Granny? I'm sure he'd like that."

Emma shook her head. "Granny's not allowed," she explained. "She did that the last time we boarded Archie, and the other animals went nuts. Seems the other dogs wanted to play with Granny, too. The kennel owners had no idea what caused the pandemonium, but they were sure Archie was the root of it. Told us if it happened again, he'd not be welcomed back."

Emma turned back to Granny. "I'll be home tomorrow, Granny. I'm picking Archie up on the way back to the house. Then you two can have a nice long visit."

The ghost was not mollified. "Just foolishness, that's all." Granny's scowl deepened before she disappeared.

"From the look on your face," Phil said, after taking a deep swallow of coffee, "I'd say we're alone again."

Emma threaded an arm through his and leaned into him. "That we are, and maybe for the rest of the trip if you're lucky, cowboy."

"But?"

"What but?" Emma looked at him. "Did I add a but?"

"Not in words, but I can see your mind whirring like a turbine engine. We may be alone physically, but Tessa and her problem are with us mentally. You're thinking about the movie connection, aren't you?"

"Guilty, counselor." Emma looked out at

the sea and sighed. "I just wish I'd brought my laptop."

"Had you, I would have thrown it into the ocean. Hell, I'm a lawyer, and I didn't bring mine."

Emma looked sheepish. "I know, but I'd love to take a peek at IMDB."

"Okay, I'll bite. What's IMDB?"

"The Internet Movie Database. A website containing information about movies, actors, directors, TV shows — anything and everything put on film."

"Won't Jackie check that site?"

Emma hemmed and hawed. "Of course she'll check it," she finally admitted.

"I see, but you don't want to wait for her. You want to check it now. Doesn't your cell have an Internet connection?"

"Yes, but websites are sometimes difficult to read because of its size." She shrugged. "Guess there's no harm in waiting until either Jackie calls or I get home tomorrow."

"Except that you'll have ants in those fancy pants of yours."

Phil stood up. Pulling out his wallet, he dug out some bills and left them with the check. "Come on, let's see what we can do about satisfying your curiosity."

Phil took Emma by the hand and guided her back to their hotel. Once there, he approached the front desk.

"Do you have a business center with computers for guest use?" he asked the clerk, a young Latino in an impeccable suit and slicked-back hair.

"No, sir, I'm sorry. We have a business center but no public computers." When they started to walk away, the clerk added, "But you might try the library. They have public computers with Internet service."

Emma perked up. "Would the library be open today?"

"Yes, ma'am. It's open every Saturday until five o'clock. You'll find it a few blocks over on Sumner, right next to the police station. Do you need a map?"

Phil smiled at the young man. "We know where the police station is. Thanks for your help."

At the library, Emma logged on to the IMDB website and did a search for Tessa North. Her name yielded a hit. Emma clicked on the link.

"It says here she was in five movies and two TV shows, all bit parts."

Phil looked over her shoulder. "Any personal information?"

Emma moved the mouse over another link. "Here's something interesting. Seems Tessa was born Theresa Nowicki on May

26, 1946. Doesn't give a city, just Nebraska."

"That would have made her twenty-two-years old at the time of her death." Phil picked up a stubby library pencil and a scrap of notepaper from a supply kept on the desk. He started scribbling down the information.

Emma went back to the short list of films, opening each link and studying the information. On the third film, she saw a name that made her freeze. "Phil, I think I found a lead."

"To her death?"

"I hope not, but it might lead to more information."

With an index finger, she stabbed at a spot on the screen. It was a list of people connected with the movie. Phil read the entry out loud in a quiet voice. "George Whitecastle, director." He turned to look at Emma, his eyes wide. "Hey, isn't that —"

Emma cut him off. "It sure is."

It was Phil who broke the awkward silence brought on by the discovery on the computer. "Just because your ex-father-in-law directed one of Tessa's movies doesn't mean he knows anything about her. She was a bit player. He might not even remember her at all."

"I know, Phil, but maybe he *will* remember her. And if he does, he might remember someone named Curtis. I know it's a long shot, but it's worth a try. The Whitecastles are very nice people. I'm sure George will help me if he can. And look here." She pointed to another name connected with the movie. "Paul Feldman produced this film. He's a very close friend of George's. I've known him for years, too."

After seeing George's name, Emma got an idea. Methodically going down the list of people involved with each movie and TV show in which Tessa appeared, she looked for someone named Curtis. Nothing showed up. But Emma knew not all people involved with films were listed. There were always people behind the scenes, money people, as well as worker bees.

As soon as they left the library, Emma called the home of her former in-laws. A maid answered and informed her that the Whitecastles were not expected home until Monday afternoon.

"Now what would you like to do, Emma?" They were standing on the sidewalk on Crescent Street. Ahead of them was the bay; behind them, the town. People walked past them in both directions. Soon it would be sundown.

Emma gave him a suggestive glance. "It's our last night on Catalina. I say we watch the sunset, put the hot tub to good use one last time and, if so inclined, head out for a romantic dinner." Before he could respond, she added, "The ghosts are only invited to the first part."

"Fancy Pants, I like your style."

"But first, there's one last errand I need to run."

As the sun went down on their last night on Catalina, Phil and Emma joined Sandy Sechrest on her bench. With her was another ghost, that of an elderly man whom Sandy introduced as her husband, Howard. The two couples, living and dead, sat companionably side by side and watched the sun disappear. The women were in the middle.

"I bought your painting today, Sandy," Emma told the spirit. "Just before I came to watch the sunset."

"The one with Tessa?"

"That's the one. I'm going to put it in my office to remind me of you and my time here on Catalina." The ghost smiled with pleasure.

After waiting a moment, Emma asked Sandy, "Did Tessa ever tell you she was an actress?"

The spirit knitted her brows in thought. "Can't remember exactly. She talked a lot about the movies, but I thought it only the star-struck fancy of a young girl."

"Seems it was more than that. She appeared in a handful of films and a couple of TV shows. Nothing major, mostly bit parts in silly things. I'm wondering if that was how she knew Curtis."

"I'm afraid I can't help you, Emma. Sorry."

"It's okay. I have connections in Hollywood through Grant's family. I'm going to check with them." Emma looked at the ghost, not caring if any live people noticed. "Sandy, it has been a pleasure getting to know you. I hope we meet again. Feel free to come visit me and Granny on the mainland."

The ghost smiled at her and placed a hazy hand on top of one of Emma's. Emma couldn't feel the hand but was touched by the gesture. "You'll have to come here for those visits, Emma. Except for minor surgery about six years ago, I haven't left my beloved island in over fifteen years."

Emma glanced at Phil and smiled. "Guess we'll just have to come back, then."

EIGHT

Even though she knew the way, a uniformed maid led Emma upstairs and into George Whitecastle's private study. It was the Tuesday after Thanksgiving. Emma had called George that morning, hoping to get a green light for an unplanned visit. A little over an hour later, she was kissing her ex-father-in-law on his sunken cheek.

"Thanks for seeing me, George."

He smiled warmly at her, then shifted his frail body in his large leather chair until he found a comfortable spot. The chair was dark red and had been his favorite for as long as Emma could remember. Across his lap was a blue and gold throw sporting the UCLA Bruins logo. Like both Emma and Grant, George was an alumni of the university. Sprawled on the floor next to George's chair was an elderly Golden Labrador, its muzzle as white as its owner's remaining hair. The dog greeted Emma with solid whacks of its tail against the floor but didn't get up.

Emma squatted and scratched the old dog behind its ears. "How are you, Bijou? Still standing guard, I see." The animal licked her hand and thumped its tail a few more beats. Unsure of how Bijou would react to Granny, Emma had asked the ghost not to tag along. They would rendezvous later at Milo's place.

The Whitecastles lived in a small mansion in Bel Air, a very wealthy section of Los Angeles just off Sunset Boulevard near the UCLA campus. Like most rooms in the home, the study was large and filled with tasteful, expensive furniture. Two of the four walls of the study were lined with floor-to-ceiling bookshelves stuffed with books, memorabilia, and awards, including two Oscars, from George's long and illustrious career in the film industry. Beyond the bank of windows that looked down over the estate's manicured lawn, Emma could hear the sound of a mower.

"How are you feeling, George?" Emma asked as she took a seat on the sofa closest to George's chair.

"Eh." George held his hand out flat and tilted it back and forth with a slight movement. "So-so."

George had been diagnosed with lung cancer three years earlier, right after his last film was released. He'd held his own for a time, but in the last year the cancer had spread, taking no prisoners in its march to dominate his body. He'd once been a big man, strong and broad shouldered. Grant took more after his mother, whose build was slender and refined. It broke Emma's heart to see how the disease had ravaged George's body, leaving him a bag of bones and skin.

"Would you like something to drink, Emma? There should be some sodas and water in the fridge. Or I can have Helen bring you something else, like coffee or tea." George indicated a small wet bar located to the left of a large wall-mounted flat screen TV. The TV was currently turned to CNN, the sound muted.

Emma got up and crossed to the wet bar. "Water's fine. Can I get you something, George?"

George declined with a slight shake of his head. Emma pulled a bottle of sparkling water from the small refrigerator. She poured it into a crystal tumbler and returned to her seat on the sofa.

"Is Celeste home?" she asked.

"Not right now. She's out for an afternoon of lunch and shopping with her friends. I think there's even a trip to the spa planned somewhere in the mix." He sighed. "The sicker I get, the more she shops. As if it's a celebration."

Emma felt awkward. Although she knew no marriage was perfect, in the years she'd known the Whitecastles, she'd seldom seen or heard a cross word between them. She passed off George's remark as a bitter comment from a sick man. "I'm sure it's just her way of coping with everything, George. Everyone has their own particular way of dealing with stressful situations."

"And is your way going on TV with your own show?"

Emma studied George Whitecastle. His body may have been reduced to rubble, but not his quick mind and sharpshooter tongue. His days of directing movies were over, but he was still involved with the business, as evidenced by the stacks of scripts littering the desk and table next to his chair.

"Actually," Emma explained, "the producers approached me about the show, not the other way around. A friend referred me to them. It never occurred to me until then to have anything to do with show business."

"And how are the ratings?"

Having no doubt that George had been following *The Whitecastle Report*'s progress,

Emma flashed her ex-father-in-law a smirk. "I'd be surprised, George, if you didn't know them better than I do."

The sick man let out a weak snort that deteriorated into a ragged cough. Emma stood up and went to his side. She picked up a glass of water from the table next to him and offered it, balancing the glass while he held it with shaking hands and took several long drinks from a straw, sputtering slightly between each one.

"Thank you, Emma," he said when he was finished. He wiped his mouth with a large cotton handkerchief clutched in one hand.

"Should you be here alone?" She remained hovered in concern over the man who'd been like a second father to her.

"The maid's here, and a nurse comes in twice a day — all day on the maid's day off." He pointed to a small buzzer attached to a cord next to his chair. "I just have to hit this and someone will come." His voice was raspy. "Just that the coughing knocks the shit out of me."

"Maybe I should come back another time?"

George shook his head. "No, my dear, no. I've always enjoyed your company. Damn son of mine is a fool. Should have had two daughters, not one of each. Think it's too late to trade Grant to the Millers in exchange for you?"

Emma laughed. "Not sure my parents would find that an equal exchange. Grant's not exactly a favorite topic with them." After patting the old man's arm, she sat back down on the sofa. "And how is Deirdre?" she asked, referencing Grant's older sister.

"Fine as ever. We all went up to their home in Santa Barbara for Thanksgiving. Celeste and I stayed the weekend. Grant and his brood returned to LA Thursday evening." His final words drifted off, as if he wished he hadn't said them.

"Sounds lovely." Emma tried to keep her voice even to assure George that whatever Grant did, it didn't matter to her anymore.

"Very tiring for me, but worth it to see everyone together, even if Grant and Deirdre don't get along that well. Deirdre's family asked after you and Kelly. Celeste happily filled them in on Kelly's schooling and your show." He paused to take a breath.

"I'm tiring you."

"Nonsense." He waved off her concern. "Most days I sit here alone. Feels good to have an intelligent conversation with someone I care about." He took another deep breath, this time keeping the cough at bay. "You still seeing that guy from Julian?"

"Yes, I am. In fact, Phil and I went to Catalina over the holiday."

"Catalina." George said the word softly, tasting it like a long-forgotten favorite food.

He closed his eyes and leaned his head, with its thinning white hair and translucent skin, back against the fine grain of the leather — his skull a pale yolk in a pool of dried blood. For one startling moment, Emma thought he'd died. Then he smiled and opened his eyes.

"It's been a long time since I've been to Catalina. Used to go there on fishing trips with buddies, mostly from the industry. Decades ago, it was the scene of many wild parties." George gave a little cough into the handkerchief before continuing. "Later, we went there as a family. With you and Kelly, too. Remember that?" Emma nodded. George closed his eyes again. "Happier times, that's for sure. Or at least healthier ones."

After giving George a moment to rest, Emma opened up the topic of Tessa North. "George, do you remember a young actress from years ago named Tessa North?"

George remained still. Emma wondered if he'd heard her. She was about to repeat the question when he asked, "Should I?"

"She was in one of your movies from the

sixties. A film called *Beach Party Prom*."

The mention of the film's title caused George Whitecastle to give off a strong but short laugh, followed by more coughing. "Now there's a title I'd hoped never to hear again." He looked at Emma, his tired eyes circled with mirth. "Where in the hell did you ever uncover that asinine thing?"

"When I was on Catalina Island, the name Tessa North came up. Research on her connected me to that movie, then to you."

George adjusted himself in his chair before answering. "Everyone was doing those awful teen beach movies back then. They were moneymakers, no matter how bad they were."

"Do you remember Tessa? Her real name was Theresa Nowicki. She was a bit player in the movie — one of the beach bunnies."

He knitted his brows and thought a minute before answering. "Sorry, neither name sounds familiar. But then I never remember extras from current films, let alone . . . damn, what was that . . . thirty-five, forty years ago?"

"Just over forty."

George fixed his aging eyes on his former daughter-in-law and studied her. "Why the interest in a nobody from the sixties?"

Emma wasn't sure what to tell George.

She didn't know how much he knew, if anything, about her clairvoyant activities. Grant and his family might not know at all, unless Kelly told them, but she doubted her daughter would do that. Kelly had been on vacation with her father when Emma initially came face to face with the spirit world, but when her daughter returned home, Emma had sat her down and explained the situation. At first shrouded in disbelief, Kelly eventually came to understand that her mother had a special skill — her grandmother, too, though not at the same level. Elizabeth Miller could hear Granny but not see her. It'd made the girl ask if she'd discover her own clairvoyant talents in time. It was something both Elizabeth and Emma wondered themselves and discussed. Would the gift be passed along, generation to generation, like a specific hair type or nose shape? Only time would tell.

Like Emma's father, Kelly had made peace with the unusual dynamics that had come into their family, and she agreed to keep it a private matter as much as possible. But Sandy Sechrest had picked up on it while watching Emma's show. Was it because she, too, could see spirits, or because Emma unconsciously gave off a certain vibe about it? Either way, she decided to not make any confessions to George Whitecastle just yet about communing with ghosts.

"I was doing some research on ghosts that haunt Catalina Island, and her name came up as a possibility, along with Natalie Wood's. Of course, I already knew about Natalie Wood drowning just off the island."

George's mouth arched downward. "Yes, that was a very tragic accident. Left us all stunned."

"When I looked into the names of other possible spirits, the name Tessa North came up. Further research brought me to her acting career."

"What did she look like? Do you know?"

"I believe she was in her early twenties, very pretty, with a girl-next-door appeal and a great figure. She wore her blond hair in a flip."

George's mouth changed from down-turned to a half smile. "Wish I could help you, Emma," he said with a slight shrug. "But you just described two-thirds of the young girls who flocked to LA in the sixties. Take away the flip and you've described half of those who flock here now. Pretty girls with dreams of stardom are as common as dirt, no matter what the decade."

"I knew it was a long shot, but it never hurts to ask." Emma looked over at George.

He looked exhausted. "I should go and let you rest." She got up and gave George a goodbye peck on his cheek and Bijou several pats on his old head.

"Please come back more often, Emma," the old man said with genuine affection. "I miss you. So does Celeste. Come back and visit as much as you like. You're still family as far as we're concerned."

Her eye grazed over several groupings of framed photos scattered around the room. Photos of the rich and famous were clumped together with family pictures. She was in many of them, letting her know that George meant what he said about her still being family.

She smiled down at him. "I will, George. I promise."

Emma was almost to the door to the study when another thought occurred to her. She turned around. George had already returned his attention to the TV, using the remote to turn the sound back on.

"George, one last question, if you don't mind."

He muted the TV again. "Anything, dear."

She took a couple of steps toward him. "In all your trips to Catalina, do you recall a man named Curtis who used to go over there on his yacht? He might also have been involved with the film industry in some capacity."

George didn't answer right away, but Emma was sure his eyes went wide for an instant before melting into indifference. "Curtis? Don't recall anyone by that name. Curtis what?"

"Not sure. It was just a name that kept coming up in connection with Tessa. Could be his first name, or maybe his last. I only know he used to go over to Catalina on his boat in the sixties."

"Sorry, Em, but I'm drawing another blank."

Emma started to leave, but George held up a hand, stopping her. "You say this Tessa girl is a ghost that haunts Catalina Island?"

"That's what I've heard." Emma chose her words carefully. "A book on Catalina spirits mentions her. She supposedly died on the island in the late sixties."

Again, George Whitecastle's tired, runny eyes expanded for a split second, as if the tidbit of information had sent a small shock through his system. He turned his face away a moment. When he faced Emma again, he was composed. "Ghosts." He said the word with a half sneer. "I suppose that accounts for that pin on your sweater."

Emma's hand instinctively went to the

little diamond ghost pin. She'd worn it every day since Phil had given it to her. "This?" She laughed, again stepping carefully across the thin ice of half-truths. "Phil gave me this last week. It's a little joke between us."

The old man remained silent as he searched her face. "Emma, do you actually believe the hooey you discuss on that show of yours?"

Emma put her hands on her slim hips and narrowed her eyes at him in mild defiance. "George, in all honesty, there's probably less *hooey* on my show than on Grant's."

George Whitecastle tilted his head back and laughed. The sound was weak but steady before changing to a cough. Emma stepped up and again helped him with his water.

"Of that, Emma," he said when he'd composed himself, "I have no doubt."

NINE

"Do you think your father-in-law is telling the truth?" Milo asked as he handed Emma a mug of steaming tea.

After leaving the large and stately White-castle home, Emma drove to the small, compact residence of Milo Ravenscroft. They'd made an appointment to go over the information Emma had gathered so far on Tessa.

Although Jackie the Wonder Assistant had been diligent in her quest for information on Tessa North, aka Theresa Nowicki, she'd hit a brick wall. Except for the information on IMDB, the girl didn't seem to exist. But Jackie wasn't deterred; just the opposite. She was now on the hunt. She'd done searches on the name Nowicki in Nebraska and came up with a boatload of hits. She'd also run checks on several of the women who had appeared in various movies with Tessa and who were about the same age at

110

the time. Several were still in the Los Angeles area, and a couple were still acting. Armed with the two lists, she'd called Emma on Monday afternoon.

The two women decided to split the chores. Jackie would follow the leads in Nebraska, hoping to find someone related to Tessa. Emma would tackle the list of actresses. After calling three of the names on her list, Emma finally connected with a woman who remembered Tessa. She agreed to meet Emma on Wednesday morning at her office in Century City. Emma continued going down the names, calling one after the other. She struck out on four others and left voicemails for the remaining two names.

"No, I don't, Milo. At least not the full truth." Emma wrapped her hands around the sturdy mug of herbal tea and drew it to her, sniffing the aromatic blend with appreciation. "At first I didn't think anything of it, but when I mentioned Curtis, I'm sure George went momentarily bug-eyed."

"So you think he knows this guy?"

"Could be, or maybe it triggered a memory. For decades, the rich and powerful of Hollywood did a lot of partying in Catalina, and George was probably in the thick of it. In fact, I remember Grant saying something a few times about his dad being quite a playboy in his day."

"Like father, like son?"

Emma thought about that. "I always did think that Grant was trying to live up to his father's fame and reputation. George was larger than life. Still is, even though he's near death. He cast quite a shadow over his family, especially Grant."

A short silence fell between them until Emma put the conversation back on track. "When I mentioned something to George about Tessa dying on the island in the late sixties, I received the same quick, surprised look as when I mentioned Curtis."

"But he didn't say anything specific about it?"

"Nope. Just held on to his story that he had no idea who she was and that he knew no one named Curtis."

"Interesting."

"Yes. And each time, he turned his eyes away from me when he made his denial. Wouldn't most people continue staring in surprise?"

"Probably." Milo took a drink of tea. "Unless they have something to hide or are afraid of their eyes giving them away."

"Exactly." She took a sip of her own tea. "But that's not the real reason why I think George is lying."

Milo straightened his glasses and looked at her with eager expectation, waiting for the next tidbit of the puzzle. He found the machinations of the living much more baffling than the activities of the hereafter.

"When I was leaving the house, a car drove up to the Whitecastle's. Paul Feldman, one of George's closest friends and longtime colleagues, got out. He was the producer on that beach film Tessa did with George."

"Is that you, Emma?" Paul Feldman had said as soon as he spotted her heading for her own vehicle. He approached her with a wide smile. In his arms was a large white paper bag from which drifted a mouthwatering aroma. He shifted the bag so that it was cradled in the crook of his left arm and held out his right hand in a warm greeting. "What a pleasant surprise. I haven't seen you for a very long time."

She shook his offered hand and returned the smile. "I was just visiting George."

"I'm sure he appreciated it. He's rather homebound these days, the poor guy." Feldman shook his head. "Sometimes I think the inactivity is killing him faster than the cancer."

Unlike the tall, stately George Whitecastle,

Paul Feldman was a short, plump man with a bald head and close-trimmed gray beard. His rosy face and perky nose made him look almost elfin. While both men were in their late seventies, Paul Feldman was the picture of good health.

"It's nice that you drop by to keep him company, Mr. Feldman." Emma leaned forward and sniffed the white bag. "Is that bag from Nate'n Al's?" Nate'n Al's was an old-fashioned and famous restaurant and deli in Beverly Hills. Many a show-business deal had been brokered in its vinyl booths.

Paul Feldman laughed. "You know how George loves their food. I always bring matzo ball soup, pastrami, and corned beef when I visit. And pickles. Lots of pickles." He gave her a conspiratorial wink. "You might call me his dealer."

"I take it Celeste doesn't know about this?"

"Oh, she knows. Not happy about it, but she knows."

"Is it okay for him to eat this stuff?"

Feldman shrugged. "Considering his condition, what does it matter? It's one of the few pleasures he has left. That, and taking my money playing cards."

Emma smiled. As Feldman turned to make his way to the front door, she stopped him. "Mr. Feldman, you produced several of George's films over the years, didn't you?"

The pleasant man stopped and turned. "Why, yes; in fact, I produced his very first film. We were both greenhorns back then."

"Do you remember a young actress in the late sixties by the name of Tessa North? She was in *Beach Party Prom*."

Before Emma had all the words out, the deli bag nearly fell to the ground. It was only Feldman's impressive reflexes that saved it in the nick of time. "Look at me," he said shaking his head as he secured his valuable package. "Such butterfingers. George would never forgive me."

Emma was sure the fumble had less to do with Feldman's grip and more to do with the surprise of hearing Tessa's name. Next to George's display of barely discernable shock, Paul Feldman's reaction was an 8.0 on the Richter scale.

"So, you do remember her?"

Feldman studied Emma a few seconds before answering. "Yes, I remember Tessa. Why?"

Emma gave him her spiel about researching in Catalina and coming across her name.

"A ghost? Are you serious?" There was disbelief in his tone, but not mockery.

Before she could answer, he added, "Oh, but of course — George told me you were doing a show on the paranormal. He said it's quite good." It was high praise coming from either George or Paul, two giants in the industry.

Feldman shifted the large bag in his arms and held on tight. "I always wondered what happened to that girl. She was quite a beauty and very sweet."

"Considering it was forty years ago, you seem to remember her well."

He laughed, then leaned forward. The smell of warm deli meat surrounded them. "To be honest, I had a bit of a crush on Tessa. Admiration from afar, you might say. But she was very young, and I was very married."

"Do you remember anyone hanging around Tessa by the name of Curtis?"

Feldman ran his fingers over his beard. Emma wondered if the gesture was to steady his nerves or to help his thought process. "Sorry, can't say that I do. Why? Is he a ghost, too?"

Emma laughed. "No. Just a name that came up in connection with hers."

Milo put his mug down on the scuffed round table between them. They were seated in the large dark room he used for client meetings and séances. Around the room were various shapes and sizes of unlit candles and stacks of books. The books were not neatly filed onto book shelves, like in George's office, but mostly stacked on the floor in short, crooked towers, some leaning precariously.

Emma studied her mentor and smiled. Since she'd met him, Milo had spruced up his image. Instead of bent, thick glasses, he now wore fashionable ones. His hair was better cut. His clothing was updated but still casual. There was even a slight spring in his step.

"You look rested and relaxed, Milo. The trip to Chicago obviously agreed with you."

"Yes, it was very enjoyable." He smiled, but it was inward, not directed to Emma.

"So, when were you and Tracy going to tell me?"

Milo's face could have rivaled a ripe tomato. "Tracy?"

Tracy Bass was Emma's best friend and a professor at UCLA. It was Tracy who'd strong-armed Emma into attending the group séance at which the two of them had met Milo and Granny had made her first contact with Emma.

"Tracy went to Chicago over Thanksgiving, too — to see her family."

Milo shook his head in defeat. He wasn't a good liar and knew it. "I told her we should tell you, but she wanted to wait and see how things went with her family first."

Emma knew Tracy seldom introduced her lovers to her family. This meant the two of them were serious. Tracy's family were a well-to-do, ultra-conservative, and uptight bunch who considered Tracy a brick short of a load, in spite of her academic achievements. Emma could just imagine how Milo, a nerdy psychic, would go over with them. Thinking about it made her want to laugh, but she kept a rein on her giggles. On the other hand, Milo was probably the type of man they would expect Tracy to be involved with, even if not the type they would choose for her themselves.

"And how did it go?"

"Well." Milo said the word in a short release of breath. "I felt like a bull on the auction block for stud services. A skinny bull of questionable heritage, with one testicle missing."

This time, Emma couldn't hold it in. She laughed so hard tea ran out of her nose. Milo plucked a few tissues from a nearby box. "There's a skill I didn't know you possessed," he said, handing them to her.

"Sorry, Milo." Emma wiped her nose and eyes and tried to compose herself, but the giggles didn't want to stop.

"I guess Tracy's plan was if I passed muster with them, then she'd tell you. We've been friends since that trip to Julian but only recently became involved romantically." He took a long sip of his tea. "I guess the jury's still out in Chicago."

Emma shook her head. "It's not about what they think, Milo. Trust me on this. The test was if *you* didn't run screaming from the relationship after you met her family, then she'd feel safe to tell me and others."

Milo chuckled. "They were rather intimidating, to say the least. Her younger brother actually called me a freak to my face."

Emma laughed again. "Now you know why Tracy lives here and hardly ever visits them. She came to California for college and never looked back. Even my straight-laced family seems bohemian compared to hers."

"It was a true test by fire, and I have the blisters to prove it."

"But you didn't run screaming, did you?"

He gave her a nod filled with conviction. "Hardly. I'd slay dragons for Tracy."

Emma's heart swelled at the thought of Tracy finding a man who adored her as

Milo obviously did. She'd known something was up with Tracy for the past six months or so. She'd been secretive, and Emma had guessed that she might be seeing a new lover. She also had seen the early chemistry between Milo and Tracy but didn't think it had moved beyond friendship and a common interest in the paranormal. Tracy did not have any skills when it came to such things, but she was very interested in the field and taught a class on the subject at the university.

"You two going to yak all day, or are we going to help Tessa?"

Milo turned a big smile toward the ghost of Granny Apples. "Hey, Granny."

Neither he nor Emma were surprised to see her, but they had hoped she wouldn't be alone.

"Where's Tessa?" Emma asked, pulling on one of the shawls Milo kept handy for clients against the cold of the spirits. "I thought you were going to bring her here today."

The ghost set her face into its familiar scowl. "I said I'd try to bring her. Can't help it if the girl won't budge."

"She still afraid of missing this Curtis guy?" Milo asked.

"Stubborn as a goat, that girl is." Granny

paced the room, not in long strides but with graceful glides like an ice skater. "I tried to explain to her that she wouldn't miss nuthin'. That we were trying to help her find Curtis. Even that Sandy woman tried to convince her to come with me."

Emma sighed. "It's okay, Granny. We knew she might not be persuaded to come today." Her eyes followed the ghost as it crisscrossed the room. "Would you stay still, Granny? You're making me dizzy."

The ghost stopped on a dime, spun around, and disappeared. "Just give a holler," her disembodied voice told them, "when you have something useful to say."

Emma shook her head. "If Tessa's stubborn as a goat, then Granny's a mule."

"I heard that!" a voice called out of thin air.

"You were supposed to hear it, Granny," Emma called back.

"Ladies, ladies," interrupted Milo. "We'll never be able to help Tessa with all this bickering." He turned to Emma. "What exactly did you find out from your father-in-law?"

"Nothing more than what I already told you. He says he doesn't remember anyone named Tessa North or Theresa Nowicki. But he also said he hardly remembers any of his extras from movies." From the change in the air, Emma knew Granny had departed. She dropped the shawl from her shoulders.

Milo nodded while he jotted down a few notes. "Makes sense. I'm sure he's seen thousands of pretty actresses come and go during his career."

"But like I said —," Emma started, then paused. She had a notebook and pen. The notebook contained the notes she'd taken so far on Tessa North. She tapped the pen against the paper as she gave her next words more thought. "I'm sure I saw George's eyes widen when I asked about a man named Curtis who had a boat."

"Sure the question didn't simply surprise him?"

"It could have done that, too. But this looked like a spark of recognition, or even concern. I know it's not much. I mean, it's just a slight facial movement and one given by a man who is seriously ill, but something inside me sensed it was more. I just can't seem to pass it off as unimportant. And with the big reaction I received from Paul Feldman, I'm pretty sure he knew her, too. I'm also sure if I'd talked to Mr. Feldman after he'd seen George, I would have received a far different reaction from him."

"Very possible. George would have had time to warn him that you might be asking questions."

Milo closed his eyes and meditated on the situation a few moments. Emma remained still, not wanting to disturb his concentration. When he opened his eyes, he shook his head and said, "I'm not getting any grasp on this at all. Is there anyone else you can ask about this? Anyone else who might remember Tessa?"

"I've thought about asking Celeste, my mother-in-law. She might remember something about a man named Curtis hanging around George. There's also Worth Manning. He's another old friend of George's and, like George and Paul Feldman, he was involved with the movies years ago. The three of them were thick as thieves. Still are."

Milo's brows shot up. "Worth Manning? The actor turned politician?" He pointed a finger at Emma. "Didn't he retire from the US Senate several years ago?"

"Yes, that's him. Grant and I went to his retirement party. George and Celeste hosted it. His son, Stuart, is a bigshot in Washington now — a congressman with some pretty powerful friends." Emma took a sip of her tea. It was cool now, but she didn't mind.

A shadow tiptoed across Milo's thoughts like a cat crossing a grave. He closed his eyes again, inviting it to remain and show itself. "Didn't Tessa say something about the night Bobby Kennedy was shot?" He asked the question without opening his eyes.

"Yes. She said Curtis was very upset by the assassination. He was even there that night at the Ambassador Hotel. That's why he brought her to Catalina, to unwind in the days following it." She paused as Milo's line of thought occurred to her, too. "And Worth Manning was involved in politics, even forty years ago. I remember that from his retirement party. He has both the movie connection and the politics connection. He might know this Curtis person."

"He knows Curtis." The words were Milo's but said in an almost lifeless tone.

Startled, Emma stared at him. He was still seated across from her. His eyes remained closed. His body was limp. "Who knows Curtis, Milo?" she asked with caution, not wanting to disrupt Milo's concentration.

Milo didn't move, not even the flutter of an eyelid. "The politician. He knows Curtis."

It wasn't the first time Emma had ever witnessed Milo make a psychic connection. She'd seen it twice before, both times while sitting in on group sessions with clients. It was always the same. One minute he was engrossed in conversation, the next he seemed asleep, but he continued the conversation as if on autopilot. During these occasions, Emma wasn't sure if a spirit was talking through Milo or if his inner mind was seeing things his conscious mind could not. Milo believed it to be the latter.

Avoiding sudden movements, Emma slipped off her chair and made her way to Milo's side of the table in a slow, low squatting position.

"Worth knows Curtis? Is that true?" she asked in an almost whisper.

Milo, his eyes still closed, nodded. "Yes."

"Is this Curtis still alive?"

When she didn't receive an answer, Emma prodded carefully. "What is his full name? Can you tell me that?"

Milo's brows knitted over his shut eyelids. "Curtis. Curtis. Curtis. Tessa's Curtis."

"Did Curtis hurt Tessa?"

As suddenly as it had started, Milo snapped back to the present. His eyelids blinked rapidly, then flew open. He sat up straight in an abrupt movement and looked around, surprised to find Emma kneeling at his feet.

He blinked a few more times, as if assaulted by a bright light. He looked down at Emma, this time with clarity. "Worth Manning knows Curtis. I'm sure of it."

Emma stood up and patted Milo on his shoulder, knowing these events drained him physically. "That's what you said. Could you see anything else?"

"Not really. Just a lot of flashes. I tried to concentrate on all their names, but only Manning's got a hit. Even the name Curtis wasn't clear."

Emma sat back down in her chair. "That doesn't mean that George didn't know him, too."

"No, it doesn't. But as you know, these things aren't literal."

Picking up her pen again, Emma tapped the end of it against her notepad. "I've known all three of those men since I was in college, Milo. Over the years, they and their wives were at all major family events and parties hosted by Celeste and George. They were even at my wedding. They are like uncles to Grant. Considering George's reaction and what you just experienced, I'm guessing if one of them knew this Curtis guy, there's a good chance they all did."

"What's your next step?"

"Tomorrow morning I have a meeting with Fran Hyland, an actress who knew

Tessa. Then I think I'm going to have lunch with my ex-mother-in-law, if she's available. She's invited me several times now, but I've always had other plans. Seems as good a time as any to pick her brain. I'd also like to talk to Worth Manning — maybe even Paul Feldman again. That is, if George hasn't already gotten them together to compare stories."

Milo screwed up his face and stared at Emma.

"What?" she asked him, her pen in mid-tap. "I know that look. You have something to tell me that's unpleasant."

He nodded. "If Curtis killed Tessa North and these men had a hand in it, say like helping him cover it up, they might be considered accessories to a murder."

"It was over forty years ago."

"True, but there's no statute of limitations on murder. I'm not sure about any time limit on accessory."

Emma leaned back in her chair, considering Milo's words. The possibility that George might have been involved in the death of someone, even as a cover-up, settled in her gut like sour milk. She didn't want to consider it and turned away from the thought. George was her daughter's grandfather. "We don't even know if Tessa was murdered, Milo, so thoughts like that might be jumping the gun."

"Very true. If there's been no report of her death, then maybe her body was never found."

"That's the conclusion I came to after talking with the spirit of Sandy Sechrest."

"I hate to keep harping on the murder angle, Emma, but usually undiscovered bodies are the result of murder."

Milo was dragging her thoughts back into the shadows. Emma stuck out her chin. "Not always. You read about old bodies found all the time where people weren't murdered."

"From time to time, yes. But usually those folks died in a plane crash or avalanche in remote areas, not in a popular vacation spot."

Intellectually, Emma knew Milo was right. She wished for all the world that there had been no connection at all between Tessa and George Whitecastle, and maybe there wasn't beyond the fact that he had directed one of her movies. Maybe, she told herself, she'd only imagined his surprise when she'd mentioned the name Curtis.

"For now, though," she said to Milo after draining her mug, "let's just find out who this Curtis fellow is. He's the key to getting

Tessa to cross over, and that's our real goal, isn't it?"

"Sounds good to me."

Just as Milo spoke, the air in the room turned cool. Emma pulled the shawl back over her shoulders. "So, Granny," she called out, "you through pouting?"

There was no response, and the air continued to grow cooler, the draft moving throughout the room almost in a solid body. First the coldness drifted toward Milo, then shifted toward Emma.

"Come on, Granny, quit fooling around." Again, Emma received no response, nor was there any physical manifestation of the spirit. When she looked across the table at Milo, the hair on Emma's arms stood stiff as tacks.

Even though the cold draft was not visible to the eye, the trained senses of Milo Ravenscroft followed its path as it drifted with purpose around the room. It seemed to be checking them out, watching them, taking their measure.

"That's not Granny, is it, Milo?" Emma's voice was low and cautious. She hugged herself, more against the unknown than the cold.

"No, it's not." Milo didn't look at her when he spoke, but kept his eyes trained on the invisible air current, following it with his inner guides more than with his eyes. "What's more, I'm not sure it's friendly."

Emma tried to follow Milo's lead, concentrating on the moving draft.

"Whoever you are," Milo called to the spirit, "make yourself known." His voice was gentle yet commanding. "We are friends to those who have passed."

At his words, the draft picked up speed, swirling and buffeting them as if driven by a large oscillating fan. The drapes moved. Wisps of Emma's hair lifted and fell against her face. One of the teetering stacks of books fell.

Then it was gone.

TEN

Emma sat across the white linen-covered table from Celeste Whitecastle. It was the day after her visit with George, and they were at Celeste's favorite lunch spot, a small, tucked-away bistro on Rodeo Drive in Beverly Hills with an exclusive clientele. From the street it looked like a smart but tiny café, but once inside patrons could bypass the small dining room and walk toward the back to a private courtyard where more dining tables awaited. The courtyard was landscaped with well-placed potted shrubs and flowers, giving each table a sense of privacy. The centerpiece of the courtyard was a stone fountain that gurgled happily as it serenaded the toney diners. Emma loved the place almost as much as Celeste did. It reminded her of the cafés she had visited in Paris.

Originally scheduled to meet with Fran Hyland at ten o'clock, Ms. Hyland's assistant had called the afternoon before and asked Emma if the meeting could be moved until the afternoon. With the restaurant and Hyland's office only about a mile apart, Emma called Celeste, hoping to set up the luncheon before her appointment. She was pleased when Celeste quickly agreed to the date and place, and even more pleased to get a reservation. Emma had been shameless in using the Whitecastle muscle to gain the latter.

Menu in hand, Emma looked around the charming restaurant courtyard. "I haven't been here in a long time."

Celeste smiled. "I think the last time we were here together was when we took your mother out for her birthday. Remember that, Emma?"

"Yes, of course. It was a lovely day. That was what, two years ago?"

"Almost three."

Emma put down her menu and reached across the table to pat Celeste's hand. "I'm sorry it's been that long, Celeste. Really, I am."

Celeste put her hand over her former daughter-in-law's and squeezed it quickly before drawing it away. "It's understandable, dear. You've been through a lot in the past few years. But it looks like things are much better for you now." She picked up her own menu and started reading it, even though she knew it by heart. "I'll have you know, I've never brought Carolyn here, and I never will. She's more the taco truck type."

Inwardly, Emma laughed at the comment, wondering what Celeste would think if she knew that Phil Bowers had recently introduced her to the dining delights of neighborhood taco trucks. "That's not necessary, Celeste. This is hardly a competition."

Celeste set the menu down on the edge of the table and looked at Emma with the wise study of a martial arts sensei. "Oh, but my dear, it is. It's always a competition where men are concerned, and don't you forget that."

Even in her early seventies, Celeste Whitecastle was a great beauty. She'd had work done on her face, but it was not overdone. She preferred to wear just enough lines to place her in her fifties rather than stretch her face into the clownish denial of an aging woman trying to recapture her youth. Who did those women think they were kidding? The more pulled the skin, the more it advertised "scalpel at work." Celeste's breasts, however, did scream "boob job." As long as Emma could remember, Celeste's breasts were high and perky, even now. No bra was that good. And no septuagenarian could boast natural breasts that looked spectacular in a bikini top. Not many forty-year-olds could either.

Celeste's hair was the color of pale gold and worn shoulder-length. Today it was swept back tight from her face and captured at her nape with a tortoiseshell clip. She was a thin woman with eyes the color of a mourning dove and an aristocratic head held aloft by a long, stately neck. Her clothing — wool pants, cashmere turtleneck sweater, and matching coat — were by a famous designer and all in winter white. Everything about Celeste Whitecastle was impeccable and elegant, from her makeup and pearl and diamond earrings down to the nails at the tips of her ring-adorned fingers. Emma had worn gray lightweight wool slacks and a pale pink, long-sleeved silk sweater. Her own ensemble was also designer labeled, but unlike Celeste's outfit, Emma's had come off the rack.

Celeste reminded Emma of a crown jewel. She was Hollywood royalty, with all the bearing and protocol of the real royals running around Europe. Elizabeth Miller and Celeste Whitecastle had hit it off when they first met back when Grant and Emma had been college students in the first blush of love. But Emma's mother, while beautiful and elegant in her own well-kept way, also managed to exude a natural warmth toward friends, family, and even strangers. Even Grant had commented on the difference between the two women and often said he was more comfortable around Elizabeth. Elizabeth Miller could go easily between kitchen and garden, then on to a formal affair with little fuss. Celeste, on the other hand, was like a fine porcelain museum piece best shown in a glass case with a velvet lining.

Not for the first time, Emma wondered if Grant had married her hoping to marry a woman like his mother — again, possibly competing with his father. Both Emma and Celeste were slender and blond, with fine features and a flair for presentation. One of the things that broke up Emma's marriage, besides Grant's infidelity, was his insistence that Emma have breast surgery. Funny thing: when Grant cheated, none of his flings had looked like either she or Celeste. It made Emma wonder if he would have married Carolyn Bryant if she'd not gotten pregnant.

Emma was about to ask Celeste what she meant by competition when a man approached their table. He was in his late fifties, with ramrod posture and silver, wavy hair. Dressed in a stylish dark suit and tie, he looked more like an old world duke than a restaurant owner. Behind him hovered the spirit of an elderly portly man that Emma recognized immediately. The ghost playfully winked at her.

"It's a pleasure to see you again, Mrs. Whitecastle," the man said to Celeste with a courtly bow.

"Good afternoon, Peter."

He bowed in Emma's direction. "And you also, Mrs. Whitecastle."

Emma nodded back with a small sympathetic smile. "Thank you, Peter. And I'm sorry about your father. He will be missed."

A flash of surprise crossed Peter's face, but he held his considerable composure. "Thank you, Mrs. Whitecastle."

"I'm sorry," a surprised Celeste interrupted. "What about Edmund?" she asked, referring to Peter's father. "I know he's been ill lately."

Peter turned to Celeste. "I'm afraid Edmund . . . my father . . . passed away two weeks ago, madam."

Surprised by the news, Celeste pressed a hand to her heart, then quickly extended it to Peter. "My condolences, Peter, to you and your family. Edmund was a lovely and gracious man."

He took Celeste's offered hand and bowed quickly over it. "Thank you, madam. My father started this restaurant. It won't be the same without him."

Emma glanced over at Edmund's ghost and smiled. "Something tells me, Peter, your father's presence will always be felt."

"I certainly hope so." Peter quickly cleared his throat and turned to Celeste, ready to conduct business. "Today, madam, we have the cauliflower purée you like so well."

At Peter's direction, a young waiter placed thin-stemmed glasses of water and lemon in front of them and followed up with a basket of fragrant flatbreads. Then he took their orders. Celeste ordered the cauliflower purée, followed by the grilled chicken and fresh pear salad. Emma ordered the soup with a seared ahi tuna salad. Before leaving, Peter asked if they were comfortable and offered to turn on the tall space heater near their table. The two women said they were fine. With a half bow, he left to attend to the other wealthy and famous patrons scattered around the courtyard.

Celeste leaned toward Emma and whispered, "How did you know Edmund had died?"

Passing off the question lightly, Emma

answered, "I heard it somewhere."

"The restaurant was closed for a week recently, but it was never clear why. I wish they'd told someone."

Emma watched as Edmund's ghost silently supervised the comings and goings of his restaurant. "Some people are very private about such things."

After a short silence, Emma returned to their prior conversation and the question she had wanted to ask. "What did you mean by competition, Celeste? Earlier, when you referred to me and Carolyn? I certainly don't feel that way."

With a small sigh, Celeste ran a delicate finger down the side of her water goblet. "What do you think Carolyn was doing all that time with Grant?"

Emma shrugged and picked up a piece of bread laced with fresh rosemary. "I always thought she was just one of his many playmates."

"And I'm sure so did my son. But while you and Grant were playing marital tug-of-war, Carolyn was playing her own game. And she was playing to win, my dear."

"Excuse me, Celeste, if I don't find my failed marriage a suitable topic of sport and entertainment, although the tabloids certainly did." Emma took a small bite of bread, chewed, and swallowed. "If it was a game, it was one I didn't wish to play any longer, nor did I think Grant a prize worth keeping."

With her water glass held close to her face, Celeste watched Emma over the rim before taking a drink. When she put the glass down, a dainty lipstick smudge was left behind. "I hope you're not so naïve to think you were the first Hollywood wife to be cheated on. No-talent actresses like Carolyn are like barnacles. They find a sturdy ship, fasten themselves to it, and hang on. If they get knocked off, they'll find another ship." Celeste's voice was thick with amusement.

"I know it happens all the time. But if you'll recall, when Carolyn became pregnant, Grant made the choice for all of us." This was not how Emma wanted to spend lunch with Celeste, and she hated that she felt the need to add one last jab. "And quite frankly, if it was a game, I think I emerged the grand prize winner in the end."

"Son or no son, Emma, you might be right about that. Is that darling little bauble on your sweater an indication of something serious?"

Emma fingered the diamond ghost and smiled. "Phil and I are enjoying each other's company, but we're not rushing into anything."

"That's nice to hear." Celeste smiled at her briefly before dropping her head to dab the corners of her mouth with her napkin. When she leveled her gray eyes at Emma again, they were dark, like side-by-side caves. "I don't think Grant is happy with his choice."

"That's not my concern, Celeste. The only thing I have in common with him any longer is Kelly and my love for you and George."

The waiter came with their soup. The two women took their first spoonfuls in silence. The soup was the color of fine lace, with a delicate flavor.

"Speaking of actresses," Emma began, deciding to forge ahead. "Forty or so years ago, did you ever come across or hear of a young actress by the name of Tessa North?"

Upon hearing the name, Celeste Whitecastle's spoon hovered over her cauliflower soup like a hummingbird over a flower. It was a slight hesitation, no longer than the beat of Emma's surprised heart, but unmistakable nonetheless.

Celeste skimmed her spoon across the top of the soup. "Forty years ago, I was already retired from acting."

"That's true, but maybe you heard the

name. She was in one of George's films back then. The beach party one — *Beach Party Prom.*"

Celeste brought the spoon to her mouth but did not take the soup. Instead, she dribbled the creamy liquid back into the bowl and placed her spoon on the edge of the plate under it. Immediately, the young waiter appeared at their table and gestured if he should remove it. In silence, Celeste commanded him to take it away. Emma indicated for her own plate to be removed. Like magic, their salads appeared and were placed in front of them. Celeste pulled her coat over her shoulders. Emma didn't feel any change in the temperature but looked around just in case Granny or some other spirit had decided to drop in. She saw no ghosts except Edmund, and he was nowhere near them.

"Are you cold, Celeste? Should we ask them to turn on the heater?"

"I'm cold, Emma, but not with the temperature."

The elderly woman picked up her fork and started pushing pear and chicken chunks around like chess pieces. Emma took a bite of perfectly grilled tuna and waited.

Without taking a bite, Celeste put down her fork. The stately Peter floated to her side like an attentive courtesan. "Is the food not to your satisfaction, Mrs. Whitecastle?"

"It's fine. My appetite simply isn't with me today."

"Shall I remove the plate?"

"Not just yet, Peter."

Peter bowed and started to take his leave when Celeste stopped him.

"Peter, could you please bring me a martini. You know how I like them."

"With pleasure, Mrs. Whitecastle." He turned to Emma, awaiting her instructions.

"I'd like some herbal tea, Peter. Your special blend, if you have it."

As soon as they were alone again, Emma leaned forward. She could see Celeste was disturbed. "Are you all right, Celeste? Perhaps we should go?"

With a delicate hand, Celeste waved off the suggestion. "No, dear, I'll be fine. It's just . . . well. . . ." Celeste lifted her shoulders, then dropped them. "How can I put this?"

"Take your time."

Their drinks arrived. While Emma let her tea steep, Celeste swirled the olives in her delicate glass a few times before taking a taste. She followed up with a second sip, this one longer.

After putting down her glass, the older

woman looked around, making sure no curious ears were tuned their way. Then she turned her eyes on Emma. "The truth is, I never met Tessa North, but I know who she is . . . or was at one time."

Emma had just taken another bite of her salad. She paused mid-chew and stared at Celeste while sorting through her thoughts and matching them with Celeste's words. She didn't know if George had said anything to his wife about their conversation the day before or not. She swallowed her half-chewed food with a big gulp. Celeste answered the unasked question.

"George told me you were asking him about Tessa — something about her being a ghost on Catalina Island. Is that correct?" The cocktail seemed to be steadying Celeste.

Emma nodded while she washed her food down with some hot tea. She watched Celeste with eagle eyes. It was obvious the subject of Tessa North meant something to the woman. "Yes. I came across her name during some research. I just wondered if you and George knew her."

Celeste took a long drink of her martini. One more gulp and she'd be done with it. "I never met the girl in person, but I knew all about her."

She waved to Peter to prep another drink. "Why don't you eat a little, Celeste," Emma coaxed.

Like a child following orders, Celeste took a small bite of chicken and greens, chewed, and swallowed. With effort, she took another small bite. She drained her martini just as Peter appeared with her second. She swirled it around but didn't drink. Instead, she stared straight into Emma's eyes.

"Tessa North was almost my Carolyn Bryant."

ELEVEN

"What?" Emma heard Phil say through her cell phone earpiece, his voice full of disbelief.

"That's what Celeste said. Seems that not only did George know Tessa, but the two were hot and heavy, almost to the point of breaking up his marriage."

"So George lied to you. Didn't it occur to him you might ask his wife?"

"Hard to say. Or maybe he thought she'd never say anything. After all, to the world they are the gold standard of Hollywood marriages, and image is very important to Celeste. He might have thought she'd be too proud to admit she'd almost lost him to a younger woman." Emma checked her watch, making sure of the time.

"Then again," added Phil, "George is dying. Maybe he didn't care."

"Another good possibility."

Emma was sitting in her car in the parking structure next to the building that housed Hyland Staffing, Fran Hyland's company. She was a little early for her appointment, so she returned the voicemail Phil had left her while she was with Celeste.

Celeste's comment about Tessa had landed on the linen-covered table with all the crash and drama of plane debris falling from the sky. Emma's mouth hung open so far and for so long, she'd started to cough. Celeste took a sip of her fresh martini while she waited for Emma to find her voice.

Pushing aside her salad, Emma leaned across the table. "What exactly do you mean by that, Celeste?"

The waiter came toward them to whisk the salad plate away, but Emma held up a hand that stopped him and turned him around.

Celeste popped an olive in her mouth and chewed it slowly, weighing what she was about to say now that she'd opened a can of worms.

"Just what it sounded like, Emma. If George told you he didn't know Tessa North, he was lying. I never met the little tramp, but I knew all about her. She was carrying on with George, and he was totally smitten. Friends of mine saw them out

146

together quite often. Fortunately, the paparazzi wasn't relentless like it is today, so photos of them didn't show up all over the newsstand like Grant and Carolyn's affair."

"It obviously ended. Do you remember when?"

"Not exactly. But one night, George came home and announced that he'd gotten his mistress pregnant." Celeste fixed her eyes on Emma. "Sound familiar?"

Emma was so stunned she went temporarily brain dead. Finally, she forced out the next question she wanted to ask. "So George was going to leave you and marry Tessa?"

"No. I decided to leave, but he pleaded with me not to. He said he would take care of the bastard child when it was born, but that the affair was over. He said it had been a big mistake and begged for my forgiveness."

"So you did — forgive him, I mean?"

"Not fully, but in time we found our way again. We had built a life together and with our children. And the public was less forgiving of a straying husband back then. It could have hurt George's career."

Emma played with her teaspoon as she gathered more scattered thoughts and glued them together. "Celeste, I don't mean to be indelicate, but over the years there's always been rumors about George and . . ."

"And other women?"

"Yes. Grant used to tell me about some of George's activities."

Celeste pushed her martini glass away without finishing her drink. "Yes, there were others — many others. George was always falling into bed with one actress or another. But those were just flings, Emma, and for the sake of our family and for the sake of my own comfortable lifestyle, I kept my mouth shut. I knew he'd come back to me after each one. But Tessa was different. George was mesmerized by her, and the baby almost cinched the deal." Celeste leaned forward. "Tessa was playing her game, the same game Carolyn Bryant played. But I played it better."

Celeste leaned back in her chair. "Did you know that George was married when he met me?"

Emma shook her head in disbelief, wondering when the revelations were going to stop. She was getting dizzy from mental whiplash. "No, I didn't."

"Yes, I stole him right out from under his mousy wife's nose. They didn't have children and hadn't been married long, but as soon as I met George Whitecastle on the set of a movie, I knew I wanted him. Quite frankly, had it not been me, it would have been someone else. His first wife wasn't cut out to handle his future success. He needed someone who knew the business — not just the glamorous side but the hard work and ugly politics that come along with being on top in Hollywood." Celeste bobbed her head, a rueful smile stretched across her face. "Tessa North was trying to play a game I had already mastered."

"So you never knew what became of Tessa or of her baby?"

"No, and I didn't care. For all I know, she had the bastard, and George has been supporting them all these years. Or maybe she found another sorry sucker and was more successful with him."

After waving the waiter back over to clear their dishes, Celeste pulled her martini glass back toward her. "You said Tessa's a ghost on Catalina. Tell me what that means exactly."

"In my research for a future show about the ghosts of Catalina Island, I came across her name, but not much else. Further research connected her to one of George's movies."

"If she's a ghost, then she's dead. Correct?"

"Yes, that's exactly what it means."

"Do you have any idea when she died?"

This time Emma fudged the truth. "No, not exactly."

Celeste narrowed her eyes at Emma. "Don't toy with me, Emma. I'm old, but I'm not stupid. Your show, that brooch, the way you knew Edmund was dead — if there is such a thing as ghosts, then I'm thinking you've met Tessa's."

After a long pause, Emma nodded. "I have. She's called the bikini ghost. She died quite young on or near Catalina Island."

Celeste scoffed. "Catalina. Might as well have been called Sodom and Gomorrah in those days."

"And I'm pretty sure Tessa died a few days after Robert Kennedy was shot."

That got Celeste's attention. "Really?" Celeste toyed with her remaining martini olive. "Are you sure Tessa died shortly after the Kennedy assassination?"

"Pretty sure. Why?"

"Did you actually see her? Tessa's ghost?"

Emma fixed her eyes on her ex-mother-in-law, leaving no doubt to what she was about to say. "Yes, Celeste, I saw Tessa North's ghost with my own eyes."

Celeste looked around before leaning forward. "How did she look? I mean, if she'd been pregnant when she died, would her ghost look pregnant?"

The significance of what Celeste was asking alerted Emma. "I'm not one hundred percent sure, but I think so. Ghosts tend to look like they were when or just before they died. Tessa's ghost wears a polka dotted bikini and has a terrific figure."

When Celeste didn't say anything more, Emma pushed. "How long before the assassination did George tell you she was pregnant?"

Celeste's mind pushed through the booze to do the calculations. "She would have been eight or nine months pregnant around the time Kennedy was killed. Unless, of course, she was already several months along before George told me. Then she would have recently had the baby."

Emma let herself slump against the back of her chair. She needed time to let the information meld like flavors in a stew, but instead found herself cooking on her feet. If Tessa had a child, why hadn't she mentioned it? Emma recalled the ghost's figure. Even though hazy, it didn't look anything like one that had just had a child.

Peter came by and asked if they cared for dessert. After declining, he had the young waiter bring them the check. Emma put down a credit card, and it was swept away for payment.

After the waiter left, Emma decided to do more digging. "Weren't you and George at the Ambassador the night Robert Kennedy was killed? I'm sure I've heard George talk about it a few times over the years."

Celeste nodded, her eyes sad. "Yes, we were, along with many of our friends."

"I imagine the Feldmans and Mannings were with you."

"Yes, of course. We even stayed at the hotel that night. All of us were very involved in Kennedy's campaign, especially Worth and his son, Stuart."

Emma wanted to know George's whereabouts after the shooting, but knew she had to ask carefully. His name wasn't Curtis, but she wanted to make sure George White-castle wasn't in Catalina during the time Tessa died. "That must have been very traumatic — that night and the days that followed."

"It was." Celeste fingered the rim of her glass. "I don't think George or I left the house for nearly a week afterwards, we were so devastated. The TV was on nonstop. I cried for days."

If Celeste was telling the truth, then George hadn't been in Catalina. While it didn't mean he knew nothing about it, at least he wasn't there. And he wasn't the one Tessa was waiting for.

"Another name came up during my research, Celeste. Tessa was connected somehow to a man named Curtis — not sure if that's a last name or a first. Do you remember anyone by that name hanging out with George or his friends?"

Celeste took a final sip of her martini as she mulled over the name. "I don't recall anyone by that name. Maybe he was another married lover. Maybe he killed Tessa because she'd become a liability."

"Wow," said Phil when Emma finished telling him the details. "That was quite a lunch."

"Tell me about it. I'm not even sure Grant knows his dad was married before."

"But you know, Celeste might be on to something. Maybe this Curtis fellow dumped Tessa, hurt and dying, on the island to get rid of her. Didn't she say there was a loud noise and blood? Maybe he shot her and left her to die."

"Hmm, and maybe Celeste had her bumped off. I hate to say this, Phil, but with all the lies being bantered about, anything's possible, even the most unlikely."

TWELVE

Century City isn't a real city at all but an area on the west side of Los Angeles known for being the entertainment business district. Besides housing Fox Studios, Century City is also home to a mall, luxury hotels, and several well-known restaurants, and its high-rise office buildings accommodate many businesses that cater to show business in all its forms.

After finishing her call to Phil, Emma checked in with Jackie. Sandwiching calls in between her duties for the travel show, she'd been working her way through the Nowicki listings she'd found, but so far had not had any luck reaching many people. Those she did, didn't remember anyone by the name of Theresa Nowicki or Tessa North.

Hyland Staffing was located on the twenty-third floor. From a search on the Internet, Emma had discovered that it was an employment agency specializing in providing temporary and permanent staffing of all kinds, from assistants to chefs to drivers, to businesses and individuals that required a higher level of professionalism and discretion from employees.

When Emma presented herself to the receptionist in the lobby, the young woman promptly handed her a clipboard with an application. "Do you have a résumé with you?" she asked Emma.

Before Emma could answer, a very stylish older woman came out into the lobby. "I'm afraid Mrs. Whitecastle isn't here for a job, Cassie." The woman held out her hand to Emma. "I'm Fran Hyland."

After the two women shook hands, Fran Hyland led Emma down a short corridor and into a large and beautifully appointed corner office with a spectacular view of the Hollywood sign.

"You'll have to excuse Cassie, Mrs. Whitecastle," she said after Emma was settled in a chair and she had taken a seat behind her spotless desk. "We so seldom see anyone but applicants here in the office."

"You don't see potential clients here?"

"Most of my clients are very famous or powerful people. They expect me to go to them."

"Of course." Emma set her shoulder bag

down on the chair next to the one in which she sat. From it, she pulled her small notebook and a pen. "Let me get right down to why I'm here, Mrs. Hyland."

"That's Ms. Hyland, if you please. My married name is Kilgore, but I never use it professionally."

"Fine, then, Ms. Hyland." Emma cleared her throat. She had no doubt that Fran Hyland was efficient at matching employers with employees, but she worried that Fran would be too formal or concerned with protocol to dish any useful information about Tessa. Only plunging ahead with questions would tell. "As I said on the phone, I'm here about some research I'm doing on Tessa North. You knew her when you were both acting, didn't you?"

"Yes, I knew Tessa. We were both blond and pretty and, well, rather curvaceous. We often auditioned for the same parts."

Studying Fran Hyland, Emma could see that in her youth she must have been a knockout. Even in her sixties, the skin on her lined face was beautiful, and her eyes clear and bright. Her figure, dressed in an impeccable navy blue St. John knit suit, was still fairly trim, and her smartly cut hair was a glossy silver. Her only jewelry consisted of a fine gold watch, diamond stud earrings, and a gold circle brooch fastened just below her left shoulder.

"How long did you remain in acting?"

"I stopped acting shortly after I turned twenty-five. Parts became scarce when I became too old to play a sorority girl or beach bunny. Truthfully, I didn't have the talent for anything with more substance. I was a pretty face and figure, and not much more, I'm afraid. Soon after, I got married. I started Hyland Staffing nearly twenty years ago."

"Did you know Tessa well?"

"Well enough. It wasn't unusual for a group of girls to share an apartment. I didn't room with Tessa myself, but one of my best friends did, so I saw her frequently."

"Do you know whatever became of Tessa North?" When speaking to Fran Hyland on the phone, Emma had edited out the part about ghosts on Catalina Island. In meeting the woman, Emma felt it had been a wise decision. The woman definitely didn't appear to be ghost friendly. "From the records, it looks like she'd been getting steady work, then disappeared in the late sixties."

Ms. Hyland folded her hands on her desk and leaned forward, one eyebrow arched like an ash-brown rainbow. "Why the interest in a girl who was only in Hollywood a few years?"

"I'm doing research for a show, and her name came up a few times. I found it curious that she simply disappeared. Tessa was in several of the beach movies in the sixties; so were you. In fact, the two of you worked on a movie for George Whitecastle, my former father-in-law, didn't you?"

"Yes, we did." Fran Hyland leaned back in her chair and swiveled to look out the window. "I always assumed that Tessa left Hollywood and went back home. She was from somewhere in the Midwest, I believe. She talked about it all the time when we were all together."

"Was there any specific reason why she might want to leave?"

Ms. Hyland swiveled back around to face Emma. "It was a very tough business for a young woman, especially a pretty one. A lot of predators, drugs, broken promises, and shattered dreams. It's still pretty much the same way now."

"Your friend, the one who roomed with Tessa — is she still in Los Angeles?"

"Yes. She's still doing some acting, too, though mostly she waits tables. She's sixty-three years old, no family, lives in a crappy apartment in Culver City, and still thinks she's going to make it big." Ms. Hyland tossed Emma a cynical smirk. "Over the years, I've tried to offer her better paying positions, but she says she's happy where she is."

"I'd like to talk to her, if I could."

"Her name is Denise Dowd."

Emma nodded in recognition. "I believe I came across her name at the same time I found yours." It was true, Emma recognized Denise Dowd's name from Jackie's list of actresses. "I left her a message but haven't heard anything back yet."

"Doesn't surprise me that you already have her name. There was a core of us in the mid to late sixties that were always hired whenever they needed a chorus of jiggling sexpots in the background. Offscreen, many of us lived together, like our own little sorority."

"What about some of the others, Ms. Hyland? Do you know where they are now?"

Fran Hyland shook her head slowly. "The only ones I kept in touch with over the years were Denise and Cynthia Small. Cynthia died a couple of years ago. She landed a small recurring part on a soap that lasted several years. After that, she drifted out of the business, got married, and settled in the valley."

Hyland swiveled around in her chair again

and studied the view for a moment. When she turned back to Emma, she seemed to have made up her mind about something.

"Denise works second shift at a restaurant on Pico Boulevard near Sawtelle — a place called Bing's. You might try her there. She always enjoys rehashing the old days."

Emma jotted the name and location of the restaurant in her notebook. "I appreciate you taking the time to meet with me, Ms. Hyland. A few more questions and I'll be out of your way."

"My pleasure, Mrs. Whitecastle, and if you find out what happened to Tessa, please let me know. I'd love to get in touch with her again." Fran Hyland gave Emma a tight smile as she handed her an embossed business card. "And, of course, if you ever find yourself in need of hiring an assistant or other type of help, please keep me and my company in mind."

Emma took the card and nodded graciously before posing her final question. "Do you recall if Tessa was involved with anyone romantically?"

Ms. Hyland frowned, noticeably agitated around the edges by the question. "Difficult to remember anyone specific. We were all very young and attractive. There were always lots of men flocking around us."

"What about someone in power, say, like George Whitecastle or Paul Feldman?"

The frown turned ugly as Fran Hyland sat up straight in her chair. "Is that what this is all about? Are you trying to pin some ancient peccadillo on George Whitecastle? According to the trades, he's nearly at death's door. Are you planning on writing some tell-all book now that he's dying?" She stood up, sending her chair sliding backwards. "Is that your idea of revenge for what his son did to you? Or didn't you get enough money in the divorce?"

"Calm down, Ms. Hyland. That's not my intent at all."

"I've built a thriving business keeping people like you away from the rich and famous, and now you're here pumping me for information?" Fran Hyland's voice had transformed into a low growl laced with outrage. "You'd think you'd know better, seeing that you're a TV personality yourself these days. I only talked to you because you're part of the Whitecastle family."

"I promise you, Ms. Hyland, this has nothing to do with a tell-all book, movie, nothing like that. I simply want to know what happened to Tessa North."

"Get out, Mrs. Whitecastle." When Emma tried to say something more, Fran Hyland pointed toward the door, the long painted nail at the end of her index finger showing the way like an emergency beacon. "Leave now or I'll call security."

Back in the car, Emma called Phil again. "Guess what?" she asked as soon as he came on the line. "I was just thrown out of an office in Century City."

"Why are you surprised, Fancy Pants? When we met, I threw you off my property. You just have that initial impact on folks."

THIRTEEN

It was late in the afternoon, and Los Angeles traffic was turning asphalt ugly as people started leaving work. Emma calculated that if she headed home right this minute, she might be ahead of most of the freeway snarl. Another hour and she'd be crawling all the way back to Pasadena. According to her GPS, the intersection of Sawtelle and Pico wasn't far from Fran Hyland's office. Emma had a decision to make — head home and call it a day or push on to Bing's and hope to catch Denise Dowd before Hyland got to her and poisoned the well.

She turned out of the parking garage and headed south on Century Park East. At Pico Boulevard, she turned right. She gave herself until Overland Avenue to make up her mind. Turning left on Overland took her to the 10 Freeway and the way home. Going straight took her to Sawtelle. When she got to Overland, she kept her vehicle straight.

Bing's was located on the south side of Pico, just beyond the 405 Freeway overpass. Emma turned left into its parking lot. Before getting out of the car, she called Milo. When he didn't answer, she left him a voicemail with the latest updates, knowing Celeste's revelations alone were going to set his internal senses tingling like high-voltage antennae.

Bing's was an old-fashioned restaurant that, according to its sign, had been in Los Angeles for over sixty years. The inside was dark, its booths made of tufted red vinyl, and the walls were paneled. Emma stepped inside and let her eyes adjust to the dim lighting. The restaurant didn't look like it had had a makeover in those sixty years either.

Straight ahead, she saw a few booths; beyond them, a long, old-fashioned bar at which several patrons were enjoying cocktails. To her right was a large room with more booths. Even though it was a little early for dinner, the place was hopping and nearly full. Upon closer examination, Emma noted that almost every customer in the place appeared to be a senior citizen, including most of the waitresses that bustled by.

A middle-aged man came to the front

desk. In his hand he clutched several menus. "One for dinner?" he asked.

"Um," Emma stammered, not sure what to do. She had expected a diner, the type of place with a counter where she could chat up Denise Dowd while she worked. "Is Denise Dowd working tonight?"

"Yes, Denise's here."

"Would it be possible to sit at one of her tables?"

"Hold on a moment," the man told her before scurrying off to the dining section to the right. When he returned a second later, he said, "Yes, there is a small booth available in her station. Follow me, please."

Emma was led around a dividing wall inset with fish tanks to where several small booths just large enough for two were set. A few feet across from the booths was a real wall. It felt cramped yet cozy, and semi-private, which, Emma thought, might be perfect for talking with Denise away from prying eyes. She slid into the booth, which was already set for two, and took the menu. Only one other booth on this secluded side was filled, occupied by a single man two booths down, munching a salad while squinting at a newspaper in the dim light.

"Denise will be with you shortly," the host said before dashing off.

Soon a waitress, one hand holding a plate of steaming food, passed her. "Be with you in a sec, hon," she said to Emma.

Emma's mouth watered as her nostrils picked up the scent from the passing plate. She'd eaten four hours earlier, and it had been on the light side, not to mention unsettling to her digestion. Opening the menu, she scanned it. Bing's specialty seemed to be comfort food and lots of meat — prime rib, steaks, and barbeque — and most items were bargain-basement priced. Then she saw the reason for the early crowd. Every night from four thirty to six thirty, there were even more bargains on full meals that included drinks and dessert. Bing's was a senior diner's dream. Emma continued moving her eyes over the menu until she located the seafood section. A lot of it was fried, but there were several healthy offerings. Emma smiled. Phil would think he'd died and gone to heaven in this place.

After delivering the plate to the man sitting nearby, the waitress stopped by Emma's booth. The name tag fastened to her uniform read *Denise.* "Know what you want, hon?"

Denise Dowd appeared to be in her early sixties. Her hair was a light reddish-brown and stiffly styled. Her dark eyes, with their blue eye shadow and penciled brows, peered out over the top of reading glasses. She was dressed in a white cotton shirt and black pants and seemed more like an actress playing a stereotyped character waitress rather than a real waitress. Emma tried to study her face without being rude. Although they'd never met, Denise looked familiar.

"Any recommendations?"

"Tonight's special is the country pork chops. Best you'll ever have. Also have a grilled halibut that's not on the menu."

"I'll take the halibut, please."

"Salad or soup? Soups today are minestrone or chicken noodle. We make our own green goddess dressing and our own soups."

"The minestrone." Emma noticed that Denise wasn't writing any of the order down.

"Rice, mashed potatoes, fries, baked potato? It also comes with fresh steamed vegetables."

"Rice." Emma also ordered a glass of house chardonnay and some water.

In a jiffy, Denise Dowd returned with her wine. A few moments later, she put a small basket with garlic toast and a cup of soup down on the table. Emma started to say something, but Denise scampered away to say goodbye to a large table of folks just leaving. Somehow Emma had to ask Denise about Tessa, but if the restaurant continued to bustle, it was going to be difficult. She took a spoonful of soup. It was hearty and delicious.

Soon Denise delivered Emma's halibut. It was a nice piece, grilled to perfection. The side of rice wasn't plain white but more in the Spanish style. It was a good meal, nothing fancy, but filling and tasty. Emma dug in. Although she was having trouble finding time to chat with Denise, she was enjoying having a quiet home-style meal.

Denise continued to hustle orders and carry food out to tables. "Everything okay?" she asked Emma during one of her passes. Emma nodded and took another bite.

Shortly after she finished her meal, a busboy cleared the table. Emma was savoring the last bit of her wine when Denise stopped by. "How was it?"

"Excellent," Emma answered. "The rice was a nice surprise. I expected a bland pilaf."

"Folks love our rice," Denise said with pride.

"Have you been working here long, Denise?"

"Seventeen years. Most of the waitresses

have been here a long time."

It was then that Emma placed where'd she seen Denise, or at least her face. "I'm sorry if I seem rude, but aren't you on TV in a commercial? Something about arthritis medicine?"

The waitress beamed. "That's me. Also did one for adult diapers."

"So you act as well as wait tables?"

"Always had the acting bug. Did more of it when I was younger — was even in a few films when I was in my twenties. But mostly, I've done commercials."

Lining up her mental ducks, Emma was about to ask about Tessa when Denise said, "Dessert comes with your meal. We've got chocolate pudding, tapioca, or ice cream."

Emma grinned. "I love good chocolate pudding. Do you make it fresh here?"

"Just like everything else."

"Sounds good to me."

"With or without whipped cream?"

"Without." She paused. "Ah, what the heck — make it with."

While Denise headed off to get the dessert, Emma mentally chided herself. She had to start asking Denise questions about Tessa. When the dish of thick, dark chocolate pudding, topped with a cap of fluffy whipped cream, was placed in front of her, she got down to business.

"Denise, could I ask you a few questions?"

"Sure. Is it about our menu? You doing a piece on the restaurant?" She placed Emma's tab down on the table.

Emma shook her head. "Sorry, nothing like that. My name's Emma Whitecastle. I left you a voicemail yesterday."

Denise Dowd peered over the top of her reading glasses and studied Emma for what seemed like forever. "Whitecastle. Yes, I remember the call. Hard to forget a name like that if you're in the business. You're George's former daughter-in-law, aren't you? The one who divorced that sleazebag on TV."

"That's me. Do you know George?"

"I was in two of his movies when I was young. Another about ten years ago." Instead of saying more, Denise looked away for a moment, then turned back to Emma. "I'm pretty busy here."

"Please, Denise. I was just at Fran Hyland's this afternoon. She said you used to room with Tessa North. I'm trying to find out what happened to her." After a short pause, she added, "It has nothing to do with my being part of the Whitecastle family. I just want to know about Tessa North. Her name came up in some research I was doing for my own TV show on the paranormal."

The last word caught Denise's attention. "Paranormal? You mean like ESP, fortune-telling, ghosts, stuff like that?"

"Yes." Emma dug into her handbag and pulled out her business card for *The Whitecastle Report*. She handed it to the waitress. "I know you're busy, but perhaps we can meet later when you're off work or even tomorrow sometime."

Denise looked over the card, then turned her face toward Emma. It was as blank as a white bed sheet. "Eat your pudding, Emma, and I'll think about it." It sounded like something a mother would say to her child.

Emma dawdled over her pudding, but Denise never stopped by her table again. Finally, deciding she'd struck out with Denise Dowd, Emma slid out of the booth and headed for the front area to pay her check. She was almost out the door when she heard someone call her name. It was Denise Dowd. Turning back into the restaurant, Emma ran smack into a man just leaving.

"I'm so sorry," Emma said to the man, a short, balding, nondescript sort.

The man looked down at the ground and mumbled, "No problem." He scooted out past her and disappeared into the dark parking lot just as Denise reached Emma.

The waitress handed her a slip of folded paper. "I believe you dropped this." Giving Emma a professional smile, Denise said, "You come back real soon."

Once outside, Emma opened the folded note and read it under the entry light. On it was printed an address in Culver City and the words: *Tomorrow — 10 am sharp. Only chance you'll get.*

Emma was glad she'd left a nice tip.

FOURTEEN

Once she returned home, Emma called Milo and caught him up on all the latest developments in her investigation. He hadn't had any more insights on Curtis or information on the spirit that had visited them. They agreed to meet at his house following her visit with Denise the next day.

After the call with Milo, Emma settled onto the leather sofa in the den with her laptop and a glass of wine and started going through her e-mails from her TV show's account. There were notes from fans of the series, along with the usual crackpots, as well as a couple from religious zealots warning her she was on the path to hell. There were also suggestions from both fans and experts for topics for new shows. Emma deleted those that deserved deletion and wrote short thank-you notes to those who'd written to say how much they enjoyed the show. Those e-mails offering topic suggestions were put in a special folder that she and Jackie would review together to see if there were any good possibilities to pass along to the show's producers. Jackie had offered to respond to the show's fan mail, but Emma felt it important that she do it personally. She was almost done when a chill wafted through the room.

"Where have you been, Granny?" Emma asked without looking up from the computer screen. She received no answer.

The chilly current moved past her again at quick speed. Emma looked up but saw nothing. She looked down at Archie, who was curled next to her on the sofa. He was alert, his intelligent dark eyes following the cool draft, but his tail was not wagging.

"That's not me," said Granny, who materialized on the sofa next to Archie. The dog glanced at his pal and thumped his tail a few times at the familiar spirit. Just as quickly, he went back on alert, worried about the one that wasn't known.

Emma looked at Granny, then at the hazy puff circling the room. "Who are you?" Emma asked the visiting spirit. She closed her laptop and placed it on the coffee table in front of the sofa. She got to her feet, ready to face the spirit. "Please show yourself."

The spirit was still not defined, appearing only as a filmy column of steam.

Without taking her eyes off the unknown ghost, Emma asked Granny, "Do you know that spirit?"

"Can't say that I do."

"Can you describe it to me? Is it male or female?"

"I can't see her fully either, Emma."

"Her? So it's a woman."

"I'm not sure, but that's the sense I get. And I don't think she's happy."

Emma didn't think so either. Though she knew that ghosts couldn't physically harm her, it was still unnerving to come across those who were angry or disturbed.

"Have you come here for help?" she asked the strange ghost. "I'm willing to help you, but I must know who you are first."

The column circulated around the room, faster and faster, until it came to a halt directly in front of Emma. She felt the apparition nose to nose with her, as if trying to breathe in her warm breath. Archie gave off a short whine.

"Hush," Granny told the dog.

"Who are you?" Emma whispered. The front of her body was much colder than her back, and the hair on her neck and arms stood stiff like tines on a fork, but she didn't move or back down.

Granny left the sofa and faced the visitor, spirit to spirit. "Stop this nonsense and tell us what you want or leave," she demanded. "You can come back when you're ready to be civil."

After a short pause, the cold spout of air started circulating the room faster and faster, often brushing up against and around Emma. Archie whined again. This time, Granny didn't shush him. Then, suddenly, the air in the room went still, and Emma knew the spirit had gone.

Emma dropped to the sofa, mentally exhausted. "We need to find out who that is, Granny. And what she wants."

"Oh, so now you want this old mule's help, do you?"

"Come on, Granny. You know you're stubborn. It's not like it's news to you."

Granny drifted across the room and leaned against the fireplace, her arms crossed in defiance. "Seems to me it's a family trait."

Emma hung her head, knowing she should have been more sensitive and thought her words through before speaking. Granny was definitely stubborn and cantankerous, but she was also loyal as the day is long, and had very delicate feelings. Emma wasn't sure who was more tiring at the moment, Granny or the unknown ghost. Ever since Catalina, Granny had been ornerier than ever. "I'm sorry, Granny, if the mule remark hurt your feelings. You know I love you. Sometimes family members forget to be nice to each other."

The diminutive ghost sniffed, her nose out of joint. "Well, I reckon so." The spirit moved slowly around the room until she circled back toward the sofa. "And it's not like I haven't been called a mule before."

Denise Dowd lived in an older, well-maintained apartment building on a quiet street just a few blocks from Sony Studios. The pale green building had two stories, six apartments in all. Originally built with the apartments accessible to the public, in recent years it had been gated and a security call box installed. Just before ten o'clock, Emma located Denise's button on the call box and pressed it. She was immediately buzzed in. The apartment was on the second floor at the end located over the carports in the rear of the building.

When Denise Dowd opened the door, she looked like a different person. She was dressed in an exquisite flowing African print caftan. Her auburn-tinted hair had been brushed out and softly framed her face, which was scrubbed and makeup free. And while the lines on her face appeared more prominent, her overall appearance was softer and more becoming than how she'd looked the night before. Denise the waitress was ordinary-looking; Denise the actress was quite attractive.

Emma was ushered into a very spacious apartment stuffed full of furniture, photos, and knickknacks. The floor plan was the standard open style, with the kitchen and dining area exposed to the living room. Down the hallway, directly across from the front door, Emma caught sight of three open doors — a bathroom and two bedrooms. The furnishings were old-fashioned, overstuffed, and exploding with floral prints.

Before disappearing into the kitchen, Denise told Emma to make herself comfortable. The morning had arrived with a cool drizzle, forcing Emma to slip a jacket over her jeans and baby blue sweater. She pulled the jacket off and hung it on a nearby coat tree before taking a seat on the sofa. Soon Denise returned with a tray laden with china teacups and a matching teapot, which she placed on the coffee table before taking her own seat on the sofa.

"I hope you like tea, Emma. I find it the

civilized thing to serve guests, especially early callers. Later in the day, I like to bring out the booze." She winked. "You look to me like a lemon kind of gal. Me, I prefer it like the English, with milk."

"Yes, lemon, please."

After slipping a thin lemon slice into a delicate rose-patterned cup, she handed it to Emma, along with its matching saucer. "And please help yourself to the biscuits — also English."

Denise prepared her own cup of tea, then leaned back against the high back of the sofa, waiting for Emma to explain herself.

After taking a sip of tea, Emma cleared her throat and began. "Thank you for seeing me, Denise. I wasn't sure you would."

"Neither was I at first. But while you were eating your pudding, I gave Fran Hyland a quick call. She told me to avoid you at all costs." Denise gave off a short snort of laughter. "That's when I knew I had to hear what you had to say. If Fran found you objectionable, then I'd probably find you fascinating."

"I thought you two were close friends."

Denise laughed again. "Fran and I have known each other since before Noah built his ark, but I wouldn't call her a close friend. She knows the Denise from the restaurant. She thinks I'm a loser with a dead-end job, living just above the poverty line."

"I did notice quite a difference in you from last night."

"One of the benefits of being an actress is that you can easily slip in and out of character. I keep my public and my private lives very separate. Thanks to my job at the restaurant, the commercials I've done over the years, and sound investments, I've managed to buy this building. Fran doesn't know that, and I'd prefer she not."

"Is there something wrong with Fran Hyland?"

"Something you didn't already notice yourself?"

"She did seem pretty uptight."

"Uptight? I've worn girdles with more give."

This time it was Emma's turn to laugh. "Actually, the conversation with Ms. Hyland was going along smoothly until she got it into her head that I was writing some sort of tell-all book. Before then, she told me how many of the young actresses hung out together, even lived together. She mentioned that she and Tessa North often auditioned for a lot of the same parts because of their similar looks."

"Very true. Back then we banded together for both economic and safety reasons."

"And you shared an apartment with Tessa?"

"Yes, with Tessa and two other girls. Shelly Campbell was a dancer who did a lot of musicals before heading to Vegas, where the work was more plentiful and the pay better. Heard she married some rich stage Johnny. Colleen was the funny one of the bunch. She wasn't movie-star pretty like the rest of us, but I think Colleen worked more because of it. Less competition, I guess. She always landed a lot of character parts like the plain-Jane friend or the quirky co-ed. In fact, of all of us, she had the longest and most successful career. She was on a long-running Western drama for years, right up until last year, when she died suddenly from a stroke."

"Are you talking about Colleen Miles?"

"That's her."

"She played the wisecracking cook on *Wildfire,* didn't she? My family watches that show every week. I loved that character."

"Believe me, Colleen was a wiseass in real life, too, right up until the end. Being on that show wasn't exactly a stretch for her. Unlike Fran and I, Colleen and I were close friends."

Denise was quiet for a moment, then got up and retrieved a large photo album from a nearby table. "Since you're interested in Tessa, I got this old thing out for you."

She returned to the sofa and flipped through the album until she came upon several old photographs of young women cavorting in bathing suits.

"There we are," she said, pointing to a particular group shot with nearly a dozen girls, "the original Wild Bunch." She chuckled. "That's me and Fran in the first row." The two women she indicated were stunning in both figure and face. "And that's Shelly, the dancer."

Emma pointed to a girl almost in the middle of the group. She wore her blond hair in a flip. "That Tessa?"

"That's her."

Denise flipped a few pages until she came to more girls in bathing suits. They were lounging around in directors' chairs, some of them reading, a few smoking. "This was taken on the set of *Beach Party Prom.* There's me with Colleen."

As Denise had said, Colleen was not a great beauty like the others, but she had a pleasant, impish appeal about her and a lovely figure. Again, Emma spotted Tessa right away.

"Did you ever see *Beach Party Prom*?" Denise kept her eyes on Emma. "It was a real stinker, but it made a nice chunk of change for the studio."

"No. I didn't even know it existed until I checked IMDB for Tessa's information."

Denise closed the book carefully and let it rest on her lap. "Tell me, Emma, how do you know what Tessa North looked like? She didn't have that much of a career before she took off." Before Emma could hem and haw her way to an answer, Denise added, "In fact, let's get down to why you're here. You said you were doing research for your TV show. Considering your show is about the paranormal, the natural question here is, have *you* seen a ghost you believe is Tessa?"

The question wasn't posed with either sarcasm or skepticism, nor was it delivered with awe. It was simply a question with a head-on delivery — like Denise herself. Emma decided it deserved a head-on response, the same as she'd given Celeste when she'd asked the question.

Putting down her teacup, Emma turned to face Denise. "Yes, Denise, I have, flakey as it sounds."

"I see." Denise put the album on the coffee table and picked up the teapot. "More tea?"

Emma nodded, and Denise refilled her cup. This time, Emma picked up just the cup, leaving the saucer behind. She held the warm porcelain in her hands for comfort as she weighed what and how much to say. In the end, she finally decided to tell Denise everything, including her belief that Tessa died on Catalina and her body was never found. She even told Denise about Sandy Sechrest.

When she was done with the story, Denise got up and went to a sideboard in the dining area. When she returned, she held two small snifters in one hand and a bottle of Rémy Martin in the other.

"Who gives a damn if it's still before noon," Denise said, pouring cognac into each snifter. "After a story like that, I need a drink."

FIFTEEN

After Emma took the offered glass, Denise raised her own snifter. "To Tessa North, whatever and wherever she may be." They both took a drink: Emma, a small sip; Denise, a large gulp.

"So what can you tell me, Denise?" Emma asked, setting her drink on the table. The last thing she needed was to drive to Milo's half in the bag, and after everything she was learning, she could easily drain the glass as Denise was doing. "Do you know who Curtis is? Or anyone Tessa might have been involved with romantically other than George Whitecastle?"

"No matter what your mother-in-law believes, Tessa was never involved with George like that. And she certainly wasn't pregnant or had a baby that I knew of." She took another drink. "George hit on all the girls and usually won them over. After all, he was a player and quite handsome. If he

185

got into Tessa's panties at all, it was only a couple of times before he moved on. That was his M.O." Denise furrowed her brows in thought. "But honestly, I don't even recall a passing fancy between them."

"Did George ever make a pass at you?"

"Sure." Denise radiated another inward smile. "Old George found his way into my bed on several occasions over the years. He was a good time, as long as you understood that's all it was. Remember, Emma, it was the sixties. Free love. No fear of AIDS. Drugs at every party. Everyone was letting loose — especially us girls raised strict Catholic and away from home for the first time."

"Even Fran Hyland? She hardly seemed like a party-girl type to me."

Denise laughed again. Emma liked her laugh. It was hearty and unselfconscious.

"Don't let that proper, suit-wearing exterior fool you. When we were young, Fran hopped in and out of more beds than a bed bug and could drink her weight in booze."

Emma thought of the prim and indignant woman she'd met the day before and had difficulty picturing her as a wild child of the sixties.

The two women sipped their drinks companionably — Denise cognac and Emma tea — before Emma continued on with her questions.

"Celeste Whitecastle told me that several of her friends told her they saw George out with Tessa."

In response, Denise picked the album back up. She leafed through it until she found what she was seeking, then turned the album toward Emma. "Look at some of these photos, Emma, and tell me what — or, more specifically, who — you see."

Emma studied several of the photos spread over the two open pages. Several of them were group shots around a table in a club or restaurant. Scattered over the table were various cocktail glasses and even a champagne bottle and a few flutes. She pointed at one of the men in the photos. "I'm pretty sure that's George."

"That it is."

Emma pointed to a woman a few places down. "That's Colleen." She moved her finger over. "And that's Fran and Tessa on either side of George." There were three other men in the photo and a woman she didn't recognize. "Where were you and Shelly?"

"I took the photo. Shelly had already moved to Vegas. This other woman was one of Fran's roommates. I think her name was

Cindy or Candy, something with a C."

"Cynthia Small?" Emma prompted.

"Yes, that's the name. Did Fran tell you that, or are you seeing Cindy's ghost, too?"

Emma shook her head and laughed. Everyone was now assuming that she was seeing ghosts at every turn. "Fran told me."

Denise indicated another photo, but in this one Denise was wedged between Fran and one of the men. "See, I'm in this one. It was taken by a waiter. As I recall, we were celebrating Tessa's birthday. Usually, we went out in groups like this. I'm not saying there wasn't any pairing off or people meeting up other times, but generally we partied in groups. So Mrs. Whitecastle's friends might have thought Tessa and George were an item if they saw us all out, but, like I said, I'm pretty sure they weren't."

Emma studied the photos closer. "Any chance either of these two men are named Curtis?" Before Denise could answer, Emma poked a finger at the man sitting next to Denise. "Wait a minute, isn't that Worth Manning?"

"Sure is. He was starting to climb politically by then and was becoming more concerned about his image." Denise laughed. "Or at least his handlers were. Shortly after this party, he almost never came around."

Emma studied the other photos. "I don't see Paul Feldman here. He, George, and Worth Manning were close friends; still are. Did he hang out with you, too?"

"We saw Paul once in a while, but not as often as Worth and George. George always joked that Mrs. Feldman kept Paul on a short leash. I met her once at a party. Quite the stick in the mud, but it was Worth's wife who was the real bitch. Nasty as they come. It's no wonder the boys played around."

Emma thought the comment odd. She'd met Mrs. Manning on several occasions, and she'd always seemed quite pleasant and charming, although Emma thought Denise was right about Mrs. Feldman. She'd always struck Emma as being dull and inflexible.

"Who's this other guy?" Emma landed a finger on the man she didn't recognize.

"That's Tony Keller. He shot himself about a year or so after this was taken. Word was his studio cancelled his contract, but there were other rumors about him being caught in a homosexual love nest. Not sure which I believe."

"Tell me, Denise, did you all go to Catalina together from time to time?"

"Yes, though usually the men took some-one's boat over to fish and we girls went by ferry and met them there. There were some wild parties on the island."

"So I've heard."

Denise grew quiet and stared down at the group photo. "I was just remembering when this photo was taken. Tessa's birthday was at the end of May. This was taken just before she took off."

"Didn't you find it odd that she just disappeared? Weren't you concerned?"

"Until you showed up talking about seeing her ghost, I always thought she'd gone back to Nebraska. And who knows, maybe she did and this whole ghost thing is just your imagination."

Emma gave Denise a look that assured her she wasn't in the habit of having imaginary friends. "Was Tessa the sort who would leave without saying goodbye or give an explanation to her friends?"

Denise shrugged. "Colleen and I were both out of town on a shoot the week Tessa left. When we returned, her things were gone. There was just the three of us in the apartment then. About a week or so later, we got a postcard from Nebraska saying she'd decided to go home and didn't want any long goodbyes or for us to try and talk her out of it."

"Why would she think you'd try to talk

her out of it?"

"Tessa didn't talk much about her family, but from what I gathered, home was pretty miserable. She was raised by her brother and his wife, and I got the feeling they were pretty mean to her, even abusive. In the few years we lived together, she never received any mail or phone calls or visits from family members that I knew of. She seemed to be all alone in the world, except for us." Denise took a drink from her snifter. "Shame, too, because she was such a sweet thing. Rather naïve and innocent. Tessa wasn't quite as wild as the rest of us. Didn't hardly drink. Didn't swear. She was totally enamored of Hollywood. Colleen and I always thought it was a bit strange that she took off like that, but after the card came, we didn't give it much thought."

In her head, Emma replayed part of her discussion with Fran Hyland. "And you're sure Tessa never talked about going back home to Nebraska?"

"Positive. Whenever anyone asked her about her family, she'd shut right down. We wouldn't even have known where she was from if we didn't see it on her driver's license when she first came to California."

"Did you ever try to reach her?"

Denise shook her head. "Didn't know

where to start. We just knew she was from Nebraska. She never even told us her brother's name."

"And you didn't know who she was dating at the time she disappeared?"

"Not really. She didn't seem that interested in hooking up with someone steady. She seemed more intent on having fun. And she loved being an actress. She wasn't bad, either. Not Shakespeare quality, but she probably would have had a decent enough career, especially with those boobs of hers."

"According to Tessa's ghost, she and this Curtis guy went to Catalina on his boat shortly after Robert Kennedy was assassinated. You sure you don't remember anyone hanging around Tessa who owned a boat?"

"Some of the guys had boats. Not sure which belonged to who, but I'm pretty sure Worth owned one of them."

"Maybe Worth and Tessa were seeing each other before she disappeared."

Denise gave the idea some solid thought. "You know, Worth and Tessa did have something going for a short while, but I'm pretty sure it was over long before this photo was taken."

"Denise, would you mind loaning me one of those photos? I'd really like the one taken at the club, the one with all of you."

In response, Denise unstuck it from the album page and handed it to Emma, who turned it over. On the back was printed in faded blue ink: *Tessa's B'day 1968.*

"Thank you. I'll return it as soon as I can."

Denise flapped her hand gently at Emma. "Oh pish, no hurry. I haven't looked at these old photos in more than twenty years."

Emma stood up and stretched her long legs. Grabbing her jacket, she slipped it on. Denise rose with her. "Thank you for your time, Denise. I really appreciate it." She held out her hand to Denise Dowd, who took it and shook it with a hearty pump.

Emma was almost out the door when she paused and turned back. "Are you sure, Denise, that George Whitecastle didn't have a specific mistress, or maybe one woman he saw more often than any of the others?"

"Not that I knew of, unless he was very discreet about it. Seemed to me, he bounced from flower to flower too often to have someone on the side in addition to his wife. And he was a very busy man. Where would he find the time and the energy?"

"And you didn't know of any of the women in your group, or maybe on the fringes of it, becoming pregnant?"

"Colleen had a scare once, but, thankfully,

that's all it was."

"You have my number. If you remember anything you think might be helpful, please don't hesitate to call."

"And if you find out what happened to Tessa, please let me know. She was a sweet kid. And although I believe what you're saying about the ghost, I want in my heart to believe that Tessa didn't die so young."

SIXTEEN

On her way to Milo's house, Emma called Jackie. "Hey, Jackie. Can you rustle up the phone number for Worth Manning for me?"

"The ex-senator? I'll do my best."

"I haven't seen Mr. Manning for several years. You might have to remind him that I'm George Whitecastle's ex-daughter-in-law. Feel free to say I'm the one looking for the number if you need to." Emma paused, then added, "Also find me the number for Paul Feldman. He used to be a big-shot producer. I'm not sure if he's still in the game or not."

"You got it. By the way, I was about to e-mail you about those Nowicki numbers. I was almost through the list when I got a hit. Some guy just outside Lincoln said he had a cousin named Theresa. Said her parents died when she was young, and she went to live with her older brother and his wife until she graduated high school and took off for California. No one's heard from her since. The brother's name is Jack Nowicki. And get this — according to the cousin, Jack and his wife were these crazy religious zealots who beat on her pretty often. The cousin said Jack lives in Arizona now in a retirement community — probably why he wasn't on my call list. I found a number for him in Arizona. Do you want me to call him?"

No wonder, Emma thought, Tessa never talked about her family and home. Still, she wondered why Fran Hyland had said she did.

"Yes. Simply ask him when was the last time he saw his sister." Emma paused, thinking of something more for Jackie to say to Jack Nowicki. "Tell him you're doing background research for a nostalgic piece on the old teen beach movies and would like to find her. It will be interesting to see what he says, given his background."

"Will do."

"And, Jackie, great work. I have no power to give you a raise, so how about a trip to a day spa?"

"Woo hoo, the other assistants are going to be jealous."

"Don't tell them."

"Are you kidding? Of course I'm going to

tell them."

As soon as they disconnected the call, Emma thought of something else. She buzzed Jackie back.

"Oh, and Jackie? One more thing. Could you look up a Tony Keller? Might be Anthony Keller. I think he was an actor in the sixties. Died in 1969 or 1970, around there, possible suicide."

When Emma arrived at Milo's, Tracy Bass opened the door dressed in jeans and a sweater with stars appliquéd across her chest. "Hey, pal," she greeted Emma.

"Hey yourself." Emma shrugged off her jacket before giving her friend a big hug. "What a nice surprise, on many levels," she added, alluding to the recently disclosed romance between Tracy and Milo.

Tracy pantomimed an *aw shucks.* "Milo told me you two were getting together. I had just one early class today so was free to horn in on your meeting. I hope you don't mind, but I'd love to see what goes on when you two talk ghosts."

Emma chuckled and rolled her eyes. "As long as you don't trot me out for show and tell in one of your classes."

"Nah, my sweetie will do that for me."

Milo and Emma settled around the old table in the back room, Milo on one end,

Emma just to his right. Emma noticed that Milo had restacked the books that had fallen during their last meeting, though the new stack was tilting as badly as the previous one. Milo offered coffee or tea, but Emma declined, citing she was filled to the gills. Shortly after they sat down, Granny appeared.

"Still no success in getting Tessa to come here?" Emma asked Granny.

"Not a lick. No new information, either. That gal's stuck on the same old tune. Curtis is coming for her and she needs to wait."

Emma glanced over at Tracy. Her friend was curled up in a large leather chair pulled close to Milo, her hands wrapped around a warm mug of tea. Her eyes were as wide as saucers and her ears fairly hummed in their attempt to pick up any smidgen of ghostly chat. Milo was whispering to her the conversation with Granny.

"What about the ghost that visited us yesterday, Granny? Any news about her?"

Milo turned to Emma in surprise. "Was it the same one who came here?"

"I think so. She — Granny thinks it's a woman — dropped by my home right after you and I talked yesterday. Didn't say anything, just spun around the room like a whirling dervish. But this time she came face to face with me, literally. I couldn't make out any image and she didn't say anything, but we were definitely nose to nose."

In her chair, Tracy shivered with excitement.

Emma continued. "I couldn't tell if she was upset or trying to tell us something."

"Humph," said Granny. "I told her to go away and come back when she could act civilized."

Milo turned to Granny. "And you have no idea, Granny, who this mystery spirit is?"

"Nada."

Emma frowned at the ghost. "Nada?"

"It means *nothing,*" Granny explained to Emma.

"I know what it means, Granny. Just when did you start saying that?"

Milo didn't need to translate to Tracy. She'd picked up the gist of the conversation and was chuckling into her mug.

"I may be dead, Emma, but I'm not too old or too stupid to learn new things." The spirit sniffed in annoyance. "I learned it from Alma."

Alma Ramirez was the Miller housekeeper. She came three times a week and had been with the family for seven years. So far, they'd been able to keep Granny's presence from Alma, and the entire family had voted to keep it that way. They didn't want to lose her.

"Granny, you know you're supposed to stay away from Alma."

"I'm not bothering her. I just like the way she talks — and sings. She's always singing along with that contraption she wears in her ears."

"Please, Granny. If Alma leaves, my mother will skin us both alive."

"I ain't alive."

Laughter erupted from Tracy as Milo filled her in on the bickering. "It's like this all the time," Milo whispered to her. "It's a wonder we get anything done."

In frustration, Emma turned away from Granny and started filling everyone in on what she'd learned from Denise Dowd. Pulling the photo she'd gotten from Denise out of her bag, she placed it in the middle of the table and pushed it toward Milo. Tracy moved forward to study it over his shoulder while Emma pointed out the various people.

Tracy was the first to comment. "Did Tessa look like this in ghost form?"

Emma nodded. "Pretty much, except she's wearing a bikini."

Milo pointed at Tony Keller's image. "So

you think this Tony Keller might have known something? Is that why you're having Jackie follow up on him?"

"I haven't a clue if he's involved or not, but I thought it wouldn't hurt to look into his death. My plan is to check out everyone who ran in that tight little group."

"Good idea," said Milo. "You never know what's going to turn up."

"I'm also having Jackie track down the numbers for both Worth Manning and Paul Feldman."

"Isn't Manning a friend of your in-laws?" asked Tracy. "Couldn't you ask them?"

"They are both close friends, but I have my reasons for not wanting to go to the Whitecastles." Emma picked at the wax on the large unlit candle in the middle of the table while ideas circled her head like orbiting planets. "George said he didn't know Tessa, and asking for these numbers would only raise further suspicion about my purpose, although I'm pretty sure if George and his pals know anything about her disappearance, they've synchronized their stories by now."

Milo fingered the photo. "But why would George lie to you, considering there's physical evidence that he did know Tessa? Even if he counted on his wife saying nothing."

"Simple," Emma answered. "He probably thought I'd take him at his word and never thought for a million years I'd be doing research into it, or that it would be important enough to me to pursue."

Tracy chuckled. "Poor guy. He underestimated you. Just like his son did."

"Could be, or he thought it would be easy enough to explain away should the truth of their acquaintance come out. After all, it was many years ago. He could simply say he didn't remember at the time I asked him. As for Celeste, she wouldn't lift a finger to help Tessa, not even in death. And if Celeste thought for a moment that George got rid of Tessa, she'd never help me find out what happened to her. Can't say I blame her. He's sick and old — and her husband. And she'd do anything to avoid a scandal."

Tracy leaned forward. "But I thought you said Tessa wasn't George's mistress."

"From what Denise told me, she wasn't, but I doubt Celeste would believe me."

Milo scratched his head and adjusted his glasses. "Wonder why George would tell his wife she was?"

"Maybe he didn't," Emma answered. "Celeste could have assumed she was from what her friends told her, and George didn't say anything because he wanted to protect the woman who was."

"And what about you?" asked Milo.

"Me, what?"

"If you find out your former father-in-law is connected to Tessa's death, are you going to say something to the authorities or let it slide to protect the family?"

It was a question that had plagued Emma's mind ever since Milo first said something a few days before about George being involved in a possible murder.

"Am I legally bound to say anything?"

Tracy shook her head. "No, I don't believe you are."

Emma pushed the candle away. "Then I guess I'll cross that bridge if and when I come to it. Might be that Tessa wasn't murdered. And it might be George wasn't involved."

Tracy gave her a look of skepticism. Milo himself had doubt written all over his face. Only Granny said what was on everyone's mind.

"If that child wasn't murdered, then I'm Barack Obama."

Milo turned to Emma, fighting to keep a straight face. "At least Granny keeps up with current events."

Emma covered her face with her palms and groaned with frustration. What she really wanted to do was rub her hands up and down over her face, but she knew it would only serve to destroy her makeup. When she removed her hands, Milo, Tracy, and Granny were all staring at her — Tracy with amusement, Milo with concern, and Granny with annoyance.

"Okay," Emma said, giving in to the popular theory. "Let's go with the assumption that Tessa North was murdered, or at least gravely injured and left to die on purpose."

"What if this Curtis did come back," Tracy added, "but it was too late?"

"Phil and I discussed that possibility," Emma told them. "If Curtis did come back and it was too late to save Tessa, then why was there no body or report of a death in the news? If he returned and she was dead, there's a very good chance he covered it up."

"Or covered her up," added Granny.

"Very true," said Emma. "We're pretty sure whatever happened to Tessa, her body was never recovered. This Curtis would know where he left her and why. We just have to find him."

Tracy raised her hand like a dutiful student. "I have a question. Say you do locate Curtis. What do you intend to do? Have you thought that far ahead?"

It was the same question Phil Bowers had asked her the night before when he'd called to say good night and see if she'd learned anything new. He'd advised her not to be like a dog that chases cars, only to have no plan once he catches one.

"Somehow, we need to get him to Tessa. If she sees him, she might feel assured and cross over, as she should. That's really my goal, to help Tessa cross over." Emma paused to think, then added, "And if she was murdered, I want to bring her justice. She deserves it."

Tracy still wasn't satisfied. "And if you do find him and he is involved in her murder or cover-up, how do you propose to get him to come along with you to Catalina?"

Granny bounced around the room in excitement. "We can hog-tie him and smuggle him aboard a boat."

Emma looked at the ghost in astonishment. "I am not going to kidnap anyone, Granny."

"I'm not exactly in favor of Granny's plan," Milo commented, "but how else are you going to convince Curtis to go over to Catalina and face the ghost of Tessa North?"

Everyone was quiet while silent ideas bounced around the room like a runaway pinball. There were so many variables still up in the air — a plethora of what-ifs.

"How about this," Emma said, breaking the silence. "If we do locate him, we can say he won a trip to Catalina. Make it two nights at a nice hotel with transportation. Who can resist that?"

Tracy sat up straight. "Hey, I've heard of cops using that to catch people with outstanding warrants. They send them bogus prize notices, and when they come to collect, they nab them. Could work."

Milo wasn't so sure. "If this guy is wealthy, it might not be something he'd bite. And how would he have won it if he didn't enter anything? Not to mention, if he left a dead or near-dead woman on Catalina, there's a good chance he's never stepped foot on the island since, and he might be shy about going back."

The last bit of Milo's comment caught Emma's attention. "I just thought of something. George Whitecastle has been to Catalina many times in the past forty years. I know, because I've been over there with him when we went as a family. If George was involved with Tessa's death, you'd think he'd be a bit put off about going back to the island. Instead, he went over often." She frowned, more to herself than to her companions, unwilling to believe the thought that had just crossed her mind. "Unless he felt no remorse or guilt."

"More to the point," said Tracy, "if he was Curtis, Tessa would have seen him during one of the trips and made her peace. I think it's safe to assume from the information you've gathered that George isn't this Curtis guy."

Emma smacked her head. "Tracy, you just opened up another possibility — one we should have thought of before." They all turned to her, waiting for an explanation. "We've been looking for a man named Curtis. What if he was only going by the name Curtis, but it wasn't his real name?"

"The girl was involved with him romantically," Tracy pointed out. "Don't you think she'd know his real name?"

Granny shook her hazy head. "Tessa's not exactly the sharpest tool in the shed."

"Granny," Emma admonished.

"Well, she ain't, and you know it as well as I do."

SEVENTEEN

Emma was not in a good mood.

Ever since returning from Catalina, she felt like she was spending all her time on the freeways shuttling between Pasadena and the west side of Los Angeles. It seemed like everyone she needed to speak with lived on the other side of the crowded metropolis area. But things went from bad to worse when she stepped out of Milo's home and found her vehicle had been vandalized. Across the side of her glossy white Lexus hybrid SUV, someone had spraypainted in black *Leave The Dead Alone.*

"How," she'd asked Milo, her voice climbing to a near shriek, "could this have happened in broad daylight?"

"It's a work day, Emma," he'd told her. "Few people are home, and the weather isn't nice today. Most people would have been inside."

The police had felt the same way when

they came to take a report. "It only takes a kid a minute to do something like this, ma'am," the young patrolman had said. They were all standing on the sidewalk in front of Milo's house, inspecting the damage. The light drizzle coming down dampened everyone's mood even more. "Though we seldom see stuff like this in this neighborhood."

The police had been courteous though doubtful that they would be able to find who'd done the painting. They'd asked about the significance of the words and, when told about Milo's profession and Emma's TV show, were surprised it hadn't happened sooner.

"This was not done by kids, Milo," Emma said after the police left and she went back inside Milo's house to calm down.

"I agree," he'd said.

They were in Milo's living room. Emma was on the sofa with Tracy next to her. Milo paced. Granny had disappeared before they'd discovered the crime.

"And I don't think this had anything to do with me," Milo told them, stopping just long enough to get his words out. "I've lived in this house over fifteen years, and nothing like this has ever happened before."

"My gut is telling me you're right, Milo."

Emma ran both hands through her short hair. "That's two cars in two years. My insurance company's going to love this," Emma said, referring to the year before in Julian when her Lexus sedan had been driven into a tree.

Milo stopped pacing and faced Emma. "Who knew you were coming here today?"

Emma thought a minute. "No one except for you and Tracy. I didn't even tell Jackie."

Tracy patted Emma on the arm. "It looks to me, pal, like you're being followed."

Although Tracy's words made sense, Emma didn't want to hear them. She wanted even less to believe them. The idea that someone was tailing her around Southern California gave her the willies like no ghost had ever done. But how else would anyone know where she was?

Emma shot to her feet and started pacing where Milo left off. As she wore out the carpet from one end of the room to the other, she ticked names off on her long fingers. "There's George, Celeste, Fran Hyland, and Denise Dowd. Oh, and Paul Feldman. Those are the only people I've spoken with about this." She stopped in her tracks, and her shoulders sagged as she sighed. "Of course, there's no telling who any of them told."

After Emma took up the pacing, Milo had joined Tracy on the sofa. The two of them had watched Emma and did their own thinking arm in arm. When Emma noticed, she wished Phil was with them. Not just for his support, but also for his clear-headed thinking.

"I'm not sure who Fran and Denise would tell," Emma said, shaking off her thoughts of Phil Bowers, "but George and Paul probably discussed it over pastrami. And either of them could have contacted some of their friends who are still around and went to Catalina back then, like Worth Manning. But spraypainting a car hardly seems like the work of men in their seventies."

Shaking a finger in the air, Tracy added, "Rich men, Emma. They are rich, powerful men who can easily hire someone to follow and intimidate you."

Emma didn't want to hear that either.

After planning their next move, Emma had climbed into her spraypainted car and headed home, ignoring the stares she received from other drivers. Her parents were due home this weekend, and Emma wanted to spend another quiet night with Archie and her heavy thoughts.

During their brainstorming, Milo had decided that he should go to Catalina and try to talk to Tessa himself. He and Tracy were planning on leaving the next morning. They would take the ferry over and spend a couple of nights. Tracy had joked that it would be a working romantic getaway, much as Emma's had been. They had reservations at the Pavilion Lodge, a favorite place of Tracy's, directly across from the beach area where Tessa and Sandy Sechrest hung out. They hoped at least one of the ghosts would speak with Milo, though Emma was sure Sandy would. She would ask Granny to pop over and pave the way.

Emma's job was to continue digging into Tessa's friends. She was also anxious to hear what Jackie had found out from Tessa's brother in Arizona. The postcard Denise supposedly received from Tessa was nagging at her like a loose thread on a sweater. If Tessa did die on the island, someone went to a lot of trouble to send that postcard from Nebraska. She, Milo, and Tracy all felt that it was a solid piece of evidence that Tessa's disappearance and death had been covered up by someone. And whoever it was had probably also removed Tessa's things from her apartment and had known that her roommates were gone that weekend. Someone had been very busy to make sure no one thought twice about looking for

Tessa — or maybe it was more than one person. Either way, they had done a good job of making it happen, and forty years ago, without the speed and convenience of the Internet, it would have been difficult for someone like Denise to look for Tessa to check up on her.

The three of them had also hoped that the mystery ghost would make an appearance when they were all together, but she hadn't. Milo cautioned Emma that it was also possible that the new spirit had nothing to do with Tessa North. The disturbed ghost could be totally unrelated, just another spirit looking for help and trying to be heard by the living.

As he talked, Emma had watched Milo closely. When he finished, she'd asked, "Do you really believe this spirit has nothing to do with Tessa?" When he hesitated, she added, "*Really* believe, like with your spidey sense?"

Milo had blushed before speaking. "My *spidey sense,* as you put it, is screaming that this entity has everything to do with Tessa. But I don't want you chasing false ghosts, just in case it doesn't." He winked at her. "Even superpowers can misfire once in a while."

Just behind their three-car garage, the Millers had a guesthouse. It was a very large single-room apartment with a full bathroom and kitchenette. The wall facing the landscaped back yard was a bank of floor-to-ceiling windows with drapes for privacy, though the drapes were seldom closed. Even the door was glass paned. Many years ago, Dr. Miller had converted it into an exercise room with various equipment, including a treadmill, bike, and free weights. On a cabinet was a combination DVD player and TV on which her mother played her favorite exercise tapes and her father watched the news while on the treadmill. The small kitchenette held healthy drinks and snacks. Just off the main room was a roomy alcove, originally meant to be the sleeping area. In the last year, Emma had repositioned the loveseat that had been there for years to make room for a large L-shaped desk and filing cabinets, turning it into an office. When Emma got home, she changed into workout clothes and headed out to her office with Archie as company.

After her divorce from Grant Whitecastle, Emma and her parents had discussed whether or not she should move out and buy her own home. In the end, the divorce settlement from Grant had been fair to both parties. Emma had plenty of money, enough to keep her comfortable for the rest of her life if managed properly, and now she had the income from her own TV show. When she first left Grant and moved back in with her parents, she had intended for it to be temporary. But when the time came to make a decision, Elizabeth and Paul Miller had proposed that she make it permanent. The Millers were in their early seventies, and both of them were still vigorous and healthy. Deciding to make hay while the sun shined, they had become world travelers in the past few years and were gone almost as much as they were home. It made sense for Emma to stay on and keep an eye on the house and Archie. And, as her father had pointed out, the big, white stately home would be hers one day. Emma hated hearing that, even though she loved the house and all its wonderful memories.

Emma knew she was lucky. Her parents were not intrusive on her privacy and treated her as the adult she was, even though she was still under their roof. They backed all her decisions, even her decision to divorce Grant and to say yes to the paranormal television show. And as much as they had grown to love Phil Bowers, they did not pressure her about him. They seemed content to let her go her own way, but they always let her know they were there for her.

The alcove in the guesthouse had become her sanctuary when she needed alone time, although with the Millers on the road as much as they were, Emma did have plenty of privacy. But it was her special place. She did most of her research and preparation for her show here. When she needed a break or to brainstorm, she'd hop on the treadmill and give both her body and mind a workout. She had a small office at the studio, which she used when she needed to be there or to work directly with Jackie, but she preferred to spend most of her time at her home office.

When she had returned home, Alma was gone for the day but had left a note on the kitchen table alerting Emma that the package she'd been expecting had been delivered. Alma had put it in her office, as Emma had asked.

The large, narrow rectangular box was propped against the kitchenette counter when Emma entered the guesthouse. In it, securely packaged, was the painting she'd bought on Catalina — Sandy Sechrest's painting of the beach, the one with Tessa North's image amongst the sunbathers. Doing quick and careful work with a knife, Emma released the painting from its bondage and stepped back to admire her purchase.

Even without the significance of Tessa's presence, it was a beautiful painting. Picking up the painting, which was heavier than it looked with its gilded frame, Emma propped it first against one wall, then another, until she figured where it best fit.

"That's Catalina," said Granny, floating in. Archie thumped his tail at the sight of his best buddy.

"Yes. Sandy Sechrest painted that." Emma studied the painting, imagining it hung on a wall. "I'm thinking I'll hang it just above the loveseat. That way, I can look at it while I work at my desk."

"For inspiration about the case?"

"The case?"

"You know," said Granny, moving closer to the painting to get another look, "Tessa's murder."

"You make me sound like I'm Sam Spade."

"Who?"

"Sam Spade, the PI from *The Maltese*

Falcon." When Granny still looked puzzled, Emma added, "I know my dad has the DVD of the movie. I'll pop it in for you sometime. Better you watch that than those old, tacky sitcoms."

Granny sniffed. "If those shows are good enough for Dr. Miller, they're good enough for me."

Since Granny had disappeared before they'd discovered the spraypaint job on Emma's car, Emma filled the ghost in on what had happened.

"Sounds to me like someone wants you to mind your own business. Makes a body wonder why." The ghost moved closer to the painting and pointed. "That's Tessa."

"Yes. The painting is of what Sandy remembered from her first meeting with Tessa's ghost. She met her years ago, when she herself was alive and Tessa first dead."

Before Emma could say anything else, a cold gust blew through the guesthouse. Archie, who'd curled up on the loveseat, whined and hunkered down.

Emma looked at the door, but it was shut tight. "I don't think we're alone, Granny."

"That we're not." Granny moved closer to Emma.

EIGHTEEN

The angry spirit swirled through the room as it had the night before, but this time with a specific purpose. Its target: the painting. The strong current of cold air buffeted and shook the painting, threatening its stance against the wall. In two steps, Emma reached it before it could crash facedown to the floor.

"Is this about Tessa North?" Emma asked the ghost as she clutched the painting against the swirl of forceful air.

"Tell us what you want," Granny demanded. "Or at least have the decency to show yourself."

"I know you're upset about something," added Emma. "But we can't help if you don't let us."

"Noooooooooooooooooooooo." The sound came from the air like wind whistling through a tight space.

"No, you don't want our help?" Emma

leaned the painting back against the wall but stood in front of it to keep it from falling. "Or no to the painting? Did you know Tessa North?" She hugged herself against the cold created by the presence of both ghosts and wished she was dressed in more than a snug knit tank top.

"Noooooooooooo!" The word was clearer this time, accompanied by a strong gust that pushed against Emma like storm blasts from the sea. She held out her arms against the force and took a step back, careful not to crush the painting. Papers from the desk took flight and scattered. Mugs lined up on the kitchenette counter rattled. The drapes lifted. Archie jumped off the loveseat and tried to cower behind it.

Granny moved to the center of the room. "Behave yourself or leave," she said to the spirit. "I'll not have you frighten Emma this way."

"No, don't go," Emma called out to the strange spirit. She turned to Granny. "It's all right, Granny, I'm not frightened." Emma turned her head, rotating it to scan the room for any sign of the spirit. Focusing on what appeared to be a hazy cloud, she ventured, "We're here to help you. You have to trust us."

The churn in the air calmed to a mild

breeze. As if thinking it over, the almost-invisible cloud moved through the room, wafting back and forth. At one point it approached Emma, getting once more close to her face. Emma felt her cheeks grow cold, as if she'd stuck her face into the freezer to scout ice cream possibilities. When the spirit pulled back, Emma's face warmed again.

Archie poked his nose out and whined. The misty cloud moved toward the animal. Granny moved protectively between the spirit and Archie.

Emma held her breath. "Please," she begged quietly, "don't frighten him anymore."

"Don't worry, Emma," Granny said, sticking her chin out in defiance. "I won't let her."

The hazy apparition started taking shape but still did not reveal itself. Emma could now see the outline of a female, but no details. The strange ghost stood in front of Granny, facing her, then tilted its head down to look at the unfortunate Archie.

"I would never harm a dumb animal," the ghost said in a barely discernable whisper.

"Archie's not dumb," Granny snapped.

Raising its head, the ghost studied Granny, then bluntly dismissed her by turning around and drifting over to Emma. "She doesn't need you," the ghost said.

"Who doesn't need me?" Emma wasn't sure if the ghost meant Granny or Tessa.

"The girl. The picture."

"You mean Tessa North?"

"Leave her be."

"Who are you? How do you know Tessa?" Emma moved closer to the spirit but didn't want to stray too far from the painting.

While the unknown spirit remained blurred in its appearance, its message was distinct and sharp. "Forget about her!" This time, the ghost's voice rattled the windows of the guesthouse. Archie whimpered. Emma stepped back, nearly falling onto the painting. "She's dead, and nothing you can do will change that."

Bracing a hand against the wall, Emma straightened herself and stood her ground, letting the apparition know she would not be bullied. "She needs to cross over. You have, haven't you? So why not let her do the same? Let her rest in peace."

The ghost floated away. When it reached the door, it swirled in a gust and swooped down on Emma and the painting again. More papers flew through the air. When the spirit was once again nose to nose with Emma, it snapped, "It's the living, not the girl, who need peace."

Emma was about to say something when her cell phone, which was sitting on the desk, rang. She inched over to it, afraid to leave the painting lest the ghost try to damage it. She grabbed the phone and quickly resumed her place wedged between the painting and the ghost. "Hello."

"Emma? This is Worth Manning. I was told you were looking for me."

"Why, Senator, what a surprise." Emma kept a wary eye on the ghost as she spoke. The spirit, done with trying to scare Emma, drifted around the room, restless and agitated. Granny stayed by Archie.

"A nice one, I hope." He chuckled, his deep voice resonating over the phone line.

Emma wondered how he'd gotten her number. She knew Jackie would never give out her private line. It had to have been George. "Yes, of course, a nice surprise. You must have heard from my assistant."

"Yes, she called my office and left a message that you wanted to set up an appointment." There was a slight pause on his end. "I hope you don't mind, but I asked George for your number."

"Did George also tell you what it was about?" As the visiting ghost disappeared into thin air, Emma sighed with relief.

Granny cooed to Archie, "The big bad ghost is gone, little fella. Come on out."

Manning chuckled. "He said something about Tessa North and ghosts. Is that correct?"

"Yes, it is. Do you remember her?"

"It was a long time ago, but I do recall a young woman by that name."

Emma wasn't surprised by his admission. Sure the three men had by now met and decided upon a mutual story, it seemed the senator had been chosen as the one to spoonfeed it to her. She left her post by the painting and sat down at her desk. "Do you have time to meet with me tomorrow, Senator?"

"How about now? I'm right in front of your parent's home."

This she hadn't expected, and it caught her off-guard.

"Emma, you there?"

A small cough escaped her lips. "Yes, Senator. Sorry. Frog in my throat." She stood up. "You're here? Right now?"

"I hope you don't mind, but I had business earlier in Pasadena so thought I'd swing by before going home. I tried the doorbell, but no one answered."

"I'm out back, in the guesthouse. Give me a minute and I'll come to the front door."

After disconnecting the call, Emma looked at the painting. She was worried the ghost would come back and try to damage it, and Granny couldn't protect it like she could. Finally, she decided to slip it back into its shipping box and lay it flat on the floor. That way, it couldn't fall if the ghost decided to cause a small tornado.

When she opened the front door of the house, Worth Manning stood on the other side. Of the three men — George, Paul, and himself — he'd been the most elegant in his appearance. At just over eighty years old, he still stood over six feet tall, with ramroad posture only slightly bent by age. His hair was white as snow and worn back away from his angular face, which was furrowed with wrinkles. Unlike George's once-beefy build, Worth was slender with wide, strong shoulders. It looked to Emma like the man still worked out to keep his physique.

Archie, at Emma's side, barked at the stranger. "Hush, Archie," Emma commanded.

Worth Manning looked Emma up and down with a predatory eye, taking in her form-fitting exercise clothes. For the second time in less than an hour, she wished she'd worn something less revealing, but this time for a different reason.

Dressed in dark slacks, a dress shirt, and sports jacket, the former senator looked confident and collected. Emma looked beyond him to where his black Mercedes was parked at the curb under a streetlight. He appeared to be alone. The drizzle that had fallen most of the day appeared to have stopped.

"Please come in, Senator."

As Emma stepped aside, Worth Manning entered the Miller residence and followed Emma and Archie into the formal living room.

"Can I get you anything?" she asked, indicating for him to sit anywhere he'd like.

"I'm fine, Emma. Thank you." Manning lowered himself into an upholstered chair with a high back and crossed one long leg over the other. Archie sniffed at the shoe remaining on the carpet. Manning reached down and let the animal nose his hand before moving to scratch the dog behind his ear. Archie's tail wagged.

"Please excuse me a moment," Emma said. When she returned, she had on the cardigan sweater her mother kept in the kitchen against drafts. "Thank you for waiting. I was a bit chilly." She took a seat on the sofa.

"Working out?"

"I was about to. Our guesthouse was converted into a home gym. I'm afraid we can't hear the doorbell out there."

"Then it's a good thing I called." He gave her a slow, assured smile — the type of smile that comes naturally to people used to being in power.

Keenly aware that coming to her home was an offensive move meant to keep her off-balance, Emma sharpened her senses and prepared herself to hold her ground. It also made her think more seriously about the three friends being behind the painting of her car.

"I was sorry to hear about Mrs. Manning. My mother told me she passed away last fall."

"Thank you, Emma. Nasty stroke. We never saw it coming. Fortunately, Linda did not linger." Manning looked around. "Where is your charming mother?"

"She and my equally charming father are on a cruise."

The comment netted her a smirk. Emma felt awkward. She'd met Worth Manning many times while married to Grant, but she'd never spent time alone with him. And now she was about to ask him some uncomfortable and very personal questions. Deciding she might never get the same opportunity, she met the situation head-on.

"As George might have told you, Senator, I came across the name Tessa North doing some research for my show."

"Something about a ghost on Catalina Island, that correct?"

"Yes. Supposedly Tessa's ghost haunts Catalina. Seems she might have died there some forty years ago."

As the room started growing cooler, Emma pulled the sweater closer. Archie moved away from the senator and curled up in a corner of the room. Glancing over, Emma spotted Granny. She was glad Granny had retreated to a far corner, taking the coldness with her. From there, she could hear and see everything without making the immediate air around the living chilly.

Emma returned her attention to the senator. "You said you remember her."

"Vaguely, yes."

"I understand some of you saw each other socially — that there were several men, including you and George, who hung around a specific group of young actresses back then."

"Did the ghost tell you that, Emma?" The question was gift-wrapped in sarcasm and tied with a wink.

"No, the ghost did not, Senator." Emma's

228

words were pointed. "But others remember."

A small sardonic smile crossed his lips. "There were always willing young actresses — one of the perks of the business, both show business and politics."

Emma fixed him with a stern, no-nonsense look. "I'm not judging you, Senator, or anyone. I just want to know what you remember about Tessa."

Manning leaned his head against the back of the chair and closed his eyes. "Tessa, Tessa, Tessa." The words came out like a mantra.

"I don't like this man, Emma," Granny whispered to her as if Manning might overhear. "And I don't like that you're here alone with him."

While Manning was lost in contemplation, Emma glanced over at the corner and shook her head a little, trying to convey to Granny that she'd be fine.

"As I recall," Manning began, opening his eyes and looking at Emma, "Tessa was a very sweet thing. Blond, I believe. Whatever became of her, I have no idea. I remember hearing that she'd returned home."

"Did you have an affair with her?"

"Yes, I did. It was fun but short-lived."

The blunt honesty surprised her, and her

reaction was noticed by Manning.

"Don't look so shocked by my confession, Emma. Especially since you already knew the answer before you asked the question." He uncrossed his leg and leaned forward, his forearms resting on his thighs, his hands clasped casually between them. "My wife is dead. I'm no longer in the Senate, and the fling was over more than forty years ago. So what's the harm now in owning up to it?"

"Emma," Granny whispered, moving closer with Archie on her heels. "Maybe that cranky ghost is his dead wife."

Emma's eyes popped open. "Of course," she said out loud toward Granny before catching herself.

"Excuse me?" asked Manning.

Turning back to him, Emma did some quick damage control. "I meant, of course, it wouldn't matter now about an indiscretion that took place so many years ago."

She focused on the senator, trying not to look in Granny's direction. The possibility that the unknown ghost might be Linda Manning buzzed through her nervous system like a nest of disturbed hornets, making her antsy to make contact with the spirit again.

"But I'm not concerned about that, Senator. I just want to know what you remember about Tessa North, such as when was the last time you might have seen her."

Manning laughed and straightened up. "Forty years ago. That exact enough for you?"

"He knows something, Emma." Granny moved toward Worth Manning. "I just know it."

As Granny drifted in the direction of Manning, Archie followed. Manning put his hand down, inviting the dog to enjoy another scratch, but as soon as the dog was within reach, Granny spun and drifted off in another direction, with the animal following. She paced the room, oblivious to the zigzag motions Archie made while tracking her across the carpet.

"What's wrong with your dog?" asked Manning.

"Archie," Emma called to the animal. "Stop that and come here." Archie stopped, puzzled by the decision before him — follow Granny or listen to Emma. In the end, the confused animal went to the person who fed him. He trotted over to Emma and settled at her feet, knowing he wasn't allowed on the living room sofa, just the one in the den.

"Don't mind him," Emma said, reaching down to pat the dog. "It's a silly game he plays with my father."

Worth Manning looked at his watch, then at Emma, giving her a wide smile. "Why don't you change and let me take you to dinner?"

"Dinner?"

"Yes, of course. One of my favorite restaurants is here in Pasadena, and I happen to have a reservation for eight o'clock. We can discuss Tessa North further over good food and fine wine." Once again, Manning's eyes scanned Emma's body.

Emma's first reaction was to wrap the cardigan sweater around herself several times and padlock it, but she resisted, knowing he would take pleasure in her discomfort.

Granny zoomed in close. "No, Emma."

"Thank you, Senator," Emma said. "That's a lovely offer."

"I forbid you." Granny stomped her booted foot silently on the carpet. Archie stood up, his ears alert, his eyes wide.

Emma fought the urge to snap off a few choice words in Granny's direction. Instead, she smiled sweetly at Manning. "But I'm afraid I've already made plans for the evening."

Emma glanced at the antique clock on the mantle across from the sofa. "I just have a few more questions, but I'll make sure you get to your dinner reservation on time."

Nineteen

"She actually forbade me. Can you believe it?"

On the other end of the phone line, Phil Bowers laughed with gusto. "You tell Granny that next season, I'm taking her to see a Chargers game in person. Best seats in the house."

"Very funny."

"You can come along, too, if you like, Fancy Pants. Unless, of course, Granny forbids it." He laughed again.

Emma squinted in annoyance at the phone, giving Phil an evil eye he couldn't see. "I'm glad you're so amused."

"Hell, this is priceless." He paused, and Emma could hear him taking a deep breath. "But seriously, Emma, I'm rather concerned about you."

"Because some old codger hit on me?"

"Let me remind you that that old codger could be involved in a murder — or the cover-up of a murder, at the very least. And I think you're right about his little visit. No doubt the three Musketeers got together and planned how you were to be handled. And who better to do the handling than a suave, seasoned politician?"

"Well, Mr. Bowers, I did not allow myself to be manipulated."

"That's my girl. But while I'm proud of you, I'm also more concerned. From what you've told me so far, especially about Tessa's things being cleaned out of her apartment and someone sending her roomies a postcard, forty years ago Tessa's death was important enough to hide. It could still be important to some folks to keep it hidden. The more you go nosing around, the more danger you could find yourself in. Remember what happened in Julian last year? Someone actually tried to kill you . . . twice."

Emma was tucked into bed. She'd been reading when Phil called, as he almost always did, to tell her good night. After Worth Manning left, she'd gone back to the guesthouse to pick up the scattered papers and shut it down for the night. She looked at the treadmill, then decided talking to Manning had been a workout enough. She was pooped. The mystery ghost had not made another appearance, even though Emma had called out to her several times, even trying the name Linda Manning to see if that got the spirit's attention. Before locking up, she put the painting, still in its box, in a closet for safekeeping.

Granny followed Emma to the guesthouse, hanging around protectively until she was positive Worth Manning was gone and stayed gone, though Emma wasn't sure what the ornery ghost could have done had Manning made a physical move on her. In the guesthouse, Granny voiced her doubt about going to Catalina.

"What if that snake comes back?" she'd argued with Emma. "It might be more than just painting the side of that fancy wagon of yours."

"First of all, we don't know if the spray-painting had anything to do with Worth Manning." Emma arranged some of the disrupted papers on her desk and placed a stapler on top to make sure they stayed put. "And what would you be able to do if he did come back?"

Emma could see that Granny was going over the options in her head and not coming up with much. "I would tell Milo," she'd finally said with a determined jerk of her chin. "He'd get help. It worked before."

"And by the time he got here, I'd be done for. That is, if that was the senator's intent." Emma stopped fiddling with the stuff on her desk. "Granny, you're needed in Catalina tomorrow to help Milo with Tessa. And don't worry, I'll be fine. I'm going straight to bed after I finish here. And look, you're fading by the second. You need to rest yourself."

"The dead don't need no rest. That's why it's called eternal sleep."

"Well, then you need to recharge your batteries."

It was true. Granny's physical presence was fast growing faint. "I'd feel a lot better, Emma, if you had a gun in the house. In my day, we'd never be without a rifle."

"I don't need a gun, Granny. I'll make sure I set the alarm, and besides, I have Archie." They both looked down at the little black dog curled up on the loveseat. As they watched, Archie twitched and let out a series of loud snores.

"You need a gun," Granny said with sturdy punctuation. "Better yet, I wish Phil was here."

"But he's not, Granny. And I don't need him here. I'll be fine."

Granny's image drifted off like mist on a breeze. "Yep, Phil *and* his gun. That's the ticket."

Emma didn't feel particularly threatened by Worth Manning, but she was wary of him. Like the snake Granny thought he was, he had slithered through her final questions slow and steady, all the time eyeing her as if she were an unsuspecting field mouse.

"Grant used to tell me how George and his buddies would go over to Catalina to fish and drink, often with female company."

Manning had offered a slick smile. "That we did."

"Did you go on your boat?" Emma asked, remembering that Denise had told her that Worth had owned a boat.

"Sometimes. If there were a lot of us, we'd take two boats."

"Did you ever take Tessa over on your boat?"

"She might have gone over with me and the others. Hard to remember, Emma. It was a long time ago. But usually we guys took the boat and the ladies joined us later."

His answer jived with what Denise Dowd had said, that the women joined the men on the island.

"What are you driving at, Emma?"

The senator's voice was starting to take on an air of impatience, alerting her that she was losing his attention. She decided to jump in with both feet instead of just dipping a toe.

"Senator, Tessa is still on Catalina Island. She's waiting for someone named Curtis to return to her. Only then will she be at peace."

Manning tilted his head back and laughed. When he stopped, he aimed dancing dark eyes at her. "You really believe that, Emma?" Before she could answer, he added with a slight shake of his head, "You were always such a smart, level-headed girl. I must say, I'm a bit disappointed."

Ignoring his comment, Emma pressed on. "Who's Curtis, Senator? And where can I find him?"

"There was never anyone by the name of Curtis in our group. Tessa North was a pretty girl with a lot of suitors. Just because she had a few laughs with us doesn't mean we were the only ones she kept company with."

Emma noticed Manning tapping his fingers on the arm of the chair, a signal he was about to cut her off. "You were at the Ambassador Hotel the night Robert Kennedy was shot, weren't you? You and Mrs. Manning were there with George and Celeste and several of your other friends."

Manning was noticeably surprised by the sharp turn in the questioning. Tilting his head slightly, he studied Emma, wondering what she was up to. "Yes, a lot of us were there. As a politician in the Democratic Party, it was also my duty to be there."

"That must have really shaken you up, Senator. Your political career was really starting to take off about then, wasn't it?"

He gave a hearty laugh. "What? Now you're going to insinuate I had something to do with Kennedy's death?"

Emma smiled. "No, of course not. It's just that Tessa disappeared shortly after Robert Kennedy was murdered."

"So you think maybe she had something to do with the assassination? Who knows, maybe she was Sirhan Sirhan's accomplice and lover." His amusement was as solid as a brick.

"After Kennedy's death, what did you do?"

"We were all questioned by the authorities. Horrible night; absolutely horrible — for us, for the entire country."

"What about the days following the murder? You would have been very upset. Maybe you went over to Catalina to relax, to try to forget for a few days what had just happened?"

Manning stood up. "I must be going, Emma. Sure you won't join me for dinner?"

Emma stood with him. She had other questions but could see she was being dismissed. Unless she followed him to dinner, she would have to end her interrogation. "Thank you, Senator, but I do have other plans." Out of the corner of her eye, she could see Granny giving her a thumbs up.

At the front door, they exchanged a handshake, with Emma thanking him for his time. But Manning did not immediately let go of her hand. Instead, he held it firmly, enclosing it in a two-handed grasp.

"I always heard, Emma, that Tessa North packed it in and went back home — another Hollywood dream dashed. Now, don't you think that's a much more reasonable explanation than all this ghost nonsense?"

"Tell you what, Emma," Phil said in an inviting tone. "Why don't you come on down to Julian tomorrow and stay the weekend? You can work on your cabin. Start decorating it so it's ready for your family for Christmas. I'm sure Aunt Susan would love to make plans with you for everyone's visit."

"I know you, Phil. You just want me to

cool things down with my Tessa research."

"Yes, I do. But I also want to see you. Unless you already have plans with a certain former US senator."

"Phil, please. He's more than thirty years my senior."

"Maybe, Fancy Pants, but he recognizes quality female flesh when he sees it. Remember, he was a big time alpha wolf in his day, and it sounds like he still enjoys baying at the moon."

"As inviting as a trip to Julian sounds to this quality female flesh, I have to take care of my car tomorrow."

"Something wrong with the SUV?" Alarm slipped into Phil's voice. "Did you have an accident of some kind?"

Darn, Emma thought. She didn't mean to let anything slip about the vandalism. In bringing Phil up to speed on everything she'd uncovered and about her exchange with both the unknown ghost and Manning, Emma had carefully edited out the spray-painting of her SUV. She knew it would worry him.

"No, no accident. Just some vandalism. Kids probably." She cringed as the half lie escaped her lips.

"What happened?"

"Nothing really, just a little spraypaint."

"Fancy Pants." He stretched the two words out into a full sentence.

"Someone just sprayed a few words across the side of the Lexus. That's all."

"What words?"

"Nothing."

"If it's really nothing, you'd tell me. Do I have to drive up there tonight and see it for myself?"

"Don't be ridiculous."

"Then you stop being evasive."

Emma knew good and well that Phil Bowers was stubborn enough to jump into his truck and drive all the way to Pasadena tonight from San Diego just to see what she was avoiding telling him.

"All right," she said in frustration. "Cool your jets." She took a deep breath and held it as if jumping into deep water. When she released it, she said in a series of nonstop words, "When I was at Milo's today, someone spraypainted the words *leave the dead alone* across the side of my car."

There was a short silence on Phil's end, then the sound of a throat clearing. "And you consider that *nothing?*"

"I realize it's not nothing, but I'm not sure what to make of it."

"It's a warning, Emma. A big one. Surely you know that."

"Of course I do. But it doesn't make me want to stop looking into Tessa's death — just the opposite. Now I want to know *exactly* what happened and who's involved."

TWENTY

Jackie Houchin looked Emma's SUV over in silence, her eyes wide pools of ink. "That's some tag job. You sure it has something to do with this Tessa ghost? Could be about you in general."

"About ninety percent sure," replied Emma. "Milo Ravenscroft is ninety-nine percent positive."

"Can't argue with stats like that." Jackie handed a large, thick, brown envelope over to Emma. "Here's the latest mail. There's also some stuff from the producer in there that he wants you to look over for next season."

Emma took the envelope, and together the two women headed into Emma's office in the guesthouse. The day was overcast and gray, but no rain fell like the day before.

"Thanks for bringing this over, Jackie. And for helping me with the car."

When Emma told Phil that she was going

to call her insurance company in the morning, he'd asked her to reconsider.

"I don't know what your deductible is, Emma, but you might be better off getting a new paint job on your own, even if it's more than your deductible. You had a loss on your insurance just over a year ago. This could make your premiums go through the roof. Get an estimate or two, then crunch the numbers before calling your insurance company."

It was sound advice. With Tracy on her way to Catalina, Emma called Jackie and asked if she'd come to the house and help her with the car. She told her they could work there and threw in the offer of a nice lunch. Seeing that it was Friday, she sweetened the pot with Friday afternoon off. She'd already called a few body shops recommended by her dealership and settled on one her father had used before.

Jackie, a young African-American woman in her mid-twenties, shrugged off her bomber jacket as soon as she entered the guesthouse. "No problem. Always happy to get out of the office for a field trip." She looked around the guesthouse-turned-gym-turned-office. "And this is a lot nicer than my cubicle at the production office."

"There's juice and water in the little

fridge," Emma told her. "Help yourself."

While Emma sorted through the papers in the envelope, Jackie grabbed a bottle of water and settled onto a nearby recumbent stationary bike.

"The numbers for both Senator Manning and Paul Feldman are in there," she told Emma as she started a slow, relaxed pedal. "Look for a blue sheet of paper."

Emma picked out the blue page. On it were printed three phone numbers for Paul Feldman and one for Worth Manning. Feldman's were his cell, home, and office. There were addresses for both men.

"Wow," Emma said to Jackie. "You hit the mother lode with Paul Feldman."

Jackie gave her a sly smile. "Turns out my boyfriend's cousin works in the administration office of the studio that handled his last two projects. Feldman is only semi-retired. The number for Worth Manning is actually the office of Kenmore Holt, his agent or manager — not exactly sure which. But Holt handles bookings for peeps on the speaking circuit, including Manning."

"So it was Holt or his office that would have told Senator Manning that we were looking for him."

"That's who I left a message with. Sorry I didn't get you hooked up directly to the senator."

"No problem." Emma held up an elegant ivory business card. "The senator gave it to me last night himself. He said his office told him I was looking for him. He must have meant Holt's office."

Jackie stopped pedaling. "Last night? You saw him last night?"

"Sure did. He showed up here, right on my doorstep. My ex-father-in-law is a close friend of the senator's. He gave him both my address and my cell phone number."

"Okay," the young woman said, leaning forward and fixing her eyes on Emma with laser accuracy, "level with me. Do Feldman and Manning have anything to do with this Tessa ghost? Or is this something else?"

It was a delicate question. Emma wasn't sure what to share with Jackie. She trusted her with the show's research and even with her own personal information, but she wasn't sure she wanted to connect George and his friends to a possible murder beyond her own circle of friends. Yet she didn't want to lie to Jackie either. She also knew Jackie was resourceful and that one minute on IMDB and she'd make the same connection to George and his buddies that Emma had. And then there was the whole question of Jackie's disbelief in ghosts. Would she think Emma nuts if she told her? It was a tough call.

"I've discovered that they knew her at one time," Emma admitted. "And I've been asking them some rather personal questions."

"So you think your own father-in-law and his friends had something to do with your ride being tagged?"

"I'm not sure, Jackie. It could have been one of Tessa's other friends I've talked to in the last few days." Emma put her elbows on her desk and cupped her face in her hands. "It seems unlikely though. Everyone I've talked to is in their sixties and seventies. The senator is eighty."

"That doesn't mean a thing, Emma." Jackie made a scoffing sound. "There's any number of fools who'd wield a paint can for twenty bucks. Forty will get you artwork. It's just a matter of giving them the cash and location of the vehicle."

Jackie dismounted from the bike and came to stand in front of Emma's desk. She was almost as tall as Emma but not as slim. She dressed very hip and wore her mahogany-colored hair clipped close to her skull, which accentuated her high cheekbones and long, graceful neck. Her large eyes studied Emma from behind trendy rectangular-shaped glasses. "Something about this has been bothering me."

Emma looked up and knew Jackie would never buy any half-baked story. In spite of her youth, she was savvy and could read people too well. But Emma didn't want to offer anything up until she knew what was on Jackie's mind. "And that is?"

Jackie moved over to the loveseat and plopped down next to Archie. The animal nudged her for attention and she complied, rubbing him behind the ears while she spoke. "I thought you wanted to do a story about ghost sightings on Catalina Island."

"I do. That's what all this is about."

"No, it's not. The only ghost you've mentioned at all is this Tessa girl. You've not had me look into any other sightings, just background on Tessa North — who she knew, her family. I'll bet even that Tony Keller guy you asked me to research is tied to her, isn't he?"

"Yes, he was one of her friends," Emma admitted. "By the way, did you find anything on him?"

"Yes, I did. It's in a folder in the package I gave you."

Emma sorted through the mail until she found a thin folder. Inside were a couple printouts of news articles.

"There's not much," Jackie reported.

"Seems like a straightforward suicide. Guy shot himself. Left no note, but friends and his agent claimed he'd been despondent for quite a while. Had been drinking heavily and unable to work. Too bad, too, because he seemed to have a promising career."

Scanning the articles, Emma took note of the date of Tony Keller's suicide. "Hmm, says he killed himself in early February of 1969. That was just eight or nine months after Tessa died." She looked up at Jackie. "And what about Jack Nowicki?"

"I reached him and fed him the lines you gave me." Jackie shook her head. "What a poor excuse for a human being. He started screaming that his sister was a whore. Said only whores go to Hollywood. When I asked if he'd seen her since she left or did he know where she was now, he said no but added as a footnote that if he ever did see her again, he was going to beat the evil out of her."

Emma pursed her mouth in disgust. "Lovely."

"Which brings us back to my original question."

The young woman's boldness made Emma want to smile, but she didn't lest Jackie interpret it as condescension. Jackie's demeanor demanded that she be taken as an equal, and Emma was thrilled to treat her as such. Other TV hosts and producers had found it off-putting, preferring assistants with a more subservient nature. Jackie didn't believe in cowering before demanding celebrities and TV personalities, and it had caused her to be shuffled between several shows until she landed with Emma and the travel show. Emma had no doubt that while Jackie's forthcoming personality might be causing her some difficulties early in her career, down the road it would serve her well when she was running her own production company. It was just a matter of time before Jackie Houchin made a name for herself in television.

In answer to Jackie's inquiries, Emma got up and went to the closet. She pulled out the box containing the painting and uncovered it, displaying it to Jackie.

"This is a painting of the beach in Avalon."

Jackie nodded. "I recognized it immediately. I've been over there many times."

Emma pointed to a figure in a pink polka dot bikini. "That is Tessa North."

After gently moving Archie aside, Jackie got off the loveseat and kneeled in front of the painting for a closer look. She ran her dark fingers with their neon nail polish lightly over Tessa's image, as if reading her history in Braille.

"Are you sure?" Jackie said, looking up at Emma.

"Yes." Emma went to her desk and produced the photo Denise had loaned her. "See, this is her back in 1968. And here is George Whitecastle and Worth Manning." Emma moved her finger to another man. "And this is Tony Keller."

"But this is just a painting with a girl in a bikini. Her face isn't clearly defined. Could be anyone." Jackie's eyes scanned the painting, taking in every detail. "Guess black people didn't go to the beach in those days."

Emma smiled, but before she could say anything, Jackie pointed at the date and signature in the corner. "And look at this. This was painted in 2006. There's no way the artist, this Sechrest person, could know that was Tessa North." Jackie turned her eyes back on Emma. "So how could you?"

This was the fork in the road Emma dreaded. She could either tell Jackie the truth or fabricate something that sounded more reasonable than the truth, followed by feeling bad for lying.

Emma propped the painting against a wall. "Jackie, we need to talk."

While Emma rolled her desk chair closer to the loveseat, Jackie resumed her place next to Archie. The animal was happy to have her back. In Emma's hand was one of the books she'd bought in Catalina.

"This painting was done by a woman named Sandy Sechrest," Emma explained. "The scene is from the summer of 1968, about the time Tessa North went missing, and I believe she died. Sandy Sechrest could see ghosts, and she remembers seeing Tessa's ghost on the beach that summer. She set it down in a painting so it wouldn't be forgotten." Emma opened the book and handed it over to Jackie. "See here? This is a description of Sandy's sighting of the bikini ghost, or Tessa North."

Jackie read the piece in the book noted by Emma. "So you met this Sechrest woman on Catalina and she told you about Tessa?"

"Kind of."

"Kind of?"

"Sandy Sechrest is now dead." Emma scooted her chair closer to the suspicious Jackie. "Jackie, when Phil and I were on Catalina Island last week, I met both the ghost of Sandy Sechrest and the ghost of Tessa North."

In response, Jackie hopped up from her seat and strode to the wall of windows, where she stood looking out at the Miller back yard. Emma let her be, knowing the intelligent woman was processing the information like a fine-tuned computer chip.

A few minutes later, Jackie said, without turning around, "You know, even though I don't believe in such things as ghosts, I knew there was something odd going on with you — something connected more personally to the show than just you being the host. Every now and then, I'd overhear you talking to someone who wasn't there." She turned to face Emma. "I always believed you were on your Bluetooth. Guess I wanted to believe it. That Milo guy? I always thought he was your connection to such craziness, then I started wondering if you had a direct line yourself."

When she paused, Emma leaned back in her chair like a therapist on the clock and asked, "So how do you feel about it, Jackie?"

It was obvious Jackie was not totally caught off-guard, but shock edged her like a thin outline. "Not sure. Do you believe ghosts are always around you? Do you think they're here right now?"

From her questions, Emma realized that while Jackie didn't believe in ghosts, she was taking Emma's personal revelation seriously.

"No, none are here right now." Emma wondered if she should tell Jackie about

Granny Apples but decided that tidbit of information could wait until the two of them could be properly introduced. She leaned forward. "Jackie, you don't have to believe in the existence of ghosts to work for me. I'll respect and honor your disbelief if you respect my abilities and my privacy concerning them. It's not something I advertise."

Jackie gave it several moments of thought before looking back at Emma. "Cute ghost pin," she finally said, noting the diamond brooch on Emma's shirt. "If that's the membership badge, sign me up."

Emma touched the brooch and laughed. "This was a gift from Phil Bowers. He gave it to me while we were on Catalina."

Jackie walked back to the painting and stared down at it. Emma let her be, allowing her to mull over the information at her own steady pace. After a full minute, Emma added, "She was about your age when she died."

Jackie continued staring down at the painting. "But we haven't found any information on her death."

"That's true. But, Jackie," Emma said with conviction, "she's dead, just the same."

Another long moment passed in silence before Jackie turned away from the painting and fixed Emma with a somber face. "Sounds to me like she was murdered."

"That's what we're all thinking. *We* being me, Milo, and my friend Tracy. Even Phil came to that conclusion."

"And you all are thinking this senator and George Whitecastle might have had something to do with it?"

"We don't know, Jackie. We just know that they knew her quite well." Emma showed her the photo again. "And we know she disappeared shortly after this photo was taken."

Again, Jackie retreated into her thoughts and went back to studying the painting. "What do you think she's waving at?"

TWENTY-ONE

"Milo," Emma said into her cell phone, "it's me. Have you met Sandy Sechrest yet?"

"No. We haven't been in Catalina very long. We just dropped our bags off at the hotel and are strolling down Crescent Avenue, hoping to bump into Tessa. Granny's gone on ahead to try and find her."

"I'm not sure if Sandy comes out much until sunset, but when you do see her, I need you to ask her a question for me. It's very important."

"Sure. What is it?"

"Ask her —"

"Wait a minute," Milo said, cutting her off. "Let me write this down to make sure I get it right." Emma could hear him talking to Tracy. A second later, he was back. "Okay, shoot."

"Ask Sandy about her painting — the one I bought with Tessa in it. She should remember which one." She stopped while she listened to Milo relaying her words to Tracy, who was probably jotting them down. "In the painting, Tessa is waving at something or someone." She paused again. "Ask her if that's what she remembers Tessa doing when she first saw her, or if it was her interpretation for the sake of the painting."

"That's an odd question."

"Yes, and I'm sorry I didn't notice it long before now. In fact, I didn't notice it; Jackie, my assistant, did." Emma smiled at Jackie, who was kicked back on the loveseat once again with Archie, listening to Emma's excited phone call.

"If Sandy painted exactly what she re-membered Tessa doing when she first saw her, it might help us somehow. It's a long shot, but you never know. Maybe Sandy can recall what Tessa was waving at, or maybe you can jog Tessa's memory when you see her."

"It's definitely a lead we didn't have be-fore."

Before ending the call, Emma gave Milo a sixty-second rundown of her meeting the night before with Worth Manning. At first hesitant to talk in front of Jackie, she finally decided hiding things from her at this point would only make her more suspicious. As

Emma talked to Milo, Jackie's face remained a blank, but her eyes broadcasted an intense interest. At the end of the conversation, like Phil, Milo told her to be very careful.

The plan was for Emma to drive her SUV to the body shop, with Jackie following behind her. Then they'd go to lunch, and after, Jackie would bring Emma back to the house. Emma had no doubt that their lunch conversation would be interesting. She was also glad the unhappy ghost hadn't made an appearance. She had enough explaining to do.

As Emma was backing out of the Miller driveway, a dark blue Jaguar pulled in behind her, blocking her exit. Looking in the rearview mirror, she groaned.

Grant Whitecastle hopped out of his car, slammed the door, and strode to Emma's driver's side. When he spotted the words painted on the side of her vehicle, he stopped in his tracks, pulled off his sunglasses, and stared at them.

Emma lowered her window. "What are you doing here?" Try as she might, she couldn't keep the snappishness out of her voice.

Grant looked at Emma, then back at the side of her SUV. He shook himself to get his mind back on his purpose. Tucking his sunglasses into the neck of his shirt, he moved directly in front of her window.

"I came to ask you what in the hell you think you're doing, bothering my parents and their friends with all this ghost bullshit." He pointed at the paint job. "But I see someone else has beaten me to it."

"I'm on my way out, Grant. I don't have time for one of your tantrums."

"You leave my parents alone, Emma."

"Is that an order from them or from you? Seems to me they were happy enough to see me. In fact, your mother was quite chatty. Both told me they wished they saw more of me."

Grant stared at his ex-wife, his face going scarlet with anger.

"If they tell me to go away, Grant, I will," Emma continued. "But I'm taking no orders from the likes of you. Those days are over."

Grant smacked the side of Emma's SUV with his fist. "I said, leave them alone!"

"And you leave Emma alone."

Both Grant and Emma swung their heads in the direction of the voice. It was Jackie. She stood, hands on her hips, a few feet away from Grant.

"Who the hell are you?" Grant Whitecastle roared at Jackie.

Emma shoved her door open, forcing Grant to back away. She climbed out of the SUV and faced him. Next door, a neighbor came out of her home to watch the scene unfold on the usually quiet street. Across the street, a man watched from a parked car. She didn't recognize the car, but the man behind the wheel looked vaguely familiar. The last thing Emma wanted was to put on a show for the neighborhood, but Grant wasn't the type to back down, with or without grace.

"That's Jackie, my assistant," Emma told Grant, shaking a finger at him. "And don't you dare yell at her. Yell at your own assistant, providing you can keep one long enough. How many have you been through this season, Grant? Three? Four?"

Glaring at Emma, Grant directed his words at Jackie. "This is none of your business, girl. Get lost."

"Girl?" Jackie stepped closer. "And if it concerns Emma, it is my business. So why don't you get your pompous ass back in your Jag before I call the cops."

"Okay, everyone," Emma said, holding her hands out and working hard to keep her voice steady. "Let's all calm down. There's no need to escalate this."

Grant Whitecastle sneered at Jackie

Houchin. "Hear that?"

"I was talking to both of you," Emma said, stepping into her irate mother mode.

Emma glanced over the hedge at the elderly neighbor who was standing half hidden behind one of her rose bushes. "It's okay, Mrs. Collins," she called out. "No need to be alarmed." But Emma knew her parents would get an earful when they returned. She turned back to her ex-husband.

"Grant, I merely asked your parents about an actress they might have known years ago; that's it. As for ghosts, that's my gig these days, if you haven't noticed." She drew a breath. "Besides, neither George nor Celeste seemed all that upset that I talked to them. So I don't know what they've told you."

"I didn't hear it from them, Emma. I heard it from someone else. I heard how you badgered my poor dying father until he was so upset he almost stopped breathing."

"What?" Emma stared at Grant with an open mouth. "That is not what happened, Grant Whitecastle. Your father has trouble breathing because he has cancer, and you know it. In fact, he was laughing during my visit more than anything. So who's telling you such lies?" As her voice started to climb, she fought to bring it in check, even if her blood pressure was about to blow. "I demand to know."

"Someone who is a hell of a lot more concerned about the Whitecastles than you are, that's obvious."

Emma stepped close to Grant. Being close to the same height, she could look him directly in the eye, which she did. "I have been more considerate about the White-castle family and its name than you have ever been." Her voice was a low, threatening growl. "It wasn't me who dragged our dirty laundry into the tabloids, and don't you forget it."

"Stay away from my family, or else."

"Or else what?"

Before Emma knew what was happening, Grant grabbed her by the shoulders and pushed her back hard into the side of the SUV. As she hit, she let out a cry and slid to the ground. At the same time, Jackie launched herself at Grant, landing on his back like a hungry parasite. She wrapped an arm around his neck and wrestled him to the ground. Emma was trying to pull them apart just as a police car slid to a stop behind Grant's Jaguar.

"Oh my god, I had no idea we were being filmed."

Emma sat in disbelief as she watched the video of Grant shoving her, followed by Jackie riding him like a nag at Santa Anita. The police getting involved was the icing on the rotten cake. She was watching the full uncut version of the snippet run on Access Hollywood the night before, the evening of the day it had happened. The serious news programs had run the story, too, but did not have the video because the paparazzi who'd shot it had sold exclusive rights to the entertainment news show. It was just a matter of time before still shots showed up in the tabloids. The cameraman had even managed to get several clear shots of the side of Emma's spraypainted SUV. The story had been tagged *The Whitecastle War Continues.*

"It's okay, Emma," Jackie said, putting a fresh mug of coffee in front of her boss. "You heard what the suits said. It will be good for the show. People who'd never heard of *The Whitecastle Report* are sure to watch it now, or at least give it a try. They've even picked up more episodes and might run it twice a week."

"You don't understand, Jackie." Emma ran her hands through her hair. "My daughter saw this last night, and so did her friends. It was humiliating for her."

Kelly had called her mother last night, having seen the news feature before Emma with the three-hour time difference. She'd not been amused to see her parents brawling on national TV, although she understood that the likelihood of Emma starting it had been slim. Phil had called her, too. He hadn't seen the video, but his aunt Susan had. She'd called him, upset and worried for Emma's safety.

"She'll get over it, Emma," Jackie told her, which was exactly what Phil had told her. "She's not the first kid to see her parents fight in public, and she won't be the last. My aunt and uncle once had a brawl on the front lawn that lasted so long, the neighbors actually brought out lawn chairs to watch in comfort."

"You're making that up."

"Sadly, I'm not." Jackie sat down opposite Emma.

Emma picked up her coffee to take a drink but put the mug down without doing so. So many things were happening at once. Her brain felt shattered, each shard running off in a different direction to pursue a different issue. She picked up a pen and started jotting down points to be addressed individually, thinking that by separating each problem, she'd be able to keep track of them better.

"Okay," she said, tapping the end of the pen against the first item on her list. "First of all, the video. What was that all about? I don't recall a car driving up while we were . . . um . . . *conversing* with Grant. Do you? There was a car parked across the street, but I never saw anyone with a camera."

Jackie shook her head. "No, but we were occupied." She pointed at Emma's list. "Don't you think we should tackle item three first? Isn't that the most important issue right now?"

"I'm saving the worst for last."

"I see." From Jackie's tone, Emma could tell she didn't agree with her plan of action.

Jackie took a drink of her coffee before continuing her thoughts on item one. "It's common for paparazzi to stalk celebrities. The creep probably followed Grant around, hoping he'd be his usual jerk self. And boy, did he hit the jackpot. We just never noticed his car drive up after Grant got there."

The theory sounded reasonable to Emma. Except for when she was in the middle of her messy divorce from Grant, the gossip hounds hadn't paid much attention to her. It stood to reason that this guy was following Grant and got lucky. He could probably put a kid through college for what Emma imagined he got paid for the video and photos.

"I think you may be right there," she told Jackie. "He was probably in the right place at the right time — at least for him." She moved the tip of the pen down to the second item on her list. "Next, who told Grant I was at his parents' home, if not his parents?"

"How about Worth Manning?" Jackie answered. "Of course, providing that ex of yours was telling the truth."

"He was. I called Celeste this morning. She said she and George were very upset and sorry about what happened yesterday. She also told me that neither of them had said anything to Grant about my recent visits. In fact, neither have seen or spoken with him since Thanksgiving." Emma looked at Jackie. "And I believe them." What she didn't tell Jackie was that Celeste had politely suggested that Emma refrain from contacting them until Grant cooled down.

They were at the office at the studio where *The Whitecastle Report* was filmed. Saturday or no Saturday, the special meeting with the show's producers that morning had been mandatory. And even though the studio was thrilled with the publicity the incident had garnered for Emma's show, it still felt to Emma like she'd been called into the principal's office. She seemed to be the only one not happy with the negative publicity, feeling it put *The Whitecastle Report* on a similar level with Grant's show.

"It could also have been Paul Feldman." Emma jotted both names down next to the second bullet point. "He arrived just as I was leaving. Either one of them are likely candidates."

"Was anyone else in the house when you visited George?"

Emma started to shake her head, then stopped. "A maid was there," she recalled. "She showed me into George's study, asked if we needed anything, then left. I assumed she went downstairs. Never saw her again. When I left, I let myself out."

"Was the maid someone who'd been with them a long time?" Jackie asked with interest. "If so, she could have told Grant, thinking she was looking after George's welfare."

Emma gave it some thought. "I'd never seen her before. They had one head maid for a very long time named Ivy, but she retired a few years ago. They also have a few part-time employees. I only saw the one maid when I was there. Except for her and

George, the house appeared empty."

Jackie was perched on the padded arm of a chair. Swinging a long leg over one arm, she slid down into the seat. "Do you think that Hyland woman or Denise Dowd would have said anything? Those were the only other two you've spoken to, right?"

"That's the entire list." Emma jotted Fran Hyland's name under Feldman's. She did not write down Denise Dowd's but instead circled point number three. "And that brings us to the third problem at hand."

Emma stared down at her third and final bullet point: *Denise Dowd Murdered!*

TWENTY-TWO

Denise Dowd had been murdered just hours after Emma had seen her at her apartment. The police had found Emma's business card on the coffee table. When the studio informed them that she was working from home, they'd shown up at the Miller residence to question her. After breaking up the fracas between Emma, Grant, and Jackie, they'd questioned each of them. Grant, knowing nothing about Denise Dowd, had been the first to be released, but not until receiving a stern warning to stay away from Emma.

When Denise didn't report to Bing's for her shift or answer her phone, someone from the restaurant went to her apartment to check on her. They'd found her on the kitchen floor in a pool of blood, compliments of a nasty knife wound to her chest. The knife was missing. There'd been no indication of a forced entry or of burglary, nor had Denise fought back. The attack had been swift and unexpected — a likely breech of trust on the part of someone Denise knew.

It was initially determined that the time of death had been sometime between when Emma left her, which was close to noon, and four o'clock. When a neighbor came forth to say he remembered seeing Denise around one thirty, it narrowed the time frame even more. Fortunately for Emma, that was the same time period she was with Milo and Tracy. The police checked her alibi, including checking the time the police report was made about the vandalism to her vehicle.

When questioned about why she was with Denise that morning, Emma told the police Denise was helping her research an actress from the sixties who had been a friend of Denise's. Emma said nothing about ghosts, but the detective, a tall, slender, middle-aged African-American man named Tillman, easily made the connection from Emma's occupation to the vandalism and asked her point-blank if the person she was researching had something to do with the paranormal. Emma didn't lie. She gave them Tessa's name and her theory that Tessa was a ghost haunting Catalina.

She and Detective Tillman were seated in the living room, with the detective occupying the same chair Worth Manning had used the night before. Another detective was questioning Jackie in the den.

Emma had been grilled before about murder. It had been in Julian when she was researching Granny's past. She knew that generally police took a dim view of ghost stories. In the Julian matter, one detective had been patient and listened; the other had been scornful. Emma had learned to be careful when bringing up ghosts to the authorities. At the same time, when asked who besides Denise Dowd she'd spoken to about Tessa North, Emma didn't hesitate to rattle off the names of all concerned. She might not offer up information, but she wasn't going to conceal it, especially since she had no idea what Jackie was telling the other detective. And it wasn't lost on her that one of the people she'd talked to might have been Denise's killer and the person behind the warning scrawled across the side of her SUV.

"Tell me, Mrs. Whitecastle," the detective said. "Do you have any reason to believe that the vandalism to your vehicle and Ms. Dowd's murder are related?"

Before she could answer, a gust of wind

swirled through the room. The detective took notice. "Must be a window open in here," he said, adjusting his suit jacket. "When we're done, you might want to check it out."

Emma knew there was no window left open. Even before she saw the spirit, she knew the mystery ghost was back.

"Now look what you've done," a disembodied voice scolded her from the direction of the mantle. "You've ruined everything."

Emma ignored the voice and returned her attention to the detective. "Not sure, Detective. I didn't know Denise personally, so I don't know who in her life might have wanted her dead. Could have been coincidental timing."

"Uh-huh." Tillman stopped writing in his notebook and fixed her with eyes the color of soot. "The police take a dim view of coincidences."

Before either of them could say anything more, the detective who'd been questioning Jackie stepped into the room. He gestured to Tillman, who stood up and went to him. The two detectives huddled in the corner, whispering. Every now and then, Tillman glanced back at Emma.

The unknown spirit was still in the room. Emma could see her outline several yards away. It hovered like a cloud without a breeze to propel it to its next location. As she focused, Emma could see more of the ghost, at least enough to determine that it might not be the spirit of Linda Manning. Emma had met Mrs. Manning on several occasions. She'd been built a lot like her husband, tall and slender. The last time Emma had seen her, her silver hair had been cropped close. Though not short, the outline of the ghost appeared to be of average height and a little pudgy, with shoulder-length hair.

As Emma watched, the ghost drifted toward her. She wanted to ask the image questions but didn't dare with Tillman keeping an eagle eye on her.

"Be glad I'm dead, Emma Whitecastle," the apparition said when it reached her. "Or else you'd be in the morgue next to that silly Dowd woman."

Emma sucked in her breath and went white.

"You okay, Mrs. Whitecastle?" The question came from Detective Tillman, who had moved to her side. The ghost disappeared.

"Yes." She looked up at Tillman, taken aback that he was flesh and bone, half expecting to see yet another spirit. "Yes," she repeated. "I'm fine. It's been a very trying few days."

Tillman took his seat again. The other detective moved within earshot. "So," Detective Tillman started, "when were you going to tell us that you think this Tessa North was murdered?"

Emma's surprise didn't last long, realizing that Jackie must have told them. "It's just a theory, Detective Tillman." She glanced from one detective to the other. "There's no concrete evidence that she was murdered."

"But you've seen her ghost?" Tillman asked.

Emma looked at Tillman, then at his partner, a compact white man who wore thick-rimmed glasses. Emma noted that both men wore serious looks without a hint of disdain. After a long hesitation, she replied, "Yes, I have. On Catalina. And no one seems to know what happened to her."

Taking out his notebook and pen again, Tillman leaned forward. "Do you know who she went to the island with?"

"No, only that she went there shortly after Robert Kennedy was assassinated and was never seen again. The name Curtis keeps coming up, but none of her friends from that time recall anyone by that name."

The two detectives questioned Emma

some more, taking turns as new thoughts and avenues of possibilities occurred to them. She cooperated as best she could, made easier by their open attitude. If they thought she was a nut case, they hid it well.

Before leaving, Detective Tillman gave her a stern warning. "For the time being, Mrs. Whitecastle, why don't you back off from your research on this North woman." When Emma started to protest, he added, "Until we're sure Denise Dowd's murder has nothing to do with your curiosity. If Tessa North was murdered, you could be stirring up a hornets' nest. You might even be in danger yourself."

Emma felt her knees wobble. In the shock of being threatened by a ghost, she'd forgotten about the real danger of the living.

TWENTY-THREE

Even though it was Saturday, Jackie went back to her own desk to catch up on some work. When she was alone, Emma dug her cell phone out of her purse and scrolled through her list of recently received calls. When she found what she was searching for, she hit the button to call the number. In spite of Detective Tillman's warning, she wasn't about to give up digging into the disappearance of Tessa North. With everything that had happened, she felt compelled at this point, her need to know gnawing at her like an overwhelming addiction.

Worth Manning picked up on the second ring. "Change your mind about having dinner with me, Emma?"

"I think I've had enough excitement for a few days, Senator. I'm sure you saw the news last night."

Manning chuckled softly. "I certainly did."

Emma cut to the chase. "Was that your doing?"

"I have no idea what you're talking about."

"Someone called Grant and told him I was upsetting George and Celeste with ghost talk and questions about Tessa North. Was it you?"

"You know what they say about making assumptions."

"I've already been made out to be an ass on TV. I can't see where I have anything to lose here."

"Emma, do I really seem like the type of man who would go running to Grant Whitecastle? He may be the son of my best friend, but, personally, I find him to be a greasy little worm." When she didn't answer, he gave a short chuckle and continued. "Believe me, Emma, had I thought your questions were upsetting George and Celeste, I would have told you to your face last night."

"What about Denise Dowd? When was the last time you saw her?"

"Ah, yes, the murdered woman. The police came by late yesterday afternoon. Truth is, I didn't remember her, and I told the police so. Even provided them with an alibi for the time in question."

"Denise Dowd was another one of the young actresses from forty years ago. A roommate of Tessa North's."

"So the police told me." A few seconds passed while Manning thought about it. "As I recall, Tessa roomed with a couple of girls. Was Denise the pretty one or the plain one?"

"The pretty one."

"Now I vaguely remember her, but we never got very close. I lost touch with most of those people once my political career took off. Is she now another ghost on your list?" Emma could hear his smirk through the phone. "Are she and Tessa frolicking together over on Catalina now?"

Emma ignored the remark. "Doesn't it seem strange that the same day I questioned her about Tessa North, the same day you came to visit me, and the same day my Lexus was spraypainted, someone chose to kill Denise? In fact, she was murdered shortly before you came by to see me."

"Is that an accusation?"

"Just stating the facts. I saw Denise. She was murdered. You dropped in, unannounced, at my home. All in the same day."

"Sounds like you're a busy little bee. And, like I said, I gave the police an accounting of my whereabouts."

Emma pressed on. "So when was the last time you saw Denise?"

"I honestly don't remember her much,

Emma. There were several girls who chummed around with Tessa. I remember Tessa because I had a short-lived affair with her. Had I not, she'd be just another forgotten pretty face. And it seems to me, you'd be better served forgetting her yourself."

"What about Fran Hyland? Do you remember her?"

There was a slight pause on Manning's end. "Yes, I know Fran."

"You said you know her, not knew or remember her. I'm guessing you've seen her more recently than forty years ago."

"That's because I've done business with Fran in recent years. She has a professional placement business here in LA. But being the smart girl you are, I'm sure you already know that."

"Yes, I do. I spoke with Ms. Hyland a couple of days ago."

"I've hired a few of her applicants over the years. Nothing beyond that."

"Did you have a fling with her back in the old days, too?"

The senator laughed. "Yes, as a matter of fact, I did. Everyone had a fling with Fran back then. But that's ancient history."

Emma pulled her notebook out of her purse and scanned the other names. "How about Shelly Campbell?"

This time the pause on the other end was long enough for Emma to prod. "Senator?"

"I remember Shelly. She stood out from the others because she was a dancer. She was very tall, with legs that went on forever . . . rather like yours."

Emma was glad the conversation was taking place by phone. Otherwise, Manning would have seen how nervous he was making her.

"And no," he added before Emma could ask, "I never had an affair with Shelly. I heard she got a big contract in Vegas and never saw her again after she left town."

A lot of Manning's story was fitting with Denise's information. Manning could have hired someone to spraypaint her car and to kill Denise, but he seemed like he didn't care if his past came to light. But it could be all a very good act. He was a former actor and a career politician — two backgrounds custom-made for spinning words and putting on a front.

"Now," added Manning. "How about dinner. I might think Grant despicable, but I've always found you to be rather fetching."

Emma tapped the end of her pen over and over on point three on the paper until the gathering of dots merged into a small ink-blot.

"Earth to Emma."

Standing in her doorway was Jackie, looking concerned. If being questioned by the police had rattled the young woman, she didn't show it. After the detectives left, Emma and Jackie resumed their plans, taking Emma's SUV into the body shop, then stopping off for a long lunch. But instead of an early lunch, it had been a late one. They'd used the time to go over the details, hoping to find something that might have been overlooked and might point them toward Denise's murderer and Tessa's disappearance.

"I called your name. Didn't you hear me?"

Emma gave herself a shake. "Guess I was lost in my thoughts."

"Your mother is on the line," Jackie announced. "She said she tried calling your cell, but it kept going to voicemail, so she called the studio."

While Emma was speaking with Worth Manning, two calls had come in on her cell, but she'd been so engrossed with the conversation, she hadn't bothered checking to see who was calling. Her parents were due home the next day. Worried, Emma picked up her office phone and punched the blinking light.

"Hi, Mother? Everything okay?" She hoped her parents hadn't seen the news about her fight with Grant. If they hadn't, she wasn't going to break it to them this way.

"Everything's fine, dear. We got off the ship just a little while ago and wanted to call you. Though we're a bit surprised to find you at your office on a Saturday."

"We got called in for a special meeting. I'm sorry I missed your earlier calls. Did you have a nice time?"

"Wonderful! In fact, Emma, that's one of the reasons we're calling. Your father and I met this lovely couple on the ship. They were positively raving about this little place in Key West. And you know your father, how he loves adventures. So we'd like to hop down to Key West for a few days. That is, unless you feel we should come straight home."

Emma cringed. There was something in her mother's tone that suggested they'd seen the video. "Why might I need you to come home?" She forced mirth into her voice. "I'm all grown up, and the house and Archie are fine. Even Granny's behaving herself, sort of."

"Hmm."

The single sound confirmed that her mother knew about the fight with Grant. "You saw it, didn't you?"

"If you're referring to your public brawl with Grant, no, thankfully, we did not see it. But we heard about it on the news last night. And people were talking about it at breakfast this morning on the ship." Her mother paused. "Are you all right, Emma? We heard that Grant nearly shoved you under a car."

"I'm fine, Mother. Grant didn't push me under a car, just against my SUV. Jackie was there to make sure he didn't do anything more. I'm sure you'll hear all the gory details from Mrs. Collins when you get home."

Elizabeth Miller chuckled softly. "Was she hiding behind her rose bushes?"

"Like always." Emma took a deep breath. "Mother, I'm sorry the video embarrassed you and Dad. We had no idea that bottom-feeder was filming us."

"I won't lie, Emma. At first we were a bit uncomfortable, but we quickly got over it. We're much more concerned about you than any fake scandal. There were a few people on the cruise who knew you were our daughter and, I must tell you, they really rallied in your defense. Everyone's very glad you dumped that bozo Grant when you did."

Emma didn't correct her mother that it was actually Grant who had dumped her.

"And what about your car? Something about the dead?"

Emma explained to her mother about the vandalism, suggesting that it must have been related to her show. She carefully edited out Tessa North and murder. There would be time enough to go into that when her parents came home.

"Dad and I are very worried about you," Elizabeth repeated. "We don't understand what could have riled Grant up like that."

"I'm fine, Mother. Really. I recently visited George and had lunch with Celeste. Grant was given some misinformation about both encounters. He thought I'd endangered George's health."

"Well, that's just plain ridiculous. You love the Whitecastles. You'd never do such a thing."

"That's what I told him."

Assured that Emma was fine and that Grant was no longer a threat, the Millers decided to go on to Key West. Emma missed her parents but was happy that they were having such a lovely, long vacation. And with them in the Keys, she didn't have to be concerned about them worrying about her getting involved in another murder. It was another thing on her mental list that she could scratch off for now.

"By the way, Mother — Phil and I think everyone should get together in Julian for Christmas. We can properly christen my cabin. What do you think?"

"I think it's a wonderful idea. Today, the warm, sultry sea, and in a few weeks, the coolness of winter in the mountains. It's perfect."

When she ended the call with her mother, Emma went out to Jackie's desk. "Do you have a copy of that phone and address information for Paul Feldman?" she asked her. "I left my copy at home."

After Jackie produced a copy and handed it to her, Emma told her to go home and enjoy the rest of her weekend. Then she went back into her office, closed the door, and placed a call to Paul Feldman's cell phone.

"Mr. Feldman," she began after he answered. "This is Emma Whitecastle."

"Hello." Although warm toward her a few days ago, today Paul Feldman sounded cool and distant.

"Did I catch you at a bad time?"

"I'm afraid I'm quite busy at the moment.

287

What can I help you with, Emma?"

Leading with the less controversial subject on her agenda, Emma asked, "Did you see the news last night about Grant and me?"

"Yes, I'm afraid I did. Ruth and I are terribly sorry you had to go through that. It looked to us like Grant was totally out of line." The temperature in Feldman's voice defrosted a bit.

"Did you tell Grant that I visited George and upset him?"

"No, not at all." Feldman sounded genuinely surprised by Emma's question. "I can't remember the last time I spoke with Grant. And your little visit with George seemed to have uplifted him. He was actually laughing about your ghost encounter over our lunch."

"I'm very glad to hear that." She paused, setting the stage for her next approach. "I don't want to be a pest, Mr. Feldman, but I'd like to ask you a few more questions about Tessa North. Would it be possible to meet somewhere?"

"I told you all I know when I saw you a few days ago." The frost was back in his voice. Emma could feel it through the phone line. "And this morning, I told the police all I know about both Tessa and Denise Dowd."

It was obvious to Emma that Detective Tillman was wasting no time going down her list of people connected with her research on Tessa North. George and Celeste had probably been contacted already, too, as well as Fran Hyland. It was going to be very difficult for Emma to do any deeper digging with these folks.

"I have just a few more questions. Who knows, they might help you remember something new that could help the police." Emma kept her tone relaxed, hoping it would ease her way into setting something up with Paul Feldman. "May I buy you lunch?"

"No, Emma, you may not." His voice migrated from cold to snappish. "It's time you dropped this foolishness before someone else gets hurt."

The line went dead.

TWENTY-FOUR

Following her call with Paul Feldman, Emma tried to concentrate on working on *The Whitecastle Report.* In light of the overnight interest in her show, during their meeting that morning, the producers had provided several ideas for future shows and wanted Emma to review them and do some preliminary research to see if they would be feasible. She and Jackie had also presented ideas of their own. Jackie was hot to trot about the Catalina concept. Originally planned to be a show about the various spirits haunting the historic island, Jackie felt viewers would be more interested in how the research led to solving a forty-year-old murder.

"It's a natural," Jackie had insisted before they went into the meeting. "Murder always brings in the audience. It jacks the ratings."

Jackie Houchin may still be young, but there was no denying she had a nose for what viewers liked. If *The Whitecastle Report* continued to grow in popularity, Emma planned on suggesting that Jackie be promoted.

"I know you're right, Jackie, but Tessa's murder hasn't been confirmed yet. And the producers may not know about the Denise Dowd connection; I'd rather they didn't for now, not on the heels of the Grant incident." Seeing the frustration on Jackie's face, Emma had added, "Tell you what, if it turns out that Tessa North was murdered and we have proof of it, I will *consider* doing a show about it."

The young woman had been somewhat mollified by the semi-promise, and Emma knew the cogs in her fertile brain were already planning for the show. Emma, though, wasn't so sure she'd made a valid promise. If it turned out that George Whitecastle and his friends were somehow involved in Tessa's death, Emma knew she could never do the show, no matter how spectacular the ratings might be. If it came to that, she hoped Jackie would understand.

As she went through her notes from the morning meeting, Emma expanded on them, fleshing out the one-line ideas into plausible shows. But the more she tried to concentrate on subjects other than Tessa

North and Denise Dowd, the more her brain revisited it. It was a car wreck she couldn't avoid — a car wreck with too many vehicles and unaccounted tire tracks.

Tessa was already dead when Emma met her, but Denise had been very much alive. The more Emma tried to push Denise out of her mind, the more she felt responsible for the woman's death. Slipping into the ladies' room, she entered a stall and had herself a good cry. Once finished, Emma fixed her makeup and straightened her shoulders. Now she had two murders to get to the bottom of, and she was determined to do just that.

After being rebuffed by Paul Feldman, Emma was more determined than ever to speak with him. If the three amigos were hiding something, she felt that Paul Feldman was the most likely to tip his hand. Of the three, he was the only one who had not stayed on course with his emotions, going from shock at initially hearing Tessa's name to turning cold and even hostile today. And he was the only one who had given her any direct warning to cease before someone else got injured, or maybe even worse. She also wanted to question George Whitecastle further, but knew that door was closed to her — unless, of course, she stormed their home and insisted, in which case *she* would look like the crazy and not Grant, and in the world's eyes, Grant would have grounds for his behavior the day before.

Remembering that Hyland Staffing kept half-day hours on Saturday, Emma put in a call to Fran Hyland's office. She was told that Ms. Hyland was out of the office and would not be returning until the middle of next week. When asked if she wanted to leave her a voicemail message, Emma declined, doubting that Fran Hyland would ever call her back, especially on the heels of Denise's murder.

Denise. Now there was someone Emma really wanted to speak to again, but now it was impossible. Or was it?

Emma still hadn't heard back from Milo and Tracy regarding the painting and any contact with Tessa. She had fought the urge to call them last night but refrained, knowing they weren't just on the island to help her but to have a little time to themselves. They probably had not seen the news or they would have called. Emma even missed Granny's crankiness and wished she could call her back home, if for no other reason than to talk to her about the case. *The case* — that was what Granny had called it, and Emma had rebuked her. But it was a case, at least now.

The idea of calling on Granny gave Emma another thought. She looked at her watch. It was just after eleven in the morning. Emma punched in the speed-dial number for Milo on her cell phone.

The first words out of Milo's mouth were, "Emma, are you all right? We heard about the thing with Grant."

"You did?"

"Granny told us this morning. She said she saw it on TV in one of the bars last night. We wanted to call you, but she said you seemed fine."

"I am, but how would she know?"

"She popped in on you last night. Said you were sleeping like a baby."

Yes, Emma thought, *thanks to a couple of sleeping pills,* but she was touched by Granny's concern and thoughtfulness. Had Granny arrived a bit sooner, she would have heard Emma on the phone in a heated discussion with Phil Bowers.

When Phil had called to check up on Emma after learning of the scuffle with Grant, Emma told him about Denise's murder. He'd nearly come unglued.

"That's it," he'd yelled. "I'm canceling everything and coming up there tonight."

"No, Phil, you're not. I'm fine."

"You've been spraypainted, assaulted by your ex-husband on national TV, and are now involved in a murder. You tell me, what part of that sounds fine to you?"

Although he had a good point, Emma had held her ground. "I said I'm fine, Phil, and I mean it. The car's in the shop, Grant's returned to his hole in the ground, and I'm not involved in any murder."

Even as she said the last part, Emma knew it was a fib. Like it or not, she was, in one way or another, involved with Denise Dowd's demise. Maybe not directly, but it was just a matter of time before the connection was revealed. As Detective Tillman had said, the cops didn't like coincidences. What's more, Phil Bowers wasn't the type to believe in coincidences either.

Emma had caved in the face of facts. "Okay, so I am *a little* involved with Denise's murder, but only because I visited her the day it happened."

"Am I coming up there, or are you driving down here?"

"Neither." Emma had set her jaw in defiance. "I've already been bullied by Grant today — don't you start in on me, too."

"I'm not bullying you, Emma. I love you, and I don't want anything to happen to you."

"I'm not going anywhere. I've been summoned to a meeting in the morning with my producers. They saw the news tonight like everyone else. And I'm sure you have a full day tomorrow, as well." She'd paused to calm down and could tell by Phil's silence that he was trying to rein in his emotions on the other end of the line. "What's more, Phil, I won't have you running up here like a knight on a white horse every time you think I'm in trouble."

Phil knew better than to argue with Emma. She was every bit as stubborn as he was, maybe even more so. She just swaddled it in refinement. "My horse is brown with a white blaze."

The comment had elicited a soft giggle from Emma and dampened their mutual high temper like soft rain on a campfire.

After a big, exaggerated sigh, Phil had added, "Will you at least promise me to keep a low profile and not go snooping around any more?"

Emma didn't answer lightly, choosing to be truthful over compliant. "I will promise you, Phil, to be very careful. It's the best I can offer."

Returning her thoughts to the call with Milo, Emma asked, "But did Granny know about the murder?"

"Murder?" From his tone, Emma knew Milo hadn't heard.

In the background, she heard Tracy chime in, her voice raising an octave with each word. "Murder? What murder? Is she talking about Tessa or someone else? Let me talk to her."

There was a slight scuffling noise, then Milo's voice, "Wait a minute, let me put her on speaker." A second later, Emma was talking to both of them.

"Okay, pal," Tracy said. "What's this about murder?"

Emma bulldozed ahead, knowing there was no easy way to break the news. "Denise Dowd was murdered the day before yesterday. It happened while the three of us were at Milo's."

On the other end of the phone there was silence. Emma broke it by giving them a summary of the details, including her time with the police and her subsequent chats with everyone else. When she was finished, the silence on the other end was deafening.

"We're coming home," Tracy announced.

"There's no need for you to come home," Emma said.

"You're being threatened, Emma."

"No, I'm not. Warned maybe, but hardly

threatened. Considering what happened to Denise, don't you think if someone wanted me dead, I'd be so already?"

"That is hardly a comfort," Tracy snapped.

"Ladies, calm down," Milo interrupted. "I think Emma's right, though I agree that it is not very comforting. It makes me think that maybe Denise Dowd knew something else — something she didn't tell Emma for one reason or another."

"Which is why I called, Milo. I've never called a ghost to me on my own. Is it possible for me to reach out to Denise's spirit?"

"Hard to say, Emma. You can try, but it's really up to her whether or not she wants to make contact. Often the newly dead are confused, but sometimes they're as alert as if still living."

"Any suggestions?"

"Get someplace quiet and dimly lit. You don't need candles, but I find that there's something about candlelight that helps, especially white candles."

"Do I call her name?"

"You can, but you really don't need to. Just think about her with focused intensity. Envision her as she was the day you saw her. Usually, when I'm calling spirits to me, I don't know them personally, but there's someone they know in the room, which aids me in sending vibrations to a specific entity. Your brief acquaintance with Denise may or may not help. Lacking that, you might try being somewhere familiar to her."

"Like her home?"

"Yes. She might still be lingering there, especially if she died there."

"Wait a minute," Tracy cut in. "I hate to pee on this parade, but Denise's place is a crime scene, is it not?" When no one answered, she added, "Are you telling me, Emma Whitecastle, that you're going to break into someone's home? More to the point, a place sealed by the police as a crime scene?"

"Well, it's not my first choice."

"Oh, please," Tracy continued with exaggeration. "You won't even park illegally."

"I repeat, Tracy," Emma said with annoyance as thick as Bing's chocolate pudding, "it's not my first choice. Besides, as I recall, there's a security gate, and it's on the second floor. Not exactly conducive to simply popping a screen off a window and hoisting myself in."

Milo interrupted. "I have an idea where Emma won't have to break any laws or any windows."

"I'm all ears, Milo." Emma picked up her pen, ready to take some notes.

"First, try calling to Denise from some-where neutral, like your office or home. If that doesn't work, go to either the restaurant where she worked or to the area around her home. You won't be able to use candles or dim the lights, but either place will have a stronger connection to her than somewhere she's never been."

Emma shook her head as she read her notes over. "I can see it now, guys. I'll go to Bing's, order the halibut, and hold a séance in one of their booths. They can charge extra for the entertainment."

Her comment made Tracy snort with laughter, but Milo remained all business. "Laugh if you like, Emma, but it might work, though I was thinking more of you going into the ladies' room at the restaurant. At her home, try the carport or get as close to the building and her apartment as physi-cally possible."

"Sorry for the flippancy, Milo. I really do appreciate your help."

"I know you do, Emma. Now, do you want to know what we found out from Sandy Sechrest?"

"Hit me with it." Emma leaned back in her office chair and closed her eyes so she could concentrate on his words.

"You were right," Milo began. "We found

Sandy Sechrest last night, and she remembers distinctly that Tessa was waving when she first spotted her. Told us she thought it peculiar."

"She recall what Tessa was waving at?"

"No, just that it was out toward the sea. Sandy is a delight, by the way. I wish I'd known her when she was alive." Milo sighed. "I would have liked to have given her confidence in her clairvoyant abilities. Sounds like she hid them most of her life."

"Sometimes I wish I'd hidden mine better," Emma told him. "Seems like the whole world now knows that I can see ghosts. I'm not sure I like that."

"You'll learn to adjust to it over time, Emma, and people close to you will accept it."

"I have," Tracy called out.

Emma wasn't so sure she wanted to adjust to everyone knowing about her clairvoyant talents, yet she'd just asked Milo's advice on how to expand them. She was going deeper into the spirit world, pulled by something she couldn't explain and propelled by her need to seek the truth and justice. She'd fussed at Phil for wanting to ride to her rescue, yet she herself was championing the dead and forgotten. It wasn't all that different, except that she could take care of and speak for herself, and the dead needed help from the world they'd left behind.

"We also found Tessa this morning," Milo continued. "Granny was very helpful in convincing her to talk to me. Both Granny and Sandy had to assure her I was a friend of yours."

"Did you ask her about the waving?"

"Sure did." He chuckled. "After giving me an eye roll like it was the dumbest question she'd ever heard, she told me she was waving for Curtis to come get her. Said she waves every day and that she knows that one day they'll see her."

"They?"

"That's what she said. It was specifically a *they.*"

When the missing piece fell into place in Emma's head, it was a nearly audible *clunk.* Emma shot straight up out of her chair, almost dropping the phone. "I just had a thought, guys. What if Curtis isn't a person — what if it's the name of a boat?"

TWENTY-FIVE

"You know anything about boat registration?"

"No," Phil admitted, "but if you hum a few bars, I could fake it."

Emma groaned at the stale joke. "Seriously, you interested in helping?"

Phil Bowers grunted on his end of the phone. "This mean you want me to come up there?"

"No," Emma said firmly. She fingered her ghost pin. "It means I could use your help with some research."

"Personally, I know nothing about boats, but I have several buddies in San Diego who live and breathe by them. Tell me what you need."

After her call with Milo and Tracy, Emma had left the studio and headed to Bing's, where she had lunch and tried to hold an impromptu séance in the ladies' room. Lunch was good, the restaurant not very busy, but her attempt to call Denise to her failed. From there, she went to Denise's apartment. She parked next to a dumpster in the alley, proving Tracy wrong — that she *could* park illegally. Getting out of her mother's car, which she was using while hers was in the shop, Emma stood in the carport directly under Denise's apartment and tried again. This time, however, she only succeeded in calling attention to herself when someone came out the back gate and demanded to know what she was doing. Mumbling something about looking for her lost cat, Emma pretended to scout the area for the nonexistent feline before finally climbing into her car and taking off.

Now she was in her guesthouse office. Before her was the Sandy Sechrest painting. She was hoping that somehow Sandy's subconscious had caused her to put names on the boats she'd painted moored in the harbor. To her dismay, no names on the boats were clear. All Sandy had touched in with her brush were some flicks of black to indicate names on the sterns.

"I need," Emma explained to Phil, "to know if ownership of a private boat can be traced through the boat's name if you don't know the registration number. And, if so, how far back we can search."

"Meaning, if it is searchable, do the records go back, say . . . forty years?"

"You read my mind, cowboy."

Emma leaned back in her desk chair as she explained to Phil the possible theory that maybe Curtis was not a person but the name of a boat. "It's a long shot, but we really don't have anything else to go on."

"The thing about Tessa waving toward the boats does add come credibility to the idea, but it still doesn't give us a clue as to who might have been on the boat or who brought Tessa there in the first place."

"Not unless we can identify the boat's owner."

At that moment, a spirit entered the guesthouse. Emma went on alert, ready to protect the painting. When Archie, who was in his spot on the loveseat, started whining with excitement, she relaxed. Soon Granny materialized. Emma tossed her a smile and wave before returning her attention to Phil.

"If Curtis isn't a real person, George and his pals would have been telling me the truth when they said they knew no one by that name."

Again, Phil grunted. "They may not have been lying, but they weren't exactly telling you the truth. From the reactions you received, I'll bet one of them either owned or was connected to that boat."

"Denise did say that Worth Manning owned one of the boats that they took to Catalina. I'd love to find out the name of his boat."

"I'll see if I can research his vessel ownership while tracking down the Curtis lead. At least we have his name. Curtis may not be the full name of the boat. Ever think of that? There could be millions of variations on it."

"Yes, I did think of that, but it's all we have to go on for now."

Emma glanced over at Granny. The ghost was sitting next to Archie but her attention was fixed on Emma, and she didn't look happy. Her hazy jaw was set, and the scowl she shot Emma's way could sour fresh milk. Emma turned away, wanting to finish up with Phil before addressing Granny's ill mood.

"But doesn't *Curtis* seem like an odd word to have as part of a boat name, no matter what the variation?" she asked.

"Could be a name that has meaning to the owner, like a kid's name or a family name."

"You're right. I hadn't thought of that."

Phil chuckled. "Given time, I'm sure you would have."

Going through the recesses of her memory, Emma searched for what information she had stored on Feldman and Manning. "The Feldmans didn't have any children that I can recall. And the Mannings only have one son. His name is Stuart. George and Celeste only had Deirdre and Grant. I don't know much about other family names, but I'm sure it doesn't show up connected with the Whitecastle family unless it goes very far back." Emma gave a little sigh of relief. The further her investigation took her from her in-laws, the happier she would be.

"Well, let me get to work on it, Fancy Pants." Phil laughed. "That's what I'd call my boat if I had one — Fancy Pants."

After the call, Emma turned to face the still-cranky Granny Apples. "I really appreciate that you looked in on me last night, Granny. Thank you."

"If I'd known about the murder, I'd never left ya."

"There was nothing you could have done, Granny. I had a good night's sleep and spent most of today at the studio office. Milo needed you much more than I did. I understand you were a great help to him."

"That Sechrest woman was more of a help than I was." Granny sniffed. "You'd have thought she was the Queen of the Apple Festival the way Milo carried on about her."

Granny had been acting crabbier than ever lately, and a reason for it suddenly occurred to Emma. She got up and went to the loveseat, perching on the arm next to the ghost. "Granny, are you jealous of Sandy Sechrest?"

"Jealous? Of that paint-splattered baby ghost? That's outlandish, even for you." Granny fled to the opposite side of the room, where she hovered near the stationary bike with her arms crossed and her back turned to Emma. Archie raised his head from his nap, unsure of what was going on.

"Granny, it's true," Emma said to the image. "Both Milo and I really like Sandy Sechrest. But you're my family. I love you."

"You can't love a ghost, Emma. Any fool will tell you that."

"A fool may not believe it possible, but I do." Emma got up and went to Granny. "Besides, what about *The Ghost and Mrs. Muir*?"

Granny, her lips pursed in wariness, looked at Emma. "Who's Mrs. Muir?"

Emma smiled. "When all this is over, I'll introduce the two of you. In the meantime, you need to remember that you are an important part of this family. Even my father, who can't see or hear you, thinks of you as family. Phil thinks of you as family, and he's not even family."

In spite of her foul mood, Granny offered up a half-wink. "At least, not yet."

Emma rewarded the remark with a frown. "Never mind that. My point is, you're a very valuable member of this family, ghost or not. Both my mother and I would be lost without you, Granny. So would Archie."

Granny turned her back again to Emma.

"Look at me, Granny," Emma said softly.

With reluctance, the spirit turned back around. Emma could see from Granny's expression that, had the ghost been able to produce tears, she would have been crying.

"The way things are going with my spiritual gifts, I'm going to meet a lot of ghosts. Some I'm going to like, some I won't — just like living people."

Granny's face furrowed with worry. "You can ask me to go away any time you like, you know. I'd honor your request."

"Yes, Granny, I know that, but I'm not going to." Emma tried to place her hands on Granny's shoulders, but they slipped through the gauzy image. "You are my family, Ish Reynolds. Your blood is in my veins, and I love you very much. We all do. And no one, living or spirit, will ever take your place."

For several moments the two women, one long dead, the other alive, stared into each other's eyes, welding tight the connection started generations before.

"So," Granny said with bluntness, her face set with determination, "what's the scoop on this Dowd woman? Got any suspects yet? My money's on Manning."

Emma shook her head in wonder at Granny's resilience. "I was just about to address that when you popped in, Granny." She moved back to her desk and fussed with a bag she'd brought in earlier. "I want to try to contact Denise's spirit. I need to ask her some questions. You can help."

As she talked, Emma pulled out a variety of white candles from the bag. Having failed in her first two attempts to contact Denise, she was pulling out all the stops for her next try. She set several candles on the desk, then scattered a few on nearby surfaces. Satisfied with the arrangement, she moved to the bank of windows and closed the drapes. The guesthouse fell into darkness save for a lamp on Emma's desk.

Granny repositioned herself on the loveseat next to Archie. "You going to hold your own séance?"

"I'm going to try." Emma started lighting the candles. "And maybe with you here, it might work better."

Once the candles were lit, Emma sat back down at her desk and tried to relax. Even though she'd gotten used to having spirits around her, she'd never intentionally conjured one up on her own. They usually came to her without an invitation. She told herself there was nothing to be afraid of. Denise would either come or she wouldn't. She wiped her damp palms on her jeans and got started.

The room was already a bit cool with Granny present, so Emma slipped a cardigan sweater over her shoulders. Then she closed her eyes and concentrated on her mental image of Denise Dowd as she'd last seen her.

After a minute of concentration, she took several deep breaths. "Denise," Emma called softly. "Denise, can you hear me?"

Nothing.

"Denise, I need to speak with you."

"Maybe if you said please," Granny interrupted.

Emma opened one eye and cast it in the direction of the love-seat. In the darkened room, Granny's presence shimmered like sparkly fabric. Looking around, Emma couldn't see any other spirit images.

"Shh, Granny, I'm trying to concentrate."

"I'm just saying, even ghosts appreciate a little courtesy."

Emma closed her eye and went back to concentrating on Denise Dowd. "Denise, I really need to speak with you." After a few heart beats, she added, "Please."

"Why not add 'pretty please with sugar on top'?"

The voice was breathy, the words sarcastic. And it wasn't Granny.

Both of Emma's eyes popped open, but it took her a few seconds to locate the spirit who'd spoken. It was the mystery ghost of before — the one who'd wanted to kill Emma. She was on the other side of the room, drifting like a swaying palm frond.

Granny left the loveseat and moved closer to the image. "Are you the dead wife of that Manning skunk?"

The unknown ghost cackled with laughter. Archie jumped off the loveseat and scurried under Emma's desk.

"That's not Mrs. Manning, Granny." Emma leaned forward, careful not to make any sudden moves that might anger or threaten the spirit. "I don't know who you are," she said, addressing the ghost, "but I know for sure that you're not Linda Manning."

"You are fifty percent correct, Emma." The ghost drifted closer, her image becoming more distinct as she approached. Granny positioned herself between Emma and the aggressive spirit. "I'm not Linda Manning, but I am Mrs. Manning. The *first* Mrs. Manning."

Emma felt her face bunch as she thought about the ghost's revelation. "I recently found out that George Whitecastle had been married before. Now you're telling me that Worth Manning was, too."

The ghost of the first Mrs. Manning emitted a cold, calculated laugh. "Today we would be called starter wives." As she moved even closer to Emma, a portion of Mrs. Manning drifted through Granny.

"Hey," Granny snapped.

The other ghost ignored Granny as if she weren't there, keeping Emma in her sights at all times. Granny drifted to Emma's side. Emma fought hard not to show the fear growing inside her like bubbly stomach acid. Although the ghost of the first Mrs. Manning couldn't harm her physically, her intimidation skills were fearsome.

"Why so surprised, Emma? You were a starter wife. It's a rather common practice in Hollywood."

Emma straightened her shoulders and set her jaw, refusing to get drawn into the spirit's web of mind games. Quickly, she assembled her mental notes and threw out a possibility. "Senator Manning was going to divorce you and marry Tessa, wasn't he? That's why you're so determined that I not help Tessa."

The ghost's smile was outlined with malice. "No, Emma, not even close. Worth wanted to divorce me; on that you're correct. But the public didn't vote for divorced men, and Worth was more caught up in political lust than romantic lust. So we came to a marital truce. No divorce, but he could have his chippies and I my own affairs, as long as everything was kept quiet."

"But he told Tessa he loved her, didn't he? That's why she's waited all this time on the island. He told her he'd return for her."

The ghost spun three hundred sixty degrees, returning to face Emma with a superior grin. "Wrong again, my dear. Worth might have dallied at one time with the stupid little tramp, but it was long over, I can assure you."

Pulling her confidence around her like a shield, Emma stood up and walked around the desk, past Mrs. Manning, to where the painting leaned against the wall. She studied it, hoping for a clue to reveal itself in the mixture of blue and green sea. The ghost came up beside her but made no move toward the painting. Granny moved close to Emma, keeping watch on the unsavory spirit.

"There's some reason you don't want me to help Tessa." Emma said the words more to herself than to the ghost. She turned to face Mrs. Manning. "What does this have to do with Denise Dowd?"

"Who?"

"Denise Dowd." Emma put her hands on her hips and matched the apparition eyeball to eyeball. "She was one of Tessa's old roommates. She was murdered two days ago, right after speaking to me about Tessa. I was trying to reach her spirit when you came in."

"I have no idea who that person is — or was."

"So you have no idea who killed her?"

"None. But if she was part of that group of harlots, she probably deserved to die."

Emma wanted to throttle the meanness out of the ghost standing beside her. She was so different from Manning's second wife, Linda, the one Emma did know. Like herself, Manning had traded up.

"It's out of my hands now anyway. I'm sure the police will be able to find a connection between the two deaths."

The ghost of the first Mrs. Manning backed away from Emma. "What exactly does that mean?"

Emma advanced on the spirit with Granny by her side. "It means that the police are now involved in this, Mrs. Manning." Emma's voice was firm, almost harsh. "It means they are going to start looking into Tessa North's disappearance to see if there is a tie-in to Denise Dowd's murder. Everything you're working so hard to keep buried may soon come to light."

"No!"

"Yes, Mrs. Manning." Emma continued pushing her own agenda, keeping the bullying ghost as off-balance as she'd done to her just moments before. "It's just a matter of time. Senator Manning, George Whitecastle, and the others may be able to sidestep me, but they won't be able to dance around the police — at least not for long."

The ghost looked horrified. "Make them stop! Tell them you made it all up about Tessa North."

"I can't, Mrs. Manning. Their investigation is already going on."

Emma didn't know how much energy

316

Detective Tillman was going to put into the disappearance of a woman over forty years ago on the say-so of a clairvoyant, but she was playing every card she had, hoping to force information out of the spirit.

"Tell me what you're hiding, Mrs. Manning. Maybe it will help."

The spirit spun again. This time, when she returned to face Emma, her hazy features were contorted in anguish. "You foolish, foolish woman! You have no idea what you've done."

TWENTY-SIX

Once again, Emma was being led into George Whitecastle's study, and by the same maid as before. She was a frumpy Asian woman whose powder blue uniform hung on her thin frame like sacking on a scarecrow. The only noticeable shape was at the waist, where it was cinched by the ties of her white apron.

"Thank you for coming, Emma," George greeted her from his chair.

As before, Emma bent down and kissed his lined cheek and patted Bijou on his loyal head.

"Is there anything I can get you, Mr. Whitecastle?" the maid asked as she stood by the door.

"Nothing, thank you, Helen."

The maid stood a few more seconds at the doorway studying Emma. "I'm fine, also," Emma told her, noticing the woman's hesitation. The maid left.

Emma took a seat on the sofa. "George, how long has Helen been with you? I don't remember seeing her before my last visit."

George Whitecastle knitted his brows in thought. His complexion was dull and gray, and the dark circles under his eyes were more pronounced than when Emma had seen him last.

"Six months, maybe less. Since Ivy retired, Celeste has gone through several head housekeepers, trying to find a good replacement." He shook his head. "Not sure this one's an improvement over the last, but she's quiet and does her work."

Emma thought about Jackie's idea that it might have been the maid who'd called Grant. "George, do you think it was Helen who might have told Grant I was here last time?"

"Why would she have done that?"

"She might have thought she was looking out for you."

"Can't see it. She would have told Celeste, not Grant. And she doesn't seem terribly interested in my well-being or that of the family. She's like a robot: does her job, period." He shook his head. "We sure miss Ivy."

A short silence fell between them. Emma could sense that this visit would be different. George seemed restless and uncomfortable in her presence, something she never recalled him being in all the years she'd known him.

"I wasn't sure if I should come today," Emma said, breaking the stillness. "Celeste thought it best that I not contact you two until the thing with Grant simmered down. I was very surprised when you called."

George Whitecastle had called Emma the day before, shortly after the ghost of the first Mrs. Manning disappeared in a rage. He asked if she would come by their home in the morning. He didn't say why, just that he wanted to clear the air about some things. She agreed to be there at ten thirty.

After the call from George, Granny and Emma had tried several more times to reach the spirit of Denise Dowd, but each attempt failed. Mrs. Manning didn't show again either. Finally, Emma gave up. After changing into workout clothes, she told Granny to come back around suppertime for a surprise. Then she hopped on the treadmill and tried to beat the stress out of her system. For dinner, Emma fixed herself a simple sandwich and a glass of wine. Then she and Granny settled in the den, where Emma plugged her mother's copy of *The Ghost and Mrs. Muir* into the DVD player.

Granny loved the movie.

Considering what Emma had learned from the ghost of the first Mrs. Manning, George's call had been perfect timing. Certain the ghost was hiding something about Tessa's death, Emma wanted to know more about Worth Manning and his first wife. She also wanted to ask George about Denise Dowd and more about Tessa, provided he was strong enough. In his call, he hadn't said what he wanted to discuss with Emma, but he had opened the door to further contact, and she was going to walk through it as far as she was allowed.

George sat small and trampled in his chair, his illness keeping him company like an ill-mannered guest. Every time he started to say something to Emma, he stopped himself. She decided to give him a prod. Reaching into her handbag, Emma pulled out the photo Denise had given her. She handed it to him. George took the photo and held it in shaking hands.

"We were something, weren't we?" he said after studying it. "I always thought we were bold, brash, and beautiful. All of us. We worked and played equally hard. The girls, too." George leaned his fragile head against the back of the chair, his eyes fixed on the ceiling. "Started out innocent enough. Just

321

a few drinks with the cast and crew during the filming of *Beach Party Prom.* Worth started coming around. He was transitioning from actor to politician about that time. Paul, being the producer, was already part of the group. Tony Keller was in the film, too. Over time, people dropped away until it was just this small, solid band that continued to hang out together."

He tilted his head and looked at Emma, a tragic smile tugging at the corners of his mouth. "We were the 'it' crowd of our time. Living for the moment, regardless of the consequences to ourselves and to others." George let out a ragged cough. "We played with fire and all got burned."

"Why did you tell me you didn't know Tessa North when you obviously did?"

"It was a long time ago, Emma. And she was a touchy subject in this house."

"But she wasn't your mistress, as Celeste thinks, was she? She wasn't the one who had your baby?"

"No, she wasn't." George's voice trembled, each word having its own separate vibration. "Celeste told me about your conversation with her. Guess I should have known my lie would be found out in short order."

"Your mistress — was she Shelly Campbell?"

George looked surprised. "Why would you think that?"

"From what Celeste said, the baby would have been born about the time that photo was taken. Shelly's the only one in your group who isn't there. Did she go away to have the baby?"

"No. Shelly left LA, but not to have a baby. She got a job in Vegas." He ran his fingers lightly over the photo, as if trying to remember through his fingertips.

"I could tell you another lie, but what's the point?" He took a deep breath, which morphed into another cough. "My mistress never had the baby." He looked up at Emma with wet eyes. "I made her get an abortion. It was illegal back then, except in special cases. We went to Mexico." He stared down at the photo again. "I should never have forced her. She wanted that baby so bad."

A cool flow of air entered the room. Bijou let out a small whine. Emma looked around but saw no spirits. Getting up from her seat, she went to George and tucked the throw draped across his lap up higher against his chest. "It's getting drafty in here," she said to him with a warm smile.

George clutched her hand and held it. "I

loved her, Emma, but I also loved Celeste. I was so torn between them. It was the most difficult decision I've ever made. And to this day, I'm not sure I made the right one."

It was then that Emma saw Granny. Next to Granny, another spirit was coming into view. Just a flicker at first, soon it materialized into a shimmering pillar of shape. Emma stared at the ghost with surprise before looking to Granny for confirmation.

"I fetched her for you," Granny told Emma, pleased with herself. Emma mouthed a word of thanks in her direction.

The new spirit smiled at Emma and approached, coming to within a few feet of George Whitecastle. Bijou let out a short couple of barks and went on alert.

George looked down at his faithful companion. "What's the matter, old boy?" The dog looked up at its master and responded with a few soft whacks of its tail against the carpet. Then the animal went silent.

Emma knelt down in front of her former father-in-law and took both of his hands in hers. She glanced at the spirit, then up at George. "I was wrong, George. I know now that your mistress was Denise Dowd."

George nodded. "I made her get the abortion, Emma. After, she found out she could never get pregnant again." Tears flowed down his sunken cheeks. "I ruined her life. I helped support her financially for years, but in reality, I ruined her life." He let loose a sob. "And now she's dead."

"Do you have any idea who killed her, George?"

Emma handed him a handkerchief that was on the table next to him. He wiped his eyes and nose with the cloth. "No. But sick or not, I'll kill the bastard with my bare hands if I find out."

The spirit of Denise Dowd moved closer, beaming. "That's my George."

Emma stood up. Staying by George's chair, she addressed the ghost. "Who killed you, Denise?"

George Whitecastle looked up at Emma, then off in the direction she was looking. He saw nothing.

"Tell George I've forgiven him, Emma. I did many years ago."

Emma looked down at George, who was staring up at her, his tired, red eyes wide with surprise. "Denise wants you to know that she forgave you years ago."

His shock turned to a deep, bitter scowl. "Don't jerk around an old, sick man, Emma. It's inhumane."

"I'm not, George. Denise's spirit is here right now, standing in front of you."

With a slow, cautious movement, George turned his head away from Emma and faced forward. "There's nothing there. I knew there wouldn't be."

"She's there, George. I can see her." Emma placed a hand on his frail shoulder. "Just as I could see Tessa North."

Denise Dowd's ghost floated in front of them. "Tell him when we went to Mexico for the abortion, at the last minute he asked me to run away with him."

Emma relayed the message. George remained frozen, a cadaver waiting for his last breath to make it official.

"He said we would live near the sea. Somewhere near Zihuatanejo, just because he liked saying the name."

Again, Emma repeated the ghost's words. This time she felt George stiffen under her hand, then start to tremble.

The spirit smiled down at George. "He wanted to name our child Gabriel or Gabriela, after Gabby Hayes."

Keeping her hand on George's shoulder, Emma said to him, "She says that you wanted to name the child either Gabriel or Gabriela —"

"After Gabby Hayes," George said, finishing the sentence. Covering his face with his hands, George Whitecastle broke into deep sobs. His entire body shook with each one. "Forgive me, Denise. Please forgive me."

Denise Dowd knelt in front of the old man and put her arms around him. "Don't you remember, I said no. *I* was the one who insisted we go through with the abortion and return to LA. It was me, not you."

When Emma finished repeating the words, George said through his tears, "She did. She was so noble. Said we had obligations. Responsibilities we couldn't ignore."

The ghost looked up at Emma. "We've been lovers off and on since. George White-castle was the only man I've ever loved."

"Denise has her arms around you right now, George."

He looked up at Emma. "I want to die, Emma. I want to die right now and be with her."

Denise stood up. "Tell him not to worry. When it's his time, I'll be here."

After Emma repeated her words, George calmed down. He wiped his face again with the handkerchief and leaned back against the chair, exhausted. After a few moments, he steadied his eyes on the empty space in front of him. "Tell Emma who killed you, Denise. Tell her so we can get the bastard."

Emma patted his shoulder. "She's gone, George."

TWENTY-SEVEN

Emma, back in her seat on the sofa, studied George Whitecastle with concern. The blood had drained from his face, and his breathing was raspy.

"He don't look so good," Granny said, coming closer to get a better look at George.

"Are you sure you're up to this?" Emma asked him.

"Doesn't matter if I am or not, it must be done."

"Should I get someone? A doctor maybe, or call Celeste?"

He shook his head. "Celeste went to our condo in Laguna Beach for a few days." He drew a long breath. "I told her last night after the police questioned me that it was Denise who was my mistress, not Tessa. I told her all about it."

"Celeste left you?"

"Not sure if it's permanent or not, but at this point I've lost them both, Celeste *and*

Denise." He choked back a sob.

"And Tessa? Did you tell Celeste about what happened to Tessa?"

"No."

"How about Denise? Did she know?" Denise seemed genuinely concerned about Tessa's death when Emma spoke with her, but Emma was learning not to trust anything in this hotbed of actors and politicians.

"No, not even her. I've never told anyone. But I want to tell you."

While Emma got up and fetched George a fresh glass of water, Granny floated around the room. She came to a halt in front of a cluster of photographs on a shelf.

"Look here," the ghost said, pointing to one of the photos. "It's Curtis."

After handing George his water, Emma joined Granny. It took her a minute to notice what Granny had already seen; then her eyes and her brain clicked in unison. It was a photo of George with Paul Feldman and Worth Manning taken years before. The three men, wearing bathing trunks, were standing on the deck of a moored boat, hoisting beer bottles in the air for the camera. Across the stern of the boat was painted the boat's name: *Curtis Lee.*

Emma picked up the photo and brought it back to George. "Whose boat is this?"

George glanced at the photo, then looked away. "It belonged to Worth. He named it after his father, who died in the war."

"Tessa North's ghost is on Catalina, waiting for Curtis to return. Curtis isn't a man. *This* is the Curtis she's waiting for, isn't it? Or if she is waiting on a man, he was on this boat the day she died."

George said nothing, just continued to look away.

"Come on, you old coward," Granny said, floating in front of him. "Out with it."

Emma frowned at Granny and indicated with a toss of her head for her to move away. Granny scowled but complied.

"Did Senator Manning kill Tessa?" Emma asked George.

"Tessa's death was an accident."

"Then why all the secrecy? An accident shouldn't be a reason for a four-decade cover-up." Emma leaned forward, eager and ready to catch the answer like a thrown ball.

"We had our reasons. Even now, if this comes out, people will be irreparably harmed — perhaps even destroyed."

Emma couldn't believe George still entertained the idea of keeping Tessa's death a secret. Even the ghost of the first Mrs. Manning knew that ship had sailed. "Not if, George. *When.* With the police investigating

Denise's death, it's just a matter of time before it all comes out."

"But we don't know Denise's death is connected."

"No, but in all likelihood it is." Emma leaned against the wet bar and looked at the boat photo again. "Would the same person who killed Tessa have killed Denise?"

George moved his head slowly in the negative. "Impossible."

She looked down again at the three friends. "Because you don't want to believe it's possible or that it is truly impossible?"

"Impossible means impossible," George said, raising his voice.

"Celeste told me that after the Kennedy murder, you stayed home for days."

"That's true."

At that point, Emma's cell phone rang. She went to her bag and pulled it out. The display showed Phil Bowers was calling. "Will you excuse me, George?"

He waved a hand, indicating for her to take the call. Emma moved to the bank of windows overlooking the grounds. Granny shifted back near George, as if standing guard.

"Fancy Pants," Phil said, "it's going to be virtually impossible to find that boat based on the information you have."

"That's okay, Phil. I just found out the information I needed. Thanks though."

"What's up?"

"I'll tell you later. I'm at my in-laws' right now. We've located Curtis."

"Was it a boat like you thought?"

"Sure was."

"In-laws or no in-laws, you be careful. It's still a double murder."

"Don't worry, Granny's with me."

"Uh-huh. And when was the last time Granny threw a punch that anyone felt?"

"Understood." Emma closed the phone and went back to George.

"That your friend in Julian?" George asked.

"Yes, it was."

"So he knows about this too?" George did not sound pleased.

"He was with me when I encountered Tessa North, George. He's the one who first insisted she was murdered and dumped forty years ago."

"He sees ghosts too?"

Tessa smiled at the thought. "No, he doesn't, but he believes in them."

"And who's this Granny person? Another ghost?"

"Yes, as a matter of fact. She's the one who brought Denise's spirit here."

George started to say something sarcastic, but his recent encounter with Denise Dowd stopped him. Instead, he eyed Emma with caution mixed with awe.

Emma put her phone on the coffee table and sat back down on the sofa. Granny settled on a leather chair across from George.

"George," Emma began, "you obviously got me over h e to tell me something, but I sense you're s alling. What are you waiting for?"

"He's waiting for us." The voice came from the doorway. It was Worth Manning. The dog, familiar with the man, wagged its tail a few times but never left its post next to George.

As Emma watched, stunned, Senator Manning came into the room, followed by Helen. He addressed the maid, "Mr. Feldman is running late for our meeting. Please show him up as soon as he arrives."

With a nod, Helen retreated, closing the door behind her.

Granny drifted over to Emma. "It's the skunk. I don't like this at all."

Although she'd known these men for years, Emma now had information on something serious that they were trying to keep hidden. A trickle of fear ran down the back of her neck. Getting up, she went to stand by the wet bar again, feeling less vulnerable on her feet. Granny moved with her like a personal guard dog. George picked up on Emma's change of mood immediately.

"Please don't be afraid, Emma. No one's going to hurt you. I just felt if you heard the story, it should come from all of us. As I told you, I wasn't there. My part was to cover it up."

She looked at George. "You moved Tessa's things and sent the postcard to Denise?"

"Yes. Denise had given me a key to their apartment when we first starting dating. I knew the other girls were off for a few days filming. We moved Tessa's things out, and I personally got on a plane to Nebraska to send postcards to a few folks to make sure no one got suspicious."

George turned to Manning. "Worth, why don't you make yourself a drink. Helen brought in fresh ice earlier."

When Manning walked over to the wet bar, Emma shifted away from it. He grinned at her discomfort — a fox making a hen nervous. He poured Scotch over ice, swirled it around in the squat crystal glass, and drank half on his first drink. Before taking the leather seat across from George, he topped off the glass with more booze. Emma noticed when he crossed one long leg over the other that his foot twitched. It was the first time she'd ever seen Worth Manning nervous.

"So," she said, "someone killed Tessa by accident? If it wasn't either of you, it must have been Paul Feldman."

"No, Emma," Manning answered. "None of us killed Tessa. And it *was* an accident."

"As I told George, it's just a matter of time before the police find out about it. I've told them about Tessa."

"They will find nothing, Emma," Manning continued. His voice was cloaked in even tones despite the jiggle in his foot. "She's a girl who returned home." He took a quick sip of his drink. "Anything else is nothing more than a ghost story — something for late-night musing in front of a fire."

Granny leaned toward Emma. "His arrogance is as thick as apple butter. I bet he done that poor girl in. I'm ready to string him up right now."

"Speaking of ghosts." Emma ignored Granny and looked straight at Worth Manning. "Your first wife seems adamant, as well, that this not come to light. Any thoughts about that?"

At her words, Worth straightened up and sniffed the air like a nosey prairie dog looking for signs of danger. "My first wife? Margaret's been dead nearly thirty-five years."

"I know about the dead part, Senator. You see, her ghost has been visiting me. A very unwelcome ghost, I might add. She even threatened my life. But fortunately for me, ghosts cannot physically harm the living."

"You're insane!" Manning shouted.

Granny flew to Manning. "You stop yelling at Emma, you old snake."

George started on a deep, painful coughing riff. Both Emma and Worth went to George's side. Emma helped him take some water. Next to George's chair, the old dog moved into a sitting position, alert and worried.

Granny calmed the animal down. "It's okay, boy." Bijou settled back on the floor.

Manning screwed up his face in anger, almost baring his teeth at Emma. She could smell the Scotch on his breath. "Can't you see your nonsense is making him worse?"

"He called me here." Emma put the water glass down on the table after George's coughing lessened.

George held up a spotted hand to stop the bickering. After a few more coughs, he spoke. "I did ask Emma to come here today,

Worth. Just as I asked you and Paul." He pounded his fist on the arm of his chair. "And where in the hell is Paul?" He coughed again.

"How the hell do I know? He just called and said he'd be late." Worth left George's side and started pacing up and down the floor of the study. "This is my problem, George, not yours. You should have asked me before spilling your guts to her." He pointed at Emma.

"No. Listen to me." George picked up the cane next to his chair and stomped it on the floor a few times. "If we're going to contain this problem, we need her co-operation and help."

"Contain?" Emma backed away from her former father-in-law. "Surely you're not asking me to help conceal Tessa's death?"

Granny stood between George and Emma, her arms crossed in defiance. "My Emma doesn't roll like that."

Emma's anger was momentarily derailed by her shock over Granny's use of words, but she couldn't say anything about it in front of the men. And now wasn't the time.

Manning started to say something, but George cut him off with a look. With a growl, Manning sat back down in his chair and picked up his drink.

"Emma," George reasoned with a thick voice. "The girl has been dead a long time. It wasn't intentional, I can assure you. But people's lives will be ruined if it comes to light. Whole careers of good works down the drain. Futures destroyed." He took a minute to clear his throat. "Pursuing this will not bring the girl back, but could, in fact, be devastating on a bigger scale." He paused, waiting for the import of his words to sink in, then added, "She had no family. No one's really missed her for forty years."

Emma stared from one man to the other in disbelief. "Are you saying that Tessa North was disposable? That she didn't matter because she didn't come from money and position and wasn't earmarked for greatness?"

George Whitecastle shifted in his chair. "Sometimes, Emma, sacrifices must be made for the greater good."

"I highly doubt, gentlemen, that Tessa North knew that her death, accident or not, was for the greater good." Emma could feel her rage boiling, her face growing hot to the touch. "Maybe you should have asked her if she wanted to make that sacrifice before you killed her!"

"You tell them, Emma." Granny bounced from one booted foot to the other like a prize fighter.

"No one killed her intentionally!" Manning shouted, quickly getting to his feet.

Bijou emitted a low growl at the sudden elevation of emotion. Emma communicated to Granny with her eyes to handle animal control. The ghost knelt beside Bijou and cooed, and the animal quieted.

"There was an argument on the boat," Manning started to explain. He turned down the volume on his voice after glancing at the old dog. "A very heated argument. Someone took a swing at someone else with a gaff — you know, the hooked poles used to pull fish into the boat. The gaff hook caught Tessa, who was trying to stop the fight, in the side of the head. As she fell, she struck her skull hard on the railing." Emotionally drained, he dropped into his chair and took a long drink. "You happy now?"

To Emma, the story wasn't complete. "So who swung the gaff?"

The two old friends looked at each other, but neither offered up a name.

"Was it Tony Keller?" asked Emma. "Was that why he committed suicide several months later?"

George answered, "Tony's suicide had nothing to do with this. He was in the hospital when Tessa died, drying out."

"He was an alcoholic?"

"Booze, drugs, even gambling," Manning added. "Studios wouldn't work with him anymore. He'd tanked his entire career."

Eyeing Manning with suspicion, Emma tried another avenue. "Boats moored in Avalon Bay are pretty close together. Are you saying no one saw or heard all this?"

"We had taken the boat out for the day on the far side of the island. It was pretty deserted."

"And you couldn't find your way to a doctor?" Emma's eyes popped in disbelief at what she was hearing.

"She died quickly, Emma. By the time we got the anchor up to go get help, she was gone."

Emma stood in front of the former senator, her hands on her hips. "I don't believe you."

"Neither do I, Emma," offered Granny, still at her post by Bijou.

"Were you there?" Manning shot back.

"No, but Tessa North was." Emma looked from Manning to George Whitecastle. "According to her, she was left. Someone told her they were going for help, but they never came back." She turned back to the senator. "You left her there to die, didn't you?"

The two men looked at each other, locking eyes briefly before George cast his down toward his lap.

Worth cut his eyes to Emma. "You don't understand anything, Emma, or else you wouldn't be hurting innocent people to chase a ghost story."

Emma moved back over to the wet bar. She walked back and forth in front of it like a caged animal, wanting to tear the two old men into bits.

"Which one of you scumbags told her you loved her, then left her to die?" Emma shouted, refusing to be intimidated.

Without warning, Emma ran her arms down the short length of the wet bar, clearing it of crystal glasses and the ice bucket. The room filled with the music of fine glass breaking. The ice bucket crashed to the floor, coming to rest on its side, ice strewn across the luxurious carpet. The Scotch bottle hit the floor, too, but remained intact, its cap on tight. Bijou went behind George's chair, where Granny continued to comfort him.

"Emma!" George yelled in a strained voice. "What's gotten into you?"

But Emma didn't answer. For a long time, she stared down at the ice bucket. Finally, she bent over and picked it up. Turning it upside down, she spilled the remaining ice to the floor.

"Emma," George said again. "What the hell?"

Emma took the bucket to George and showed it to him, pointing to the small object stuck to its bottom. "We're being bugged," she mouthed.

After handing the bucket to George, Emma dashed out of the room and flew down the staircase to the main floor of the Whitecastle home. Bijou was on her heels, following her without knowing why. Granny was following the dog. Behind them, moving much slower but with the same intent, was Worth Manning. Emma entered the kitchen, but it was empty. Turning down a hallway off the kitchen, she headed for the maid's quarters. That room, too, was empty, looking like it had been recently and quickly vacated.

Dashing to the front door, Emma checked the large circular driveway. Earlier there had been an older Toyota in the driveway. It was gone now.

"Nothing?" Worth Manning asked, catching up to her.

Emma shook her head and started back up the stairs to George's study. Manning followed. Taking the ice bucket back from George, she plucked the bug from the bottom, put it in a glass, and added water.

"I don't know if that will work or not," she said. Then, to be on the safe side, she stuck the glass inside the bar refrigerator.

"Where's Bijou?" asked George.

Granny answered. "I sent him outside through his doggie door. Ordered him to stay there."

"He went outside," Emma told George with a satisfied nod to Granny.

"Good," George said. "This is upsetting him."

Emma turned to George. "Where does Helen live, George?"

"Why, here, of course."

"All the time? She doesn't have a real home?"

"No, not all the time — mostly she stays just during the week. Celeste would have that information."

Emma walked back and forth. "Did Helen know I was coming? Or the senator?"

"Yes. I told her you were all coming by this morning."

"Why would your maid want to bug us, George?" The question came from Worth.

"I have no idea. Do you think she's been listening to me the whole time? She's only been here a few months."

"The last time I visited, there wasn't an

343

ice bucket on the counter," Emma said, going back and studying the wet bar. "I took a bottled water from the mini fridge and poured it into a glass. But there wasn't any ice." She looked at George. "Did you ask her to bring up fresh ice today?"

"No. She just brought it up, shortly before you arrived."

Plopping down in a side chair, Emma ran a hand through her short hair. "Gentlemen, your secret just hemorrhaged. And it serves you right."

TWENTY-EIGHT

"Celeste," Emma said into her phone, "it's me, Emma."

She was standing in the upstairs hallway, just outside George Whitecastle's study, calling Celeste Whitecastle on her cell phone.

"Hello, dear. What can I do for you?"

"Domestic question for you." She said the words with forced casualness. "My mother and I are thinking of adding to our household staff; can you recommend a good agency? I remember meeting Helen last time I was at your house, and she seemed efficient."

Emma was lying to her mother-in-law and didn't care one whit. She'd learn the truth soon enough without getting riled up before they knew anything concrete.

"She's better than the last few, though no one will ever replace Ivy."

"Do you remember which agency you hired her from?"

"It was a place I'd never used before, but Linda Manning referred them to me shortly before she died. Said their people are very discreet."

So discreet, Emma thought, *they're trained to use bugging devices.*

"Let's see," Celeste continued. "I have the name and number right here in my book." Emma could hear pages being flipped, then Celeste said, "Helen came from Hyland Staffing."

For some reason, it didn't surprise Emma. She was becoming desensitized to surprises. The next call she made was to Jackie Houchin, hoping Jackie was around on a Sunday and wouldn't mind being bothered.

"Jackie, I'm sorry to bother you on a day off, but it's an emergency. I'm at the Whitecastles' and need you to look up the home address for Fran Hyland."

"The Hyland Staffing woman?"

"Yes. She's out of the office for a few days, and I need to contact her, preferably face to face. Her married name is Kilgore."

"Kilgore? You sure about that?"

"She told me herself. Why?"

"Remember how you asked me to try and find out the name of that skank who took and sold the video? Well, his name is Mike Kilgore."

"You're kidding!" Emma leaned against a papered wall and realized that she could still be surprised.

"Hang on, I'm running a search right now to see if such a couple comes up." From Jackie's end of the phone came the clack of a keyboard in use.

Considering the bugging, Fran's husband being the creep who'd taken the video and sold it to TV made sick sense.

"You there?" Jackie said from the other end.

"Yes."

"We got a hit. There's a Frances and Michael Kilgore listed in Sherman Oaks. The wife's middle initial is *H*."

"Could stand for Hyland."

"Very likely. I just found a photo of them on Google images. Let me send it to your phone."

After a few moments, Emma was staring at a photo of Fran Hyland and her husband, Mike Kilgore. Kilgore looked familiar. It took her a minute, but Emma finally placed him. He'd been the man she'd bumped into leaving Bing's the day she first met Denise Dowd. No doubt Fran had sent him there in case Emma showed up. He was probably following her out the door when she'd suddenly turned around when Denise called her name. Emma was also ready to bet he was the man in the car parked across from her home the day of the fight with Grant.

"What's a bug?" Granny asked when Emma got off the phone.

"A tiny listening device," Emma explained in a whisper. "People use them to eavesdrop on other people. Our entire conversation in there today was probably being recorded by someone."

"Seems like a handy thing — not very honest, but handy." Granny looked at Emma. "You ever use them bugs?"

Emma gave Granny a small smile. "I don't need to. I have you."

Emma walked the hallway, thinking. "I want you to go back to Catalina, Granny, and talk to Tessa. Convince her that Curtis is never returning. Let her know that you know Curtis is a boat and that the boat is long gone. I imagine that Senator Manning got rid of it shortly after the incident — at least, that would have been the smart thing to do."

"Snakes are smart."

"Yes, he's a very smart snake," Emma agreed. "Talk first to Milo. Tell him everything you learned here today. Maybe the two of you together can convince Tessa to cross over."

After Granny left, Emma went back into the study. George looked weaker. The day's events were obviously taking their toll.

"Should I call a nurse or someone, George?" she asked. "Someone needs to be here with you."

"Thank you, Emma, but I just called Grant. He'll be here soon."

"Then let's make this quick," she said, "because I don't want to be here when he arrives. No telling what I'd do if he gets in a snit again." Emma sat back down in the side chair.

The two men, both used to giving orders, must have agreed, because for a change they sat and listened, albeit reluctantly, waiting to hear Emma's plan of action.

"Helen came from Fran Hyland's agency, Hyland Staffing," she announced. "I doubt Helen acted on her own. Is there any reason why Fran would want to do something like this?"

From the way the two men looked at each other, Emma surmised that they could think of at least one reason. She directed her next question at Manning. "Was Fran Hyland with you when Tessa died?"

"No," Manning answered with bluntness. "She was not."

"And, by the way," Emma added. "It

seems that Celeste was referred to Hyland Staffing by your wife, Linda. So, if I were you, Senator, I'd make sure Fran doesn't have any bugs or spies in *your* home. In fact, I just found out that it was Fran's husband who shot that video of Grant and me fighting."

The two men looked shocked. George broke the silence. "I do recall that Fran married a photographer years ago. She met him on a publicity shoot, I believe."

Emma paused and took a breath. "Which leads me to my next question. What does Fran Hyland have to do with all this?"

Again the two men looked at each other, this time making eye contact for a long time, discussing without words whether or not they should talk. Emma could feel her frustration headed for another meltdown.

"No more playing games," she demanded, her deep voice threaded with disgust. "Or I swear I'll hand you two over to the police right now and let them sort it out."

George broke eye contact with Worth Manning and turned toward Emma. "Fran Hyland has been blackmailing us for years. All of us." He looked over at his friend, signaling him to continue the story he'd opened.

Senator Manning rubbed his hands over

his face several times before speaking. "Fran was supposed to go over with Tessa and join Paul and me on the boat, but she came down with a cold. Soon after we returned from Catalina and the story circulated that Tessa had returned home to Nebraska, Fran approached me and said she knew what happened on the island. No details, just a general statement that she knew Tessa was dead. Of course, I didn't believe her. There was no way she could have known such a thing. But she persisted. Said she knew Tessa would never have returned home to Nebraska under any circumstances. Fran threatened to go to the police if we didn't pay her." Manning got up and started pacing again. "Of course, we couldn't take the chance, so we started paying her and have been since."

"Fran Hyland was right," Emma told them, growing more disgusted with the men by the minute. "If you had taken the time to get to know Tessa instead of spending that time pawing at her, you might have learned that she ran away from an abusive family. There was no way she would ever have gone back to Nebraska. Fran knew that. That's how she knew your story about Tessa returning home was a fraud."

Emma leaned forward in her chair, ready

to return to the real meat of the matter. "Somehow, Senator, I can't see Paul Feldman wielding a gaff at you, even in a heated argument. And if it had been you aiming at him, I doubt you would have missed and hit Tessa. The question still remains, who are you all protecting? And this time I want a straight answer."

"Noooooooooo!" came a disembodied voice, followed by the ghost of the first Mrs. Manning manifesting itself in an instant. The ghost flew up to Worth Manning and starting pounding her transparent fists on his chest. "Don't you dare tell her!"

A noticeable shiver ran through the senator's long, lean body. He batted at the air in front of him as he might have done at an unseen fly.

Emma was going to tell the men the ghost was present but decided not to, thinking she might be able to use it to her advantage. "Your first wife, Senator — Margaret, wasn't that her name? She knew what had happened, didn't she?"

As he nodded in her direction, the once-powerful politician looked beaten, as if the unfelt blows of his dead wife were having an effect. "Yes. I had to tell Margaret. She agreed that we needed to cover it up at all costs."

Emma's mind was turning to mush with all the details of the past few days smashing up against each other. In the chaos, some of them started to solidify. Fran Hyland had been blackmailing the three men for years based on her guess that something horrible had happened to Tessa on the island. Now Fran was staffing their households and listening in on their lives. Emma wondered when the bugging had started. Had it been going on all the time or just since she'd started nosing around about Tessa?

"But none of the other wives knew, did they?" she asked the men. "Not Celeste, not Mrs. Feldman? And certainly not the second Mrs. Manning."

"No," answered George. "There was no reason for them to know."

"Damn you, Worth," the overwrought ghost screamed at him. "You're to blame for this. You and your whoring around."

The ghost started moving around the room, causing a noticeable draft. George pulled his throw blanket closer to him.

Emma watched the ghost of Margaret Manning bounce around the room like an agitated pinball until the barrier in her mind shattered, giving Emma a plausible answer to her question — a solid reason for so much cover-up and concern, especially on the side of Margaret Manning.

Emma looked at Worth Manning, her face for once filled with compassion for the arrogant man. "Your son Stuart was on the boat with you, wasn't he, Senator? He was with you at the Ambassador Hotel, and he went with you to Catalina." Emma paused to let her words sink in. "He's the one who accidentally hit Tessa with the gaff, isn't he?" It was a guess, but a guess based on solid observance.

Manning froze in his tracks, his face pale and gaunt. "You can't prove that. No one, not even the police can prove that."

"Please, Worth," began George, his voice tired and strained. "It's time for the truth. We can't hide it any longer." When Manning said nothing, George turned to Emma. "It was an accident. And the boy had no part in the cover-up."

The 'boy,' Emma noted to herself, was now around sixty years old, with a big political career behind him and even more ahead of him. Even two of his children were in high-stakes politics in the East. Worth Manning had created a political dynasty. A scandal years ago could have destroyed his growing career and any plans he may have had for his son. The reason for the cover-up was becoming apparent but still did not excuse it.

Manning sank deep into his chair and drained his Scotch. He held his glass out to Emma. Though tempted to tell him to put his glass where the sun didn't shine, she cut him some slack and grabbed the Scotch bottle from the floor. After filling his glass, she started for the wet bar.

"No," Manning ordered. "Leave it."

Emma put the bottle on the coffee table and took a seat once again in the side chair, afraid the sofa would make her too comfortable and take the edge off her indignation. After all, they were not discussing sports scores but the death of an unfortunate young woman and a criminal cover-up.

After another big gulp of alcohol, Worth Manning started. "Stu came along at the last minute. He'd recently come home on break from Princeton and wanted to tag along. Seeing how upset he was over the Kennedy killing, I agreed. When Tessa showed up, Stu seemed okay with it. She was just a few years older than him. Maybe he thought she was there to keep him company — who knows."

"I can't allow this." The ghost of Margaret Manning shouted as she continued to whirl about the room in a rage, creating a forceful, cold air current even the men couldn't ignore.

"Is Denise back?" George asked Emma, his voice full of hope.

"No, George, she's not. But the ghost of Margaret Manning is with us. She has been with us for several minutes now. And she's not happy."

Manning scoffed and took a drink. "She never was happy, with me or anyone. Figures she'd haunt me."

"My boy," the ghost shouted into the face of the senator. "I was happy with my boy until you ruined him!"

"Continue, Senator," Emma told him. "She can't hurt you."

Manning shook his head. "I still think this ghost stuff of yours is B.S., Emma, but maybe George is right. Maybe it is time to talk about it." He took a big drink.

"The day on the boat went fine," Manning began, "but maybe we had a bit too much to drink. I know *I* had too much to drink. I made a pass at Tessa. Stuart caught me kissing her. He started yelling at me, calling me names, blaming me for his mother's misery. Paul tried to calm him down but wasn't successful. Even Tessa tried."

Manning started to take another drink,

then thought better of it. He put the glass down on the table next to the Scotch bottle and leaned back in his chair to finish the story. The air around them continued to move with agitation.

"Stu became so verbally abusive at one point that I slapped him. Pretty hard, too. He responded by coming at me with the gaff. Tessa stepped in to stop him." He paused, looking down at his hands. "The rest you know."

"No, I don't, Senator," said Emma in a quiet voice. "Tell me what happened after Tessa hit her head."

The old politician cleared his voice. Emma noted that George was visibly trembling even though his face remained stern.

"We panicked. It was obvious that Tessa was very bad off. There was a lot of blood coming out of the head wound where the gaff had hit her and where she'd come into contact with the railing. She was drifting in and out of consciousness. I knew my political career would take a serious hit if it got out. If she died, it might even destroy it. And Stu was planning on going into politics himself. Margaret's people were blue bloods from the East. With my attachments and their influence, and both of our money, there'd be no telling how far he could go."

"And Paul Feldman went along with this?"

"Paul had his own career to worry about — and his own marriage. His wife would not have been as tolerant as mine of indiscretions."

"Tolerance had nothing to do with it, you bastard." Mrs. Manning's ghost spun around the room one last time before disappearing, returning the air in the room to still and warm.

"Is she gone?" George asked. "Margaret's ghost, I mean."

Emma nodded.

The senator studied the abandoned glass of Scotch. After a moment he picked it back up. "What the hell." He took a healthy drink and clung to the glass like a lifeline as he continued. "Paul and I quickly put together a plan. We loaded Tessa into the dinghy and told Stu that Paul was taking her for help — that the dinghy would be faster. I stayed with Stu. We cleaned the blood off the boat and made our way back to Avalon. Stu was devastated. When Paul caught up to us, he told us that she'd been taken to a hospital on the mainland and would be fine. He said Tessa had a concussion and needed stitches."

Emma shook her head in disbelief, not understanding how these men she'd thought of as good and decent could do such a heinous thing. "But you knew different, didn't you, Senator? You knew that in reality, Paul Feldman dumped her in a remote part of the island and took off."

Worth Manning studied his drink and nodded.

"When they returned to LA, they came to me," George explained. "Together, we decided how best to proceed."

Emma looked from George back to Worth Manning. "And what about Stuart?"

Tears started down the senator's deeply lined face. "To this day, Stu thinks Tessa survived. We convinced him to keep his mouth shut about the accident for everyone's sake, especially his own. Even his mother talked him into remaining silent. We were never close, but a few years later, when Margaret died, he cut almost all ties with me. After law school, he settled near his mother's family. His children and grandchildren hardly know me, except by name."

The sound of a single pair of hands clapping came from the partially open doorway.

"Very nice story," pronounced Fran Hyland. Behind her was a man Tessa recognized as Mike Kilgore. In his hands was a running video camera. In Fran's hand was a gun.

TWENTY-NINE

Dressed from head to toe in Ralph Lauren, including her jacket, Fran stepped into the room. "Who knows — maybe one day it might make it to TV. At least it will if I have anything to do with it." She looked at George. "Audiences love true stories. Isn't that right, George?"

George Whitecastle was outraged by the intrusion. He grabbed his cane and stood up, ready to defend his home in spite of his frailty. The lap throw fell to the floor in front of him. "How the hell did you get in here?"

Worth Manning also got to his feet. Emma was the only one in the room under sixty and seemed to be the only one with a grasp of the whole picture. Emma answered instead of Fran. "I'm guessing with Helen's keys."

Fran flashed Emma a tight smile. "You are such a clever girl. Too bad you didn't find that bug before we got it all on tape.

Or should I say, I'm glad you didn't."

"Are you the one who spraypainted my car, too?"

Fran pointed a manicured and ringed finger at the man with the camera. "Actually, Mike here did that. But I suggested it. You see, Emma, when you came to my office, at first I was worried that you might grab the story I've been waiting forty years to get. But then I thought, why not let this crazy woman do the footwork for me? You struck me as the type who, when warned off of something, would be even more intrigued to get to the bottom of things." Again she gave Emma a smile that was anything but friendly. "And I was right."

Emma hated that this woman had her so pegged. "I was trying to help Tessa, that's all."

"Maybe, but admit it: as soon as you found out Tessa was tied in with your in-laws, you couldn't let it go, no matter what." Fran Hyland stepped closer, keeping the gun steady. "I still say there was a little bit of revenge mixed in there somewhere." She gave Emma a sly wink.

Emma wanted to spit in the woman's face. "There is no need for me to get revenge on the Whitecastles." Her eyes soaked in Fran's cold, immaculately made-up face. "If you wanted me to get to the bottom of things, why did you call Grant? It was you, wasn't it? You knew he'd get riled up and try to stop me."

Mike Kilgore laughed behind his wife. "That was a stroke of genius."

Fran smiled sweetly at her husband, then said, "It was Helen who called Grant — at my encouragement, of course."

Kilgore laughed. "Let's face it, folks, Grant Whitecastle is the paparazzi's wet dream."

Fran took her turn in the doubles game of explanations. "We knew he'd go off on a search and destroy mission if he thought you were bothering his family with all this ghost nonsense, especially if he thought it was upsetting his father. Mike just followed him, waiting for the drama to unfold. Selling that video was like money falling from heaven — like hitting a fair-sized slots jackpot just before you cash in a big winning lotto ticket."

"And this story," Worth Manning asked, "this thing with Tessa is the lotto?"

"But of course it is. It's worth millions to the right people. Surely you understand that."

Senator Manning started forward, but Fran Hyland stepped back and aimed the gun directly at him. "Not so fast, Worth. We haven't done business yet."

George Whitecastle remained standing, supporting himself on his cane. "You've drained us for years, Fran. What more do you want?"

"Ah, but George, you boys were paying me for what you *thought* I knew. Now it's about what I know for sure — what I've suspected for years — and that's that you golden boys killed Tessa and dumped her body."

"Tessa's death was an accident," Worth said, slamming his glass down on the coffee table to emphasize his point.

"Doesn't matter, though, does it?" Fran said with a smirk. "You still covered it up. It's still a crime."

Emma sat in her chair, still and listening, wondering how it would all play out and wishing she hadn't sent Granny to Catalina. Granny was right. In the event of danger, she could go to Milo for help. Milo wouldn't have to come running, he could call the cops, sending them to the Whitecastle home.

George stamped the end of his cane against the floor. It hit the carpet with a short staccato of muffled thumps but still managed to get everyone's attention. "How much more money do you want to keep quiet?" he asked Fran.

Fran and her husband exchanged a quick battery of looks before Fran said, "This isn't about keeping quiet, George. As Emma said, it's just a matter of time before the police figure it out, or before they start listening to ghost girl over there." Fran shot Emma a cynical look as she spoke to George. "I don't believe in ghosts myself, but one way or another, Emma stumbled upon the truth. I'm sure Denise's big mouth helped."

Emma pricked up her ears. "You killed Denise Dowd?"

Fran cackled. "It was an *accident,* dear. I was holding a knife, ready to butter a bagel, and she fell on it." She turned to Worth Manning. "Rather like being hit in the head by a gaff hook, don't you think?"

George took a wobbly step forward and raised his cane to strike at Fran, but he didn't have the strength to travel the short distance between them. He fell backwards into his chair and went into a small fit of coughing. "God damn you," he said from behind his handkerchief. "Denise never did anything to you."

"No, but she never did anything for me, either." Fran shifted from one foot to the other. "I went over there just for a little girl talk, to find out what she told Emma. She suspected my purpose was more serious and clammed up. I offered to pay her for her information, but she said she was going straight to you to let you know I was up to something, even though she didn't know exactly what. I couldn't allow that. I didn't have all the information I needed to put my plan in place." She studied George with curiosity. "I had no idea you two were an item all these years — another side bonus to my plan, and another forty-year-old murder, depending on which side of the abortion issue you sit."

George was too undone to speak. Noting his flushed face and continued coughing, Emma went to his side.

"Careful," Fran warned her.

"I'm just going to help him," Emma snapped, keeping her eyes on George.

Worth picked up the questioning. "If this isn't about hush money, Fran, then what is it about?"

"It's about this." She reached an arm out and gently patted the video camera. "And it's about what we have on audio. A lot of people would pay a great deal of money to get their hands on what I have. The great George Whitecastle and the equally great Senator Worth Manning confessing to a murder and cover-up, and implicating the multi-award-winning producer Paul Feldman in the bargain." Fran laughed. "And now we find out Congressman Stuart Manning was involved. That was definitely a surprise bonus." She grinned at Manning. "Your son is a personal friend of the president, is he not?"

Senator Manning was so flushed with anger, he looked about to have a stroke. Emma watched him carefully. Between Worth and George, Emma was beginning to feel like an EMT.

When no one responded, Fran Hyland continued. "Maybe the two of you would like to start the bidding to keep it out of the hands of the media."

Emma stepped away from George and toward Fran, her face twisted in anger and revulsion. "That's despicable."

"Careful, Emma," Fran said, adjusting the gun at Emma's stomach. "I'm sure with the right editing, we could implicate you, too."

Emma eyed the gun, noting that it was growing heavy in Fran's outstretched hand. "And how many of your celebrity clients have you done this to already?"

"Enough to substantially pad our retirement fund." Fran Hyland acted coy and lowered her voice as if someone might overhear. "Although my clients don't know about my little sideline. Over the years, Mike and I mostly worked behind the scenes, selling photos and leaking stories to the tabloids and entertainment gossip shows. An employment agency specializing in discreet staffing is a clever cover, don't you think? We carefully placed our spies, who were happy to get paid from both ends, and waited for something juicy to emerge. And it always did."

Everyone but Mike Kilgore glared at Fran Hyland — Worth and George with hate, Emma with anger and disbelief.

"So," Fran said in a chipper voice, "shall we start the bidding at two million?"

THIRTY

"You're insane." Emma's mouth ejected the words as if they were poison.

Worth Manning looked about to say something really nasty when his cell phone, stashed in his pants pocket, rang. He ignored it and sneered at Fran. "If this story is coming out, then let it come. I'll step up and take the punishment due me. Hell, I'll go to the chair before I'll pay you one dime more."

Hyland rolled her eyes. Behind her, her husband chuckled. "It's a good thing you took up politics, Worth," Fran said, "because you always were a lousy actor. The electric chair isn't used in California. You'd think a former senator would know that."

The phone on George's table rang next. He also ignored it. "Worth's made a good point," he said, determination coming through his shaky voice. "Enough hiding. It's time we came forward. Tessa was a nice girl. She certainly deserved better." He avoided eye contact with Emma as he spoke.

Worth's phone rang again. With his patience on a short lead, he pulled it out of his pocket and read the display. "It's Paul," he announced.

"Answer it," Fran ordered. "Ask him why he's late to the party."

When he answered the call, surprise flashed across Worth Manning's face as if he'd been branded with it. He said a few words into the phone and listened some more, his eyes growing wider with each moment of the conversation. Finally, he told the other person to calm down, saying he'd look into it and get right back to them.

"That wasn't Paul," he told the gathering in George's study in an agitated voice. "It was Ruth, his wife. Seems Paul did set out to come over here, but she just found a note on his desk addressed to her. She said it sounded like a suicide note."

"A suicide note?" The words gushed from Emma's lips. "He said he was going to kill himself?"

Worth started his pacing again, mindless of the gun being held on him. He raked his hands through his white hair until Emma feared he would pull it out.

"Not exactly," Worth told them. "Ruth

said the note said no matter what happens, for her to know he'd love her forever, but that he had to make things right. Ruth's hysterical. She wants to know what Paul meant. She said she's called his cell repeatedly, but it just goes into voicemail. She was hoping he was with us."

George shook a finger at Worth. "That doesn't necessarily mean he's going to kill himself."

Emma offered up another theory — one she didn't necessarily believe but wanted to believe. "It could mean he's going to turn himself in to the police."

Worth stopped pacing and looked up from the floor with stricken eyes. "Yes, Emma, it could, but Ruth said she checked, and Paul's handgun is gone."

A funereal silence fell over the room until Fran broke it, ready to write Paul Feldman's epitaph. "Sad, because of the three of you, he was the most decent."

"Once again, Fran," George said, full of rage, "not one red cent will you get from us. Sell the damn shit, I don't care." He looked to Worth. "We need to find Paul before it's too late."

Fran shook her head. "While I understand your concern for the little murderer, we still have a deal on the table. Maybe urgency will encourage you to close it a little faster."

"You do know," Emma said, stepping away from George and moving slowly toward Fran, "that blackmail is illegal. So is recording private conversations. You'll be in jail right along with them if this comes out."

"Not if they can't find us."

"Or extradite us," laughed her husband.

"You see, Emma, I've already sold the story. Actually, it's my story I've sold — how for years I was the confidante of Hollywood powerhouses, and how one day things went too far and a girl died. The book was bought by a big publishing house for six figures and is scheduled to come out next year. Of course, most of the stuff about Tessa was guesswork." Fran flashed a big, wide denture-filled smile at everyone. "But not anymore. Once the truth comes out, the book will sell millions."

Worth Manning shook his head, trying to clear the confusion of what Fran had just admitted. "If you got a big deal, then why are you here?"

"Greed, Senator, plain and simple; that's why she's here." Emma looked at Worth and George. "She got one big payout and another with the Grant tape, but this was the big windfall she'd hoped for."

Emma took another step closer to Fran,

noting that the bracelets on the wrist of the arm with the gun were shaking steadily. Fran used her free arm to steady her grip.

"You stay where you are, missy," she warned Emma.

"Emma, please," pleaded George.

Emma ignored him and focused on Fran. She didn't notice Mike Kilgore holding a weapon. To Emma, their only threat seemed to be the gun growing heavier by the second in Fran's aged hand. As time ticked by, Emma was getting more worried about Paul Feldman.

She engaged Fran's attention, hoping the gun would continue to become a burden. "You thought you could intimidate these guys into handing over some really serious cash to keep the video and audio tapes out of the hands of unscrupulous journalists. It never occurred to you they'd had enough."

"I could still sell the tapes, and don't think I won't."

"You're welcome to try," Emma told her, keeping her blue eyes fixed on Fran's face. "Try all you want."

"Let's get out of here, Fran," Kilgore told his wife. "We're wasting time."

"And what will we do with them?" She moved the gun in an arc covering Worth, George, and Emma.

"Leave them. We didn't get what we came for, but so what? We have enough to disappear and live in luxury for the rest of our lives."

"No!" Fran's lined face contorted. "All these years, I've waited for this moment, knowing they did something to that stupid girl, waiting for it to eventually leak out."

"Honey," Mike Kilgore implored, "come on, let's get out of here. These guys are going to spend their final years rotting in jail. I don't want to be with them."

What he said must have gotten through to Fran, because her face relaxed. "You," she said to Worth, "sit down." After a brief hesitation, the senator folded his long body back into his chair.

"And you," she said to Emma. "Get over there on the sofa by George and sit down."

"Just leave," Manning told Fran and Mike. "We won't try to stop you."

"And miss my opportunity to be a director?" Fran's smile oozed crazy. "I'm trying to decide: should the senator kill the director and the ghost hunter over being outed on the Catalina murder? Or should the psychotic medium kill both old geezers out of a sense of justice, then kill herself?" She turned to George. "Which do you think will play best in the media, George?"

Emma, who was about to follow orders and move to the sofa, froze in her tracks, her ears tuned to something she thought she'd heard.

"There's no need for violence, Fran," George told her. "Just leave peaceably. We won't tell the police you were even here."

"That's a very pretty lie, George."

"Blackmail is one thing, Fran," Kilgore said to his wife. "Murder is quite another. Let's go."

"But your wife has already committed one murder," Emma pointed out, raising her voice slightly and emphasizing the word *murder.* She kept her eyes pinned to Fran while her ears continued to hone in on the faint sounds she thought were coming from outside the room. "What's three more?"

"You're not helping things, Emma," Worth said, not looking at her but keeping his eyes on the gun.

Emma was very thankful now that Granny had convinced Bijou to go outside. Unlike the four elderly people in the room with her, the dog would have heard the sound and would have given it away. Emma was sure someone else was in the house. Then she remembered that Grant was due to arrive. She could only hope her usually obtuse ex-hubby was savvy enough to realize something sinister was going on and wouldn't make things worse.

Kilgore's eyes darted with anxiety. "I never killed anyone. She was alone on that."

Fran turned slightly toward Kilgore. "Shut up, you old fool."

"The police won't care," Emma said, trying to buy time for whoever it was to make their way to the study. If it was Grant, Emma hoped he was alone and hadn't brought Carolyn and little Oscar with him.

Doing as she was instructed earlier, Emma moved toward the sofa. When she neared George, she feigned a stumble over the fallen afghan in front of him and made eye contact, trying to convey confidence in the situation. She also took the opportunity to put her hands on his cane. Emma wasn't sure what she was going to do with it, but it crossed her mind that she might be able to whack the gun from Fran's shaky hand if things kicked into fast-forward without notice.

It didn't take long. Emma picked up muffled footsteps coming down the hall long before the four seniors in the room did.

"What the hell!" Grant Whitecastle yelled as he reached the door to his father's study. Everyone turned to look at him in surprise, except Emma. "Damn it, Emma, I thought

I told you to stay away from my family." It was obvious he hadn't caught on to the situation at hand.

"Grant," his father said. "Shut up."

Grant ignored the order and continued yelling at Emma. "Do I have to get a restraining order against you?" He barged further into the room. In his anger, he bumped into Fran Hyland, setting her off-balance.

Emma took her shot. Wielding George's cane, she came at the tilting Fran like a banshee, screaming at the top of her lungs. Grant thought she was aiming at him and jumped to grab the cane. Emma's interrupted blow grazed Fran's arm. Fran let out a scream, and the gun went off. With a cry, Grant fell to the floor. Emma gave the now-screeching Fran another chop with the cane, and the gun came loose. She kicked it out of the way and shoved the wobbly Fran Hyland onto her backside, guarding her with the raised cane. Right after the shot, Worth scrambled to his feet and threw his lanky, eighty-year-old body at a surprised Mike Kilgore.

THIRTY-ONE

"Milo," Emma yelled into her phone earpiece as she drove out of Bel Air. She was driving like a bat out of hell, heading for the Santa Monica Airport. "I'm on my way to Catalina. Have you seen Tessa today?"

"No, I haven't."

"I think the guy who left her is on his way to Catalina."

"Curtis?"

"Curtis was definitely a boat, not a person. The boat's name was the *Curtis Lee.* But the guy who said he'd get help, then left her to die — I think he might be on his way to the island. It's Paul Feldman."

"Paul Feldman killed her?"

"Not exactly, but sort of. It's a sad, disturbing story."

Emma gave her steering wheel a hard jerk, just missing the back end of the car in front of her when it decided to brake for no apparent reason. She was flying down the 405

Freeway, trying to make it to the airport in record time, and was thankful it was a Sunday afternoon and not a weekday. Fortunately, the Santa Monica Airport was much closer and much smaller than LA International. At the airport, a helicopter would be waiting to take her to Catalina. George Whitecastle had gotten on the phone and arranged it himself, saying the copter would be at the airport in fifteen minutes.

Emma didn't know for sure if Paul Feldman would head to Catalina. It was a hunch, one based on Worth Manning's confession that Paul had mentioned it to him in the past few days, saying he felt the need to go back to the island for closure.

"Please go down to the beach, Milo, and keep watch. Look for a rather short, slightly pudgy elderly man with a bald head and close gray beard. If he does go to Catalina, I don't know if he'll go to the beach or to where he left her." Emma glanced at the clock on the dashboard. "I should be there in about thirty to forty-five minutes. Have Tracy meet me at the helicopter landing with a taxi while you stake out the beach."

"Should we call the police?"

"I called Detective Tillman before I left the Whitecastles'. He's going to notify the sheriff's station on the island. And, Milo, Mr. Feldman is armed. I think he's looking to do more harm to himself than others, but still be careful."

Barely slowing down, Emma made the turn onto the Bundy Drive South exit. "There's a good chance Paul Feldman is going to or has committed suicide," she continued. "I'm thinking his ghost might meet up with Tessa's." She paused again, her mind tripping over another thought. "Milo, will the suicide affect his spirit's ability to manifest itself? I mean, in some books and movies, suicides seem to have ghost privileges stripped. Is that true?"

"No, Emma, it's not. It doesn't matter how a person dies. What matters is their desire to return and be seen."

"If you do see Mr. Feldman," she paused to swallow hard, "alive or dead, please try to hold him. I need to see him."

Finished with the call, she turned her attention to her driving. The airport was just a few minutes away.

After restraining Fran Hyland and Mike Kilgore, Emma and Worth Manning had tied them both up with cording Emma found in the kitchen. George guarded them with the gun.

Grant's thigh had been grazed by the

wayward bullet. There had been more blood than injury. He'd sat on the sofa with a towel against his wound, demanding to know what was going on and yelling at Emma that it was her fault that he'd nearly been killed. At one point, his father told him to shut up or he'd shoot him himself, and this time, it wouldn't be his leg.

Emma hadn't told Detective Tillman about her going to Catalina or about what had happened at the Whitecastles', only that Paul Feldman might be heading to the island or be there, and that she believed him to be involved in Tessa's death. She wasn't going to call him at all, but if she alerted the police, there might be a chance to stop Paul Feldman from killing himself.

George was going to give Emma at least a thirty-minute head start, then he would call Detective Tillman himself and hand over Denise Dowd's murderer, along with the full story about Tessa. They knew if they called before Emma was airborne, she might be stopped at the airport. She had to get to Catalina unimpeded. And they all knew that the police would never let her take off for Catalina until their questions were satisfied, which would take hours.

When she got off the helicopter in Catalina, Tracy was waiting with a golf-cart taxi.

Emma hopped aboard, and in minutes they were standing on the beach with Milo.

"Any sign of them?" Emma asked as soon as she arrived.

The December ocean air was cool and damp. Emma was glad her jacket had been in the car and that she'd had the sense to grab it before boarding the helicopter.

"None," Milo told her. "And we're all on the lookout. Even Granny and Sandy Sechrest."

Emma sat her weary body down on a bench. "I feel like I've lived a week in the past few hours."

Tracy came up with a cup of coffee and a sandwich. "Here, pal," she said holding it out to Emma.

Emma gladly took the coffee but turned down the food. "Thanks, but I'm not hungry."

"You're all pale and pasty," Tracy observed. "Bet you haven't eaten a thing all day."

Emma sighed. The last thing she remembered consuming was a cup of coffee shortly after she'd gotten out of bed. She'd been too nervous about her meeting with George to eat anything.

Tracy pushed the sandwich at her again. "It's cheese and grilled veggies on whole grain. Eat."

Obeying, Emma accepted the sandwich and took a bite. Her stomach did a happy dance, even if the rest of her didn't care. After she ate, the three of them sat on the bench, keeping vigil in case Paul Feldman showed in one form or another. From time to time, Milo got up and paced up and down the beach, searching in other spots. A sheriff's deputy was also keeping watch, mostly on them. Another deputy was scouting for Feldman around the island.

"You know," Milo said to Emma when he returned from one of his quick rounds, "if Feldman doesn't want us to see him, we won't."

"I know, but I think he will show himself, or at least Tessa will. She'll let us know if he's here."

"I hear you cracked the case," Granny said, showing up next to the bench. "Knew you would."

"No luck finding Tessa?" Emma asked Granny.

"None, but I did see that no-good Grant just now on the news."

Milo and Emma turned in unison to stare at Granny. Tracy turned her head in the same direction out of habit.

Granny crossed her arms and scowled.

"He's saying he jumped in front of a bullet to save your life."

Emma stared at Granny in disbelief, then collected herself. "Of course, he'd say that."

Emma knew the truth would eventually come out, but honestly didn't care if it did or not. She went back to watching the beach near the pier. When her cell phone rang, she jumped. It was Phil. Emma's heart swelled at the sight of his name on the display.

"Saw the news," he said, instead of saying hello.

"You mean my hero ex-husband?"

"The current story is that it was a home invasion at the Whitecastles' and that Grant took the bullet for you." Phil paused. "My legal nose tells me there's another, truer version, especially since Milo called me right after you called him."

"I'll tell you all the details one day, but right now I'm on ghost watch."

"You can tell me tonight. I'll be on the island soon. I'm taking a copter over from San Diego."

"But you hate helicopters."

"Sometimes a man's gotta do what a man's gotta do. Just do me a big favor, Emma Whitecastle, and don't talk to the police until I get there. Promise?"

Emma's attention was diverted when Milo gently nudged her in the ribs. As she looked up, he pointed to a spot several yards away. It was then Emma saw a bikini-clad ghost coming into view near the ocean's edge.

"Gotta go, counselor," Emma said into her phone, keeping her eyes on Tessa. "See you soon."

The ghost of Tessa North smiled and waved when she spotted Emma. In a second, she was standing next to their bench. She was alone.

"I'm so glad you came back," she told Emma with a big smile. "Your friends have been very nice to me."

"Tessa," Emma began, her voice somber. "The *Curtis Lee* is never coming back to the island. You need to understand that. It was sold by Worth Manning many years ago."

"You know Worth?"

"Yes, I do. And George Whitecastle and Paul Feldman. I've known them a long time, and I think that somehow, some way, you knew that or sensed it when you first came to me, even if you didn't know it consciously."

Tessa tilted her head in her confused-puppy way.

"I know what happened to you, Tessa," Emma continued. "I know what happened on the *Curtis Lee,* and I know Paul Feldman told you he'd return with help."

"He told me he loved me." The flirty ghost did a small pirouette in the sand. "Paul was so sweet. He had a big crush on me but was always a gentleman, unlike the others."

"I was no gentleman, Tessa."

The voice came from behind their bench. Turning, everyone — ghosts and the living, except for Tracy — spotted the ghost of Paul Feldman. Emma let out a strangled cry, knowing he'd succeeded in taking his own life. Milo reached over and took her hand to comfort her.

"I left you to die, Tessa," Feldman's spirit said, addressing the ghost in the bikini. "What I did was unspeakable."

Tessa approached him. "But you're here now, Paul. You returned, just as you said you would."

Emma got up from the bench and faced Feldman's spirit. Heavy tears streamed down her face. "I'm so sorry, Mr. Feldman. I had no idea when this all started that this would be the outcome."

Feldman smiled at her. "It's okay, Emma."

"No, it's not," she sobbed. "I wish you'd come to me before . . . before . . ."

"No worries, Emma. Really, dear. I did what I felt I needed to do. I have no regrets about my decision. My only regret is what happened years ago." He looked at Tessa, keeping his eyes on the young ghost as he spoke. "For the first time in forty years, I'm at peace."

Even without knowing what was being said to Emma, Tracy got up and wrapped her arms around her. Emma clung to her and cried.

"Hush now, Emma," the ghost of Sandy Sechrest said, appearing on the other side of the bench. "You did a good thing."

Inconsolable, Emma shook her head back and forth in disagreement. "Because of me, Mr. Feldman is dead, and the senator and George may go to prison. My own daughter's grandfather may die in prison because of what I've done."

"No, Emma," Milo stepped close and whispered. "George Whitecastle will be dead before Christmas — from the cancer."

Emma let out a painful cry. Tracy held her tighter.

Granny brushed her hand against Emma's face. "Folks have to live or die by the consequences of their actions."

The ghost of Paul Feldman came closer. "The three of us have been in prison for forty years, Emma. You've set us free; always remember that. And you've set Tessa here free, too."

Emma remained wrapped in the arms of her best friend until Milo tapped her on the shoulder. He pointed toward the edge of the beach.

She looked up just in time to see the spirit of Tessa North walking into the ocean hand in hand with the ghost of Paul Feldman.

ABOUT THE AUTHOR

Sue Ann Jaffarian is a critically acclaimed, award-winning author whose books have been lauded by the *New York Times,* optioned for film/TV rights, and praised by *New York Times* best-selling author Lee Child and Emmy award-winning actress Camryn Manheim. In addition to the paranormal Ghost of Granny Apples Mystery series, she is the author of the Odelia Grey Mystery series and the Fang-in-Cheek Mystery series that began in 2010 with *Murder in Vein.* Sue Ann is also nationally sought after as a motivational and humorous speaker. She lives and works in Los Angeles, California.

Visit Sue Ann on the Internet at
WWW.SUEANNJAFFARIAN.COM
and
WWW.SUEANNJAFFARIAN.BLOGSPOT.COM

We hope you have enjoyed this Large Print book. Other Thorndike, Wheeler, Kennebec, and Chivers Press Large Print books are available at your library or directly from the publishers.

For information about current and upcoming titles, please call or write, without obligation, to:

Publisher
Thorndike Press
295 Kennedy Memorial Drive
Waterville, ME 04901
Tel. (800) 223-1244

or visit our Web site at:

http://gale.cengage.com/thorndike

OR

Chivers Large Print
published by AudioGO Ltd
St James House, The Square
Lower Bristol Road
Bath BA2 3SB
England
Tel. +44(0) 800 136919
email: info@audiogo.co.uk
www.audiogo.co.uk

All our Large Print titles are designed for easy reading, and all our books are made to last.